"You've lived here all by yourself for four years because of this one crazy guy...that you think is me?"

Jack knelt carefully beside the rocking chair, gripping the worn armrest with both hands. "Ellen..." His voice cracked. "Am I Hank?"

His gaze was bewildered, but she saw no sign of guile or deceit. No hidden agendas. If only she could be positive.... She turned away. "I—I'm not sure."

"Look!" Jack held her chin and forced her to tilt her head and face him. "Look at me! How could you not know?"

"Because Hank threatened to undergo plastic surgery."

"Plastic surgery?"

"Yes." Ellen screamed the answer in her mind, but aloud, it came out sounding feeble and uncertain. She drew a deep breath. "He could be anybody. He could be you."

ABOUT THE AUTHOR

Born and raised in Alabama, Laura didn't discover the joys of snow until she was an adult, living in Colorado Springs. Her first fledgling experience with a heavy snowfall generated the idea for this book. Six sledding seasons and a thousand snowmen later, the air force moved Laura and her family to Leavenworth, Kansas (where it didn't snow), and a year after that, she moved to the Washington, D.C. area (where it might!).

She'd love to hear from readers at P.O. Box 10922, Burke, VA 22009

Books by Laura Kenner

HARLEQUIN INTRIGUE
263—SOMEONE TO WATCH OVER ME

A Killer Smile

Laura Kenner

Harlequin Books

TORONTO • NEW YORK • LONDON
AMSTERDAM • PARIS • SYDNEY • HAMBURG
STOCKHOLM • ATHENS • TOKYO • MILAN
MADRID • WARSAW • BUDAPEST • AUCKLAND

To my family—Mom, the real Kenner;
Dad, the real Ernest; the Bama Doctor
and our clones, Katie and Scott.
Also to Deb Stover, Pam McCutcheon and Karen Fox,
who have proven that friendship, like E-mail, knows
no state boundaries.

ISBN 0-373-22313-7

A KILLER SMILE

Copyright © 1995 by Laura Beard Hayden

Printed in U.S.A.

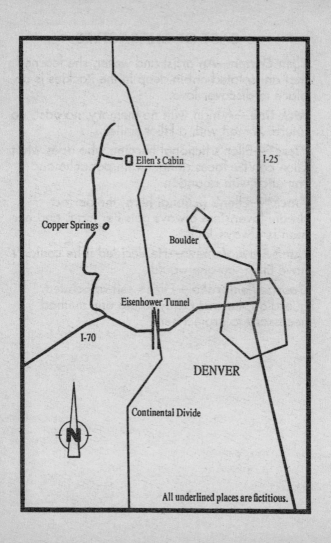

Ellen's Cabin

I-25

Copper Springs

Boulder

Eisenhower Tunnel

I-70

DENVER

N

Continental Divide

All underlined places are fictitious.

CAST OF CHARACTERS

Ellen Coster—An artist and writer, she learned that an isolated cabin deep in the Rockies is no place to discover love.

Jack Doe—A man with no memory, no past, no future. A man with a killer smile.

"Tess"—Ellen's fictional heroine who does what Ellen can't—faces danger with panache and romance with abandon.

"Jack"—Ellen's fictional hero, the perfect dream lover. Tess always gets her man, and her man is always Jack.

Hank Bartholomew—He decided if he couldn't have Ellen, no one would.

George Pembroke—Ellen's self-appointed guardian; he was ready to use any method necessary to protect her.

Prologue

"And what did the defendant say to you, Miss Coster?"

The sound of clicking knitting needles distracted Ellen, causing her to hesitate. The noise wasn't loud, but it irritated her nonetheless. She cleared her throat. "Hank said if he couldn't...have me, no one could. Shortly after that, I began to smell the smoke."

"That will be all. You may step down."

A jolt rocketed up Ellen's frayed nerves. "But what about the call I just got?"

A muscle tensed in the prosecutor's jaw. "That will be *all*, Miss Coster."

Ellen turned to the judge. "But Hank, the defendant, threatened me again. During the last break, I was paged to the public phone and—"

The defense attorney rose from his seat. "Your Honor—"

The judge cut him off with a wave. "No need to object. Will both counsel please approach the bench?"

Ellen knotted her hands into fists and hid them in the folds of her skirt. "But he—"

"Don't say anything more, Miss Coster." The judge reached up and covered the microphone, then turned to the prosecuting attorney. "Frank, you know anything about this?"

The lawyer shrugged. "I told her we couldn't bring this up now. Maybe during the sentencing hearing, but not now."

The judge turned back to Ellen. "Are you saying the defendant threatened you today?"

"Yes, Your Honor." Ellen tried not to look toward the defense table where Hank sat. She couldn't stand any glimpse at what her friends had innocently called his "killer smile." In the months since their initial meeting, the description had taken on an ominous meaning.

The black robe rustled as the judge shifted in his chair. "I think we'd better take this to my chambers. Gentlemen? Miss Coster?"

Ellen and the two attorneys followed the judge into his anteroom. Before he closed the door, he motioned for the bailiff to join them inside. Ellen sank into the soft leather chair, feeling more like a guilty student facing the principal than a key witness in a criminal trial.

The judge perched on the corner of his desk. "Norm, did the defendant leave the courtroom area at any time during the recess?"

The bailiff nodded. "Yes, sir. The defendant asked to use the restroom during the morning break. He was escorted to the facility door by two guards who remained outside, then brought back to the courtroom. There's no way he could have gotten to a phone. There aren't any in that area."

The defense attorney shook his head. "I don't see how—"

Ellen turned to the judge, pleating her handkerchief between nervous fingers. "Sir, I'm positive it was his voice."

The robed man crossed his arms. "Miss Coster, is there any way you could be mistaken? Could it have been someone else who only identified himself as the defendant, Hank Bartholomew?"

Ellen tightened her grip on the handkerchief until her knuckles whitened. "I'm positive it was Hank, not someone else. I recognized his voice... and his threats."

The defense attorney shook his head. "This is preposterous, Your Honor. There's no way my client could have made that call. Like the bailiff said, there's no phone in or near the men's restroom on this floor."

Ellen remained calm as a revelation rocked her, making her knees grow watery and her heart wedge in her throat. "I know exactly how he could have done it!" She glanced at the prosecuting attorney, who shrugged, then made a gesture for her to continue.

She took a deep breath. "Hank's father always carries a cellular telephone in his briefcase. He could have entered the bathroom shortly before Hank and hidden the phone for his son to use."

"That sounds plausible...." The judge turned to the bailiff. "Go back into the courtroom and see if the defendant's father brought a briefcase with him."

"Yes, sir." The man stepped out and returned a few minutes later, shaking his head. "Mr. Bartholomew doesn't have a briefcase with him today, although one of the guards said he brought one on the other days of testimony."

The prosecuting attorney turned to the judge. "What now? If we can't prove—"

Ellen held up a shaky hand. "Please." Inspiration arrived in the form of cold shivers sliding down her back, and she fumbled with the purse in her lap. Removing her wallet, she pawed through its contents until she pulled out a wrinkled piece of cardboard and held it out to the judge. "Can't we use this?"

The judge took the business card and studied it. A small smile flitted across his face. "Very good, Miss Coster. Let's go out there and test this theory. If it works, I want to see the looks on their faces." He gestured to the attorneys, who both released puzzled sighs but followed him back into the courtroom.

Once everyone took their place, the judge reached for the telephone on his bench and punched in the numbers printed on the worn business card. Ellen watched the courtroom observers strain to hear his end of the conversation.

Instead they heard a muffled electronic beeping sound.

The senior Bartholomew paled.

Mrs. Bartholomew jumped, pushing away the bag that held her knitting. The noise continued even when the bag hit the floor with a heavy, resounding thud.

"You bitch!"

Hank Bartholomew rose, shaking off the restraining hand his attorney placed on him. "I failed the first time, but I won't mess up again. I'll kill you yet, you bitch." An evil smile creased his all-American features, the same face she'd once thought of as handsome.

"You won't know how I'll do it!"

He straight-armed the defense lawyer, who was trying desperately to preserve the last shreds of a carefully planned defense.

"You won't know when!"

Hank lunged toward the witness stand only to be intercepted by an alert bailiff.

The judge pounded on the bench with his gavel, mimicking the sound of Ellen's heart. "Bailiff, remove the defendant from the court."

Several guards struggled with Hank, slapped handcuffs on him and pulled him toward the door. His father bellowed in outrage, and his mother began to cry hysterically.

"You won't even know who," Hank yelled from the rear of the court. "When I get through, you won't even recognize me, Ellen. Then I'll get you when, where and how you least expect. Because I can become anybody!"

His malevolent shout echoed down the corridor as they pulled him away. "Anybody!"

Chapter One

Most of the birds were gone for the season, leaving only fearless magpies to rule the skies. Ellen glanced up at the squawking black flock, flying below the ominous dark clouds that built overhead. At her feet an uneven breeze created small whirlwinds of amber leaves that rose, then drifted back to the forest floor.

She hoisted the camera to her eye and focused the zoom lens on a squirrel. Its black ears twitched as Ellen shifted against a tree trunk to steady herself. After a moment the animal returned its attention to the dinner clasped between its paws. Tufts of fur flicked once more when the camera's shutter made its first click. She took several more close-up shots of the squirrel until her subject scampered into the dense undergrowth.

"Going to snow..." Ellen's voice echoed through the silent forest. She seldom spoke aloud while photographing the beauties of nature. In fact, she rarely talked at all. Her long-suffering companion, Hermitt, possessed a Labrador retriever's uncanny way of interpreting wordless gestures and facial expressions, freeing her from the chore of verbal communication. Actually, she wasn't sure whether to credit his abilities to his breed or to the fact he had lost so much of his hearing over the years.

No matter which, sometimes she'd go an entire week without speaking a word. On those occasions when she longed for the sound of a human voice, she played a cassette in her battery-powered tape recorder or read aloud to herself while sitting in her favorite rocking chair. In the Rocky Mountains, radio reception was sporadic at best and nonexistent the rest of the time.

Dark, heavy clouds released their threat in a thin, lacy curtain of snow. Ellen blinked away a stray flake that landed in her eye. Snowflakes continued to cling to her eyelashes with annoying persistence as she trudged up the path leading back to her cabin. She shuffled down the leaf-strewn trail, acutely aware of how rapidly it was becoming a snow-covered trail. The first heavy snowfall of the season invariably caught her off guard.

I'll have to carry in some more firewood.... She looked down, riveted by the sight of a pale red splotch, marring the snow by her boot.

Blood. Ellen identified the stain with a forced detachment. She knew all too well that sometimes the survival of the fittest wasn't a pretty sight. She glanced at the tracks being masked by a filmy layer of snow.

A big animal. Playing connect-the-dots from one spot to the next, she felt her stomach churn as the blotches grew brighter and fresher. And headed toward her cabin.

Hermitt! Panic overwhelmed her for a moment, and she began to run down the trail. *Did Hermitt get out?* She looked up in dismay at the open door. *Or did something try to get in?* No animal could have turned the knob.

The answer was obvious. *A human...*

Hank!

Ellen spun around, half expecting the man to jump out from behind the low scrub oak, then she realized the biggest danger facing her was most likely *inside* her cabin.

The quiet snow continued to drift down, forming a thick, but unprotective, barrier between her and the cabin. A chill of apprehension stiffened the muscles in her face.

I'll freeze to death if I stay here. She looked around for a weapon, for anything she could use to defend herself. She remembered the large knife, resting safely in the kitchen drawer.

Inside the cabin.

Could she make it to the drawer before— *Before my imagination attacks me? C'mon, Ellen,* she chided herself. *Get a grip! Hank isn't here—he couldn't find me.* She took a deep breath and expelled it in a frosty cloud.

"Hermitt? Where are you, boy?" She stepped onto the wooden porch, noisily stamping the snow from her boots. The one thing a nearly deaf dog would react to was vibrations in the floor. Nudging the door open, she called again, "Hermitt?"

A wet trail of leaves and dirt crossed the room and disappeared beyond the bed. Ellen glanced around, letting her eyes adjust to the shadows. There were only a few places in her one-room cabin where someone could hide: the shadows near the corner pantry, the tiny curtained-off bathroom...

Or by the fire.

Just beyond the iron bed frame, a dark, anonymous mass huddled on the stone hearth. When the lump moved, Ellen released the breath she'd held. Her dog, Hermitt, grumbled, stretched his sleek black legs toward the fire and began to snore. As relief began to flow through her, she peered into the shadows closest to the bed and saw a splotch of red.

Not blood.

A red sock.

A human.

Swallowing a lump of panic, Ellen backed away, covering her mouth with her hand. When she stumbled into the edge of the opened door, she released an involuntary scream and received two muffled responses, one from the sleeping dog and the other from the uninvited guest. She pivoted and fell toward the kitchen cabinet. Pawing blindly through the drawer for the knife, she kept her attention riveted on the nameless intruder. Once she found her weapon, she held it in front of her.

"I'm . . . I'm armed! You better get back!" Her fierce warning echoed through the room and returned to her, sounding feeble and disembodied. Startled by her shout, Hermitt fell off the hearth and stumbled to his feet. He shook himself, then cocked his head toward the source of a second noise.

Ellen stood on her tiptoes, trying to see past the bars of the headboard and get a clear view of the person on the floor. She took a faltering step backward when a bare hand grasped the rail at the foot of the bed. The bloodied fingers tightened around the iron frame, and the knuckles whitened as the intruder groaned and struggled to his feet.

Streaks of dirt and blood discolored the man's pale face. Down filling escaped from a jagged tear in his dark parka. Her throat closed when she realized why the white feathers were stained a dark crimson.

He held out his blood-covered hand toward her. "P-please. D-don't be scared. I . . ." A moment later his eyes closed, his knees buckled and he pitched forward. He bounced against the mattress, then slipped to the wooden floor with a sickening crash.

Ellen stared at the scarlet imprint of blood he'd left on her pristine white bedspread. Fear and sympathy twisted through her, both sparring for control.

Hermitt padded closer to the man and sniffed at him with a brief flare of interest.

"Hermitt! Come!" The dog ignored her and dropped into an ungainly heap on the hearth, closing his eyes.

Damn you, dog! You're no protection.

She moved closer to the hearth and stared at the stranger from a cautious distance. His lack of color made his strong features seem just a little less threatening. As a fresh stream of blood flowed down his face, a pang of sympathy displaced some of her fear.

Letting curiosity overcome her initial trepidation, Ellen knelt and touched his cheek. Her unchecked imagination provided an unwanted vision of him rearing up, grabbing her wrist and shooting her a wicked smile. But in reality he merely rolled to his side and fought a painful coughing spasm.

In reality, she realized he was too busy fighting for his life to be any threat to her.

"C-cold," he mumbled without opening his eyes. "Help me..." His voice trailed away to a harsh gasp.

Braced by thoughts of momentary safety, she found it deceptively easy to say, "Don't worry. Everything will be all right. I'll help you." Yet as she spoke, she wondered whether his unconscious brain would register her words of reassurance or the feeling of uncertainty behind them.

A violent tremor rocked his body.

Ellen moved closer to the fireplace, where the smoldering embers responded to her savage efforts with a poker. A small flicker of heat penetrated the still air of her cabin. She shoved some kindling into the sputtering flames, swung the heating pot into place and hurried to collect her meager first-aid supplies. God help her if his injuries required more medical knowledge than her scant skills could address. Turning back to her patient, she forced herself to cope with the combination of concern and apprehension that filled her.

"Please, wake up," she pleaded to his lifeless features. "Help me figure out what to do." She stared blankly at the rolls of gauze and tape, momentarily giving in to her anxiety. The survivor deep within her pushed to the surface and admonished her.

Control yourself, Ellen. He's cold, so get him warm.

She unzipped his mountain parka and discovered sodden clothes beneath. Ignoring her thoughts of hesitation, she shooed Hermitt away from the hearth and hung her quilt near the fire to warm. After placing a pillow under the man's head to cushion him from the hard floor, she struggled to slide his arms out of the sleeves of his jacket. Her fingers shook as she unbuttoned and removed his wet flannel shirt. Beneath it, he wore a white thermal shirt, tucked into damp jeans that molded themselves to his muscled legs. She fumbled with the brass stud at his waistband.

Grappling with the stiff, uncooperative denim, Ellen finally peeled the jeans down, ending up with the inside-out material bunched at his ankles. She removed his single boot and fell backward when brute strength eventually won out over finesse and the tight pants slid over his dank, red socks.

His damp thermal underwear highlighted a rangy but muscular physique. She pulled up the stained knit fabric, trying to avoid the bloody spot near his temple. Dark curls bristled over his tanned chest, emphasizing the potential strength he could easily use to overpower her when he regained consciousness. She pushed away the terrifying thoughts and chided herself about her overactive imagination.

Stripping off her own coat, Ellen draped the warm lining over his upper body. Pushing modesty aside, she hooked her fingers in the wide elastic waistband of his thermal pants and slid the material down past his hips. His bright blue briefs saved her from any further embarrassment.

She began to examine his superficial injuries with a glimmer of understanding. Judging by the cuts and bruises on his knees as well as his elbows and palms, she figured he'd received his injuries in a fall. One hip seemed to be more badly bruised than the other.

Another strong tremor passed through his body, and Ellen hesitated for only a moment before retrieving the fire-warmed quilt and draping it over him. The quilt represented the only memento she had of her family, all of whom had "traveled to their rewards." Grandma Clara had made it from bits and pieces of Ellen's life: baby clothes, embroidered handkerchiefs, flannel rosebud pajamas, a piece from her confirmation dress and one from her first prom dress....

A stranger couldn't appreciate the work, the memories that had gone into the quilt. A stranger could only appreciate its warmth.

Ellen realized most of the blood came from the ragged gash in the man's forehead. She bathed the wound in warm water and cleaned the bloodstains from his skin. The uneven cut on his temple didn't appear to be terribly deep, but it bisected an angry red bruise that continued into his hairline. She cleaned the wound gently, wincing in sympathy when he reacted, even in his unconscious state, to the discomfort.

"Please . . . keep still," she pleaded as he knocked away the quilt. "You've got to keep warm. I don't know much, but I do know that."

He continued to mutter and groan and to thrash about, leaving her no option but to wrap the quilt tightly, swaddling him like a baby. With his arms pinned to his sides, he struggled against the material for a few hectic moments, then settled into what she hoped was a more normal sleep.

Who is he?

A search of his parka and clothes netted a utility-laden pocketknife, a handkerchief and a comb, but no wallet or identification of any sort.

Where did he come from?

His hiking boot looked worn and comfortable, most likely signifying an experienced hiker. His clothes were appropriate for an autumn day in the Rockies, but he evidently hadn't been prepared for the sudden Arctic blast that had blown in.

What happened to him?

Ellen had already decided he'd fallen, but why was he on her mountain in the first place? It was late in the season for a casual hike on either of the two trails that intersected below her cabin. He carried no provisions or identification, unless his backpack lay somewhere on the trail, perhaps lost in his fall.

Is someone looking for him? Only a fool would hike by himself. She looked at his solemn face and knew instinctively he was no fool. Even in his sleep the man wore a look of intelligence and shrewdness.

Who are you, John Doe? The words tasted unfamiliar. The name John Doe seemed too impersonal and much too formal for the man she'd undressed. John Does were vague copies of men, anonymous, unsure, unaware. John Does made excuses for their weaknesses, and this man exuded strength even though his battered body rested for the moment.

If nothing else, a John Doe would wear white boxer shorts.

So, she called him Jack. It made sense to give him a safe, familiar name, for no other reason than to belie a less savory nature.

His body temperature rose to normal, then his internal controls evidently overcompensated for the chill and he grew feverish. Though the quilt muffled the actions of his increasing delirium, Ellen couldn't help but share his pain as well as his confusion. She worked a braided rug beneath him, then used it to slide his body away from the crackling flames and the stone hearth.

Hermitt sniffed at the man, then retreated to his favorite spot by the fire, showing no other curiosity concerning their uninvited guest. The dog became involved only when Jack began to mutter incoherently. Ellen used one hand to hold her canine protector back and the other to try to wipe her patient's feverish forehead with a damp cloth. She tried to soothe Jack with words, but he didn't respond to her strained assurances.

"The fire!" he shouted, catching her off guard. "Good God, it'll explode! Watch out for…" His hoarse voice died away as an ugly wave of fear crossed his features. Hermitt growled in response to the man's anguished tone.

After a few moments of wordless agitation, Jack's face twisted into a grimace. "I'm not staying here. I hate hospitals!" He grew more violent, struggling against the material that pinned his arms. "Get out of my life, damn you. Leave me alone!"

At the height of his delirium, Ellen anticipated the moment when the restrictive quilting failed to hold him. Sensing her trepidation, Hermitt moved between them, effectively creating a barrier that the stranger would find difficult to cross.

She and Jack stayed on the floor together for minutes, hours—she wasn't sure which. Lacking any other knowledge, the best she could do for her patient was to treat his symptoms. She bathed his face, whispered vague reassurances and prayed. Success would mean his survival. Failure? Perhaps his death.

Moments before panic threatened to overwhelm her, Jack's fever broke with a skin-drenching sweat. He grew calmer and settled into a deep sleep, his face devoid of the emotion that had gripped him earlier.

Worrying that his temperature would spike again, Ellen fought to stay awake so she could monitor his condition. No longer perceiving Jack as a threat, Hermitt abandoned the role of protector and returned to the hearth to sleep.

The dancing shadows of the flickering fire nearly lulled Ellen to sleep, as well. To keep herself from dozing off, she found a necessary chore to take up some of her time, scrubbing the bloodstains out of Jack's clothes and hanging them to dry by the fire. Afterward, she alternated between an occasional blast of cold air and a pot of strong tea to keep her awake.

She blew into her mug, and a steamy cloud drifted up, leaving a warm layer of moisture on her face. Despite her precautions, sleep continued to beckon, and she relied on a childhood trick to stay awake. She could remember hearing Grandma Clara talking to herself, spinning wonderful stories as she made tiny stitches in her current quilting project. Ellen's grandmother prided herself on being a storyteller and for having passed her talents down to subsequent generations. Ellen was the only one left now, and rather than spin fairy tales, full of fables and folklore, she turned to popular fiction, creating a world of romance and adventure both as a distraction to life on an isolated mountain and as a potential means of living. Of course, until she sold her first book, she still had to rely on her other talent, art, a gift from her father's side of the family.

Yet, as important as her artwork was for keeping food on the table, she took her greatest comfort in the written word, and it was certainly time for a bit of such comfort. She crossed the room and pulled a rubber-banded manuscript from the bookcase. Once she found her favorite music cassette, she placed it in the tape recorder. Melodic strains of an orchestra filled the room, joining the soothing crackles of the firewood. She thumbed through the handwritten pages until a certain scene captured her attention.

"Hermitt? Time to read."

At the sound of her voice, Hermitt abandoned his warm hearth and assumed an attentive position at her feet. They both knew their roles: she was the writer and he, her best critic.

The music swelled dramatically.

"Once upon a time, there lived a girl named Tess...."

MUSIC FILLED THE ROOM, erasing all other sounds in my mind. I stood in a forgotten corner of the ballroom, enraptured by the dancers who whirled in rhythm. An orchestra commandeered one corner of the huge dance floor, and the rest of the space was filled with men in black tuxedos and women in jewel-toned satins, metallic lamés and sequins in every color of the rainbow.

Glancing down at my pale pink formal, I knew my unfashionable dress branded me an obvious impostor, not a member of this elite corps. Yet people didn't stop and stare at me. In fact, not one single person made eye contact with me at all.

It was as if I didn't exist.

Mr. Glascow, my patron for the night, had been enticed away by the sparkling wit and seductive smiles of a pair of svelte beauties. He'd excused himself and disappeared into the twirling mass of revelers, robbing me of the only friendly face I'd seen all night.

I gathered enough courage to edge toward the refreshment table. There, I gave up trying to identify any of the foods gracing silver platters and consoled myself with a cup of punch. Edging back, I hid behind the large potted plant in the corner and sipped the odd-tasting drink.

As the music came to a flourishing crescendo, the crowd erupted in applause. Between the thunderous enthusiasm and my case of nerves, I flinched, sloshing lavender punch onto the skirt of my dress. My stomach tightened as I tried to dab at the ugly stain with the small cocktail napkin.

"Here." Someone shoved a white handkerchief into my hand.

When I looked up, I was mesmerized by a pair of electric blue eyes and a sympathetic smile.

"Cocktail napkins are totally worthless. I'll never understand why our otherwise gracious hosts insist on giving us such a tiny piece of paper and try to pretend it's useful." His grin broadened, taking my breath away.

Swallowing my surprise, I tried to blot at the liquid. A purplish color slowly stained his handkerchief.

"Here, let me." He took the cloth from my shaky hands, dipped it into the clear liquid in his tumbler, then knelt beside me. "I've heard that sparkling water is good at getting out stains."

Having no idea what to say, I offered him a wan smile.

He stood, brushed off the knees of his tuxedo pants and folded the stained handkerchief into neat quarters.

"Well, how does it look?"

The spot had already begun to fade, leaving no color to mar my dress. "It's...it's almost gone. Thank you." Facing those eyes, I suddenly couldn't remember how to smile.

He demonstrated how, his grin transforming him from merely attractive to drop-dead handsome. He reached down and gently took my hand. "I hope you know how beautiful you look in that dress."

"I feel out of place." Why in the world was I opening up to a total stranger? Why was he holding my hand? And why did I like it so much?

"Nonsense!" He stepped next to me and waved toward the crowd. "Look at them. They're a cookie-cutter group of trend followers. Not an original thinker in the whole bunch. They wear whatever the current fashion guru selects as this season's haute couture. They eat only 'fashionable' foods and discuss only the 'in' topics."

I glanced at his simple black tuxedo, an anomaly in a room full of neon cummerbunds and brocade vests. He wore neither an earring nor a ponytail, unlike most other men in the room.

"On the whole, they're boring and have absolutely no vision at all." He turned and smiled at me. "But then there's you. Fresh, original. A classic beauty." He laughed at a gentleman passing near them with a plateload of indescribable food. "I even noticed you had the good sense to decline what they're peddling as food. What a revolting collection of seaweed, wheat germ, tofu. Do you know what I'd give for a hot dog right now? A real hot dog— with onions and mustard!"

I laughed in spite of my embarrassment. "The food's not that bad. I simply make a habit of never eating things I can't readily identify."

"Practical as well as beautiful! My God, woman, will you marry me and bear my children?" His grip tightened on my hand.

When a blush began to creep over my face, I was more mortified by my own reaction than his mistake.

"I'm sorry. I didn't mean to embarrass you." He ducked his head sheepishly, but kept his warm grip on my hand.

"No, I'm not. It's just..." It's just what? *"I—I don't even know your name."*

A second set of warm fingers closed over my cold, trembling ones. His heated smile seared my heart as he cradled my hand between his palms. "My name's Jack."

"P-pleased to meet you. I'm Tess." I lost my train of thought, staring into the azure depths of his laugh-crinkled eyes. I shivered with an unexpected sense of excitement.

Concern replaced his amusement. "You're shaking. Are you cold? Why don't we step outside on the balcony? It's still quite warm out there. It's actually hot."

"HOT...HOT..." Jack's moan broke into her narrative, and Ellen scrambled out of her fictional world to return to his side. His temperature was spiking again. He struggled against the swaddling as he continued to mutter the word *hot.* Pressing a wet cloth to his forehead, she wondered whether she should loosen the quilt.

"Jack, stop! You're going to hurt yourself. Please, Jack. Calm down." He thrashed and groaned, heedless of her verbal reassurances.

"It's hot...too hot! Fire everywhere. Burning... watch out!" He panted. "Oh, God. Look out! Look out!" A fist shot out of the folds of the quilt and struck her in the forearm.

Hermitt suddenly came to life with teeth bared, streaking to her side and pushing himself between Ellen and her patient. She ignored the sound and fury of Hermitt's growls as pain ricocheted up her right arm, leaving her fingers drawn up in an agonizing cramp. Shifting away from Jack, she cradled her injured arm close to her body, trying not to voice her pain in very unladylike, four-letter words.

Obeying his protective instincts, Hermitt stood at alert even after Jack's contorted features relaxed.

"Hermitt," Ellen called. "It's okay, Hermitt." The dog shot her an almost dubious look. "It's really okay. Lie down."

Hermitt growled as he stretched out, pointedly placing himself between his mistress and their intruder. But in a few minutes, the old dog's good intentions faded away as he fell asleep.

Ellen sighed and rubbed her arm, trying to bring a response into her lifeless fingers. After the sensation of feeling returned in prickly needles of pain, she wrapped the quilt tighter around her patient, wishing fervently it were a straitjacket.

Well, Mister Doe, Mr. Whoever, you're strong. Too strong. One more stunt like that and I'll haul out the ropes and restrain you for my own protec—

Protection. Protective. Protective custody . . .

Ellen eyed her sleeping guest. All her fears flooded back to her, perhaps even stronger than before. She could no longer pretend she wasn't scared to death. She glanced down at the man, feeling the panic rise in her throat.

Was he the one?

Was this the newly sculpted face of death?

Sleep softened his features, erasing the hard edge that the delirium had added to his face. His eyes were hidden behind lids fringed with thick black lashes, and a small

amount of color was returning to his cheeks. Then she
noticed a thin scar along his jaw.

Plastic surgery?

She backed away, battling the terror that engulfed her in
an ice-cold wave. Over the years, she had grown lax. Too
lax. Had she actually believed time and distance could
erect an impenetrable barrier to protect her from the ghosts
of her past?

Of course not. Yet, somehow, she *had* felt safe.

She hadn't thought about Hank in a year. For twelve
glorious months she'd forgotten about his madness and his
threats, forgotten about those who had died. She'd even
fooled herself into believing she had chosen to live in isolation for her own reasons, not for fear of his retribution.

Hank had sent her a long rambling letter soon after he
was settled in the hospital, eight years ago. The first half
of the letter accused her of all sorts of crimes against him,
for making a mockery of their "pure" love. The second
half was a precise, perverted description of what he intended to do about her betrayal.

Hank Bartholomew was crazy, considered legally insane by a court of law, but he wasn't stupid. When he began to act out the initial steps of his system of vengeance
against her, Ellen realized he meant to carry his plans to a
lethal finale. So she ran away, finding solace and safety in
her isolated mountain cabin. She'd been there a little over
four years, three years in fear, one year in feigned ignorance, an ignorance that had now shattered.

"You'll never know when," he had written, repeating
the threats he had screamed in the courtroom, "or where,
or even who."

Ellen looked down at Jack's sleeping face.

Her first instinct was to run. Again.

She pushed her fist through the sleeve of her coat, but a plaintive sound cut through her anxiety and made her stop. Jack groaned again.

What if he was Hank?

She studied his face carefully. He didn't look like Hank... didn't sound like Hank.

The important question was: what if he *wasn't* Hank? Could she live with the guilt of allowing an innocent man to die in order to protect herself? Wasn't that why she'd escaped to the mountain in the first place? So no other innocent people would die?

She stared at the thin scar.

I won't be able to help this man if I think he's Hank. I must believe he's exactly what he seems to be—a hiker who fell on the trail and hurt himself. I have to help him....

She contemplated his features. Surely no plastic surgeon could make such radical changes to a man's face.

It's not Hank. It couldn't be.

Ellen's renewed convictions succeeded in pushing the doubt to a dark corner of her mind. Tension drained from her body as she hung her jacket back on its peg and returned to the fireplace, feeling tired and just a little lightheaded. She stared at Jack's passive face, trying to hide her sympathy and lingering fears beneath a layer of curiosity.

I wonder if he has blue eyes. No... that would seem too open, too honest. She stopped herself. *Why do I assume he's not honest? I don't know anything about him. Not really.* Her mind jumped ahead, despite her self-reproach. *Amber? The right color for a man of mystery?* She shook her head as if trying to shake away the unwanted thoughts. *Any color but green... please!*

After a few minutes she gathered enough courage to touch him. Her fingers barely grazed his bristled cheek, but an uncomfortable spark of electricity rode a wave of heat from his skin. Suddenly, the entire quilt shook. A tremor rocked Jack's body. His lips trembled as he muttered something over and over.

She leaned closer. "What? Say it again, I can't understand you." She flinched when his eyes snapped open. They weren't blue like Jack's, the high-society partygoer, or amber like her supposed man of mystery. Reflecting the light from the flickering fire, his eyes were a very ordinary and murky shade of brown. She recoiled slightly when he focused directly on her.

"Am I dead?" His voice was surprisingly clear.

She tried to give him a reassuring smile, but her face wouldn't cooperate. "No...you're not." She took as much consolation as she dared in the unfamiliar timbre of his voice; he didn't sound like Hank. Definitely not like Hank.

"H-how do you feel?" she asked, stuttering under his direct gaze.

"Lousy. Who are you? Where am I?"

"I'm Ellen Coster. What's your name?"

A thin furrow creased his forehead. "My name?" His focus seemed to waver. "Uh...my name is...Jack."

Chapter Two

Lowering herself to the rocking chair, Ellen stared at the orange tongues of flame curling around the log in the fireplace.

"Jack..." As the word trailed from her lips, she felt a surge of relief start at her toes and flash up her body.

Brown-eyed Jack. Living and breathing and asleep on her floor. Jack, not Hank. Not Hank with his green eyes, the color of greed, envy, and in his case, the color of madness.

She permitted herself to stare at him, to recategorize each feature that seemed so damning. His height, the shape of his face, the breadth of his shoulders...all now seemed so very unHanklike.

Feeling a renewed sense of safety, Ellen curled up on her bed and allowed sleep to win the battle it had been raging with her consciousness all night. She had intended to awaken every few hours and check on her patient, but fatigue overpowered her and she slept soundly. What seemed to be only moments later, she woke with a start, instantly aware of the quiet chill in the air.

A fine coat of white ash covered the dying embers. Hours had passed, and night had faded away to a hesitant dawn. In the pale, gray morning light she could see the man stretched out in front of the stone hearth, still wrapped up in her grandmother's quilt. She tiptoed over the cold wooden floor to stir the coals and add more wood to the weak fire.

Ellen knew she'd soon be forced to venture outdoors to the woodshed to restock her dwindling indoor fuel. There was plenty of wood outside, split, cut and stacked, but she shivered at the thought of entering the blizzard that had raged all night.

Another chill ran up her back, and she turned, knowing instinctively that Jack was awake. Her sense of safety vanished. He might not be Hank, but he was still a stranger.

She glanced into his inquisitive eyes. "Good morning. How do you feel?"

"Like I slept in a straitjacket." He glanced down at the patchwork material tucked beneath his chin. "Would you mind?"

A hot flush of embarrassment crossed her face. She knelt beside him, struggling to unwrap the quilt. "Sorry about this. You were delirious last night, and I didn't want you to hurt yourself."

Once his hands were free, he took over the task, tugging at the material and uncovering his bare torso. His eyes grew wide as he lifted the edge of the quilt and peered beneath at his level of undress.

Ellen felt her blush deepen. "I had to undress you. It was so cold and your clothes were wet."

"I see." He cleared his throat and tucked the blanket back across his chest. "How did I get here?"

"I'm not totally sure. You must have crawled here. I came home and found you by my fireplace."

"But how'd I get inside?"

In his weakened condition, he didn't seem much of a threat. She managed the barest smile and hoped she appeared, at least, congenial. "Back in civilization, I think they call it breaking and entering." When he didn't laugh at her feeble attempt at humor, she found her tentative smile fading. "What I want to know is, why in the world are you here?"

His wary expression turned to one of confusion. "I...I don't remember." He ran a hand across the back of his neck and winced. "I'm sorry. I really don't remember much at all."

"Last night you told me your name was Jack," she offered.

"Then I guess that's my name."

Ellen felt a small seed of panic sprout inside her. Amnesia could be a sign of a serious injury, beyond her fundamental medical skills. "You don't remember your own name?"

His forehead creased in perplexity. "I'm Jack. Jack... somebody. I don't remember much of anything other than being hot and thirsty."

"No wonder." She placed her chilled hand on his bristled cheek. "You were running a fever last night. Would you like a drink of water?"

He nodded. "Please."

She returned with a plastic cup and helped him sit up before holding it to his lips. As he supported himself on his elbows, the quilt slipped to his waist, revealing powerful muscles tensed across his chest.

He took a couple of sips, then gestured away the cup. "No more...thanks. Uh—" a wave of confusion passed over his face "—I don't even know your name, or did I forget that, too?"

"I'm Ellen." She held out her hand. "Ellen Coster."

His too-warm grip revealed his elevated temperature. "Pleased to meet you, Miss Coster."

Hermitt yawned and stretched with a groan, drawing Jack's attention. He glanced at the dog. "And your companion's name?"

"That's Hermitt."

When the dog heard his name, he thumped his tail against the hearth in sleepy recognition.

"Vicious animal," Jack commented. A half smile flitted across his face. "Now if you don't mind, I'd like my clothes back."

"Your clothes—" An image of his near-naked form flashed into her mind. She felt her own temperature edge up a degree or two. She hid her momentary embarrassment by turning away. "I'm not sure your jeans and shirt are dry yet." She fingered the damp clothes draped over a chair by the fire. "It looks like your thermals are the only things dry."

He sighed and held his hand out for the underwear. "It'll do, I guess." As he prepared to flip back the quilt, he stopped and glared imploringly at her. "But first I need to—" He stopped suddenly, a slight red tinge giving him some needed color.

Ellen pointed to the curtained bathroom. "If you think you can make it, the toilet's over here. Otherwise—" she reached beneath the bed and found the object of her search "—I have this."

He stared at her in shock. "A chamber pot?"

She shrugged. "I don't have running water during most of the winter. I've had to learn how to be flexible."

He grimaced, then pulled the pot closer to him. When he straightened up, he shot her a strained look. "How about some privacy?"

Ellen glanced out the window at the swirling snow. "Shall I wait outside?"

He scanned the single-room cabin and sighed in resignation. "The least you could do is turn around, Miss Coster. Or go in there." He pointed to the curtain.

"Of course." She drew a deep breath.

Ellen waited until she'd stepped into the bathroom area before she released the breath she held. Now that he was conscious, she reminded herself not to turn her back on him. Whether he was Hank or not, he was still a stranger, and she still had to be wary of strangers.

After several moments she pretended to examine her hair while angling the antique hand mirror until she had an unobstructed view of the proceedings going on behind her back.

Jack remained on the floor as he struggled into the stretchy underwear bottoms. Inching the material up his lean, taut legs, he finally got to the point where he had to stand. He hopped over to the bookcase to brace himself while he tugged on the pants. One knee buckled, and he wore a stunned look as he clutched at the bookcase.

"Jack, are you all right?"

"N-not exactly."

She pivoted, skidded around the furniture and got to him, throwing her arms around him in hopes of providing the support he lacked. He swayed, then crumpled toward her. They dropped to the bed, a tangle of arms and legs. Ellen ended up on the bottom of the heap with Jack's bare chest pushed into her face.

For a moment the contact was...disconcerting—the warmth of his bristled skin against her cheek, the hair tickling her nose in a way which could be considered enticing, given another place, another time.

She fought back a sudden onset of emotions—not fear, but regret, anger. A sense of indignation for being forced to seek safety in isolation. She pushed at the man whose provocative contact made her question what seemed to be the only choice left to her for survival.

"For goodness' sake, Jack. Don't pass out."

"I never pass out," he grumbled. Prophetically, his arms weakened and his deadweight pinned her to the mattress. Just as she wondered if she would ever draw another breath, Jack roused, lifting himself high enough for her to squirm out from beneath.

Ellen sat on the floor in a disheveled heap. One tail of her plaid shirt hung out of her jeans, and a button had popped from her cuff. The sleeve dangled open when she wiped a few stray strands of hair out of her face. Hermitt pushed his way to her, licking her face and making a general nuisance of himself.

Jack groaned, then rolled to the edge of the bed to peer down at her. A look of concern flooded his unfocused eyes. "Are you all right?"

She drew a shaky breath and began to cough when she tried to answer him.

A gentle hand touched her shoulder. "Miss Coster... Ellen. Talk to me."

"I'm fine." She wheezed. "G-got the wind knocked out of me." She moved up to the bed and perched gingerly on its edge. "I thought you said you never pass out," she chided, taking another deep breath. She adjusted the rubber band on the end of her mussed braid. "Are you okay?"

Jack sat up slowly and ran his fingers through his hair. "I feel...dizzy." When he discovered the gauze that had pulled away from the cut on his forehead, he gaped at the small spots of blood on the tips of his fingers. "What the hell happened to me?" He glared at Ellen as if she was the source of his pain.

She stiffened under the heat of his harsh stare. "Don't look at me! All I did was find you."

"C'mon, you've got to know what hap—" Jack started to stand, but he paled and lowered himself back to the bed. He leaned forward and covered his face, failing to hide his grimace from her. Eventually he shifted upright, staring at the red blotch in the palm of one hand.

Ellen knelt beside him, trying to banish her own fears and force her voice to sound soothing and calm. "It's just a little blood. You'll be fine." She wondered if he noticed the uncertainty in her words.

He seemed to push back whatever memories the sight of blood evoked and tried to grin at her. "Yeah. Just a little blood." The pasty smile made a mockery of his strong face. "Funny... I don't remember doing this. Falling or whatever."

Ellen tried to give him a reassuring look, but found the tremor which shook his body to be disconcerting. Using her fingertips, she gently pressed the gauze bandage back in place. She reached over and retrieved his thermal shirt from the floor. "You need to put this on before you get cold." Stretching the neck opening, she guided it over his head, careful of his injury, then helped him into the uncooperative sleeves.

"Better?" she asked as she smoothed the material over his muscular shoulders.

"Uh-huh..." Jack focused on her arm, and anxiety invaded his expression. He looped the fingers of one hand around her wrist and used the other hand to pull back the loose flaps of her sleeve. He stared at the ugly discoloration that extended from her wrist to elbow. A dark wariness shadowed his words. "Did I do this?"

"Not really," she lied.

"Did it happen when I fell on you?"

Ellen pulled her arm away from him, tugging at the sleeve to cover the bruise. "No, not at all."

His penetrating stare tore through her. "I bet I did it to you sometime last night, right?"

She turned her head so she didn't have to see his clouded expression of regret. "Yes—but you were delirious." Ellen busied herself with the quilt, straightening the material as she continued. "You didn't know what you were doing."

Jack released a weary sigh. "Sorry," he whispered in a hoarse voice, lowering his head to the pillow.

Something in her hastened to assure him. "It's okay." She pulled the quilt over him, tucking it around his chest. "I'll make us some tea. How does that sound?"

"Good, I guess." He gripped the edge of the blanket and closed his eyes.

Ellen returned with two mugs of tea, hers strong and plain, his weak and sugary. "Jack?" she prompted. He responded with a soft snore.

"Oh, well..."

She filled the hours with mundane tasks, trying to recapture the normal rhythm of her day. What little momentum she achieved ground to a halt every time she glanced over and spotted the figure in her bed. Her sleeping guest represented an intrusion into a very private world. In some ways she resented his presence. Four years was a long time to isolate oneself from a bustling world, and she'd gotten used to the solitude.

Yet she still wondered how things had changed in her absence. The brief periods of clear radio reception served only to provide her with the basics and whet her appetite for more. She knew who the president was. She knew about the Persian Gulf'crisis, the dissolution of the Soviet Union, the earthquake in California, the ravaging floods.

It was the everyday things she'd taken for granted and, subsequently, missed the most. Several weeks earlier she had stumbled onto a forgotten cache, an old purse containing her expired driver's license. Ellen wondered if she could even remember how to drive.

Her only contact with the rest of the world came through an old family friend, George Pembroke, a forest ranger who lived nearby. He maintained the fragile but necessary link to civilization she needed for survival. It was George who refused to take a fee for delivering her supplies every month. He was the one who negotiated the agreement with the greeting card company for her artwork.

Perhaps a lesser man might not have been so honest. But George Pembroke, an old friend of her father's, couldn't conceivably be described as a lesser man. A man of great stature and even greater character, he dutifully, even enthusiastically, reported back each month on the popularity of her work, delivering an account statement each quarter, showing a healthy and increasing savings balance.

And like a surrogate father he continued to badger her about letting him take some of her manuscripts, having them transcribed and submitting them to a publisher. He always seemed to have faith in her even when hers lagged. She'd finally broken down and allowed him to take one handwritten manuscript as a test case.

She expected nothing; George expected everything. He was her lifeline, her staunch supporter, her friend. And if she intended to keep the link alive, she needed to get some work done.

Ellen tried to sit down and sketch, but her bruised arm made her fine motor movements erratic. It didn't matter;

what she really wanted to do was write. Artwork might pay the bills, but it was her daily quota of words that kept her mind active, alive, functioning. She pulled out her current project and stared at it.

The words refused to come.

She sharpened her pencil.

She stared out the window at the fog of snow and ice.

She reread the scene where she'd left off. The characters began to take hold of her imagination. To whisper. To move.

Ellen started writing.

JACK WATCHED HER.

She was either brave or foolish to turn her back on him. He didn't know which. Of course, he didn't know a lot of things at the moment... like his own name.

Yet, when she called him Jack it did have a familiar ring to it. But Jack who? From where? He stared past her and to the window, where the snow obscured the trees, the mountains, the horizon. Stuck in the middle of a storm... in the middle of nowhere. What a life.

Whose life? he asked himself, hoping for a prompt answer from his subconscious. The inner man remained silent. He drew a deep breath that made his head throb.

"You knocked the sense right out of you, didn'cha, boy?" He heard the voice as clearly as if it were his own. But it wasn't his. It belonged to a man, an older man.

His father?

Jack probed his mind, searching for some clue to the voice's identity, some clue to his own identity. All he found were mental cobwebs.

He glanced again at Ellen, who seemed anything but absorbed in her work. She fidgeted, fiddled and squirmed, spending more time erasing than writing. He wished she'd turn around; he wanted a better look at her face. But from his position, all he could really see was her long braid of hair, which danced against her back whenever she got into an erasing frenzy.

At the moment, he knew very little about Ellen Coster except that she had long hair, she lived in the middle of nowhere and she had a very nice voice.

And a pretty smile.

And was too trusting.

He closed his eyes. *Entirely too trusting.*

ELLEN PUSHED AWAY from the table and drew in a sharp breath at the twinge of pain that traveled to her shoulder. *Maybe later.*

Hermitt kicked his bowl across the room, signifying the approaching mealtime. Ellen relaxed as she fell into some semblance of a daily routine. After she fed her dog, she toyed with her own supper, wishing Jack were awake so she could ask him about the world beyond her mountain. Then the absurdity of her thought struck her. *What does a man with no memory know about current events?*

After cleaning her dishes, Ellen shoved another log in the fireplace and knelt on the hearth. She tried to warm her cold hands alternately above the heat of the flames and against the radiant warmth of her hot mug. Hermitt grunted a lazy warning, and she slapped the dog affectionately on the rump.

"Move over, you beast. Your fur'll start smoking if you get any closer to the fire." She sat down next to the Lab and sipped her tea. The stone made a cold and unyielding seat beneath her, but she ignored the discomfort, trying to bask in the warmth of the flames as well as fight sleep.

Sleep meant dreams, and unlike her written stories, dreams veered off into uncontrollable areas, taking her uncomfortable places where, many times, she didn't wish to go. She stifled a yawn.

Sleep? Right. Where? She glanced at her bed and its occupant. Inching closer to the fire, she soaked in as much heat as she could before charging across the cabin and retrieving her sleeping bag from the storage shelves. She spread the bag out beside the hearth, praying it would warm quickly.

After changing into her nightgown, she slipped into the sleeping bag, convinced it hadn't benefited at all from the proximity to the flames. As she settled into her makeshift bed, Ellen made a fragile resolution.

I just won't go to sleep.

She stared into the flames, her eyes growing heavy.

No sleep. No dreams.

A downdraft of wind forced a small puff of smoke into the room. *No fears.*

Chapter Three

A cloud of smoke hung over the bar.

"What'll ya have?" *the barmaid mumbled without disturbing the inch-long ash from the cigarette welded to her lip.*

I tried not to cough. "Beer." *I released a silent prayer of thanks when she slapped a brown bottle on the table instead of a foamy mug of questionable cleanliness. When I looked up, it wasn't the waitress but the bartender who stood over me.*

"This is no place for a lady," *he announced.*

I picked up the brown bottle and watched the moisture trickle down its smooth sides. "Maybe I'm no lady."

The laughter drained from his face. He slapped an iron grip on my arm, pulled me to my feet and hauled me through a back door. Pinning me against the wall, he leaned forward, his face a cold mask. "What sort of trick are you trying to play?"

"I don't play tricks." *I almost lost it when I made direct eye contact with him. He was a good-looking son of a gun in a sort of swaggering way.* "Get lost. I've got a job to do."

"A job? Good God! You're a reporter!"

"I'm not a reporter." I reached into my purse and withdrew the gun. "And you're no bartender." I sighted on the top button of his shirt.

"You're right." He started to reach into his pocket but slowed when I shook my head. Using his thumb and forefinger, he gingerly withdrew a small black wallet. The silver shield caught the harsh light from the naked bulb overhead. "I'm a private investigator."

I checked the badge, then lowered the gun. "Then maybe you've heard of the man I'm looking for. I've been after a guy named Henri Mortis for two months. He killed my brother."

The P.I. untied the apron that hung at his hips, wadded it and tossed it into the shadows. "Well, you blew it, sweetheart."

"Me?" I allowed the gun barrel to tip up for a moment.

"Yeah, you. I've been on his tail for a month and just about had him until you, Miss College-Coed, came in, reeking of 'setup' to everybody in the bar. However, I still plan to make that bastard Mortis pay for killing a friend of mine named Jeff Monroe." He crossed his arms and shot me a disgruntled glare. "This isn't the amateur hour, honey. Leave the tough stuff to us professionals."

I eyed his muscular physique, which, in my estimation, ran clear up to the empty space where his brain should have been. I pulled out my own license. "I'm a P.I., too. Name's Monroe. Jeff was my brother."

He glared at me, and his face finally softened. "You're Tess."

I nodded. "And you are . . . ?"

He gave me a faded grin. "I'm a total jackass."

I nodded in agreement. "A jackass named . . . ?"

"Blaine. Jack Blaine."

I refused the handshake he offered. "Pleased to meet you, Mr. Blaine. Now kindly put your hands up." I sighted the automatic on a dirty splotch that marred his white shirt.

"What? Wait a minute. If you were really Jeff's—"

"Shut up. You heard me, hands up. Nice and easy."

Jack's dark eyebrows drew closer as he raised his hands slowly. "You're making a big mistake."

"It's no mistake, Monsieur Henri. Up against the wall and spread 'em." I frisked him, discovering nothing except that the cocky bastard hadn't fasten the top stud of his jeans. Typical male.

"Turn around. And keep your hands on the top of your head."

"Tess, you've got to believe—" He stopped. A cold hatred emptied his eyes of all other emotions as he glanced beyond me.

I knew the ploy. "Sorry. I won't fall for that old trick." The moment after I spoke, I felt the icy cold metal of a blade press against my neck.

"I'm very disappointed in you, Miss Monroe." The real Henri Mortis wrenched the gun out of my hand. "To confuse this jerk with me? And here I thought you were a professional like your late brother. But since you've proven you're not a worthy opponent, I have no other choice but—"

I shifted my weight and threw him off balance, wedging an arm between his lethal fist and my neck. The lights went out. In the darkness, I managed to slither out of his grasp, vaguely aware of a gunshot, of someone's grunt of pain and of being slammed to the ground. By the time the cobwebs cleared from my head, the lights were back on.

"I almost had him," Blaine complained, reaching down a helping hand, which I ignored.

"We," I corrected. "And there's still a chance I can catch him."

Jack dabbed at my neck, where Henri's knife had left a small cut. "Hey, are you sure you're okay? You're bleeding."

"Fine and dandy," I snarled. "Now leave me alone."

He feigned surprise. "Is this any way to treat the man who just saved your life?"

It was bad enough he had the audacity to rest his hands on my shoulders, but to touch my cheek, pretending to remove a smudge? Some story. And in all honesty, I shouldn't have been surprised that he had the nerve to kiss me.

But what really shocked me was that I had the unmitigated gall to enjoy it. I was just beginning to relax and really get involved when he suddenly broke off. Right when it was getting good....

The next thing I knew, he spun me around and pushed me back toward the wall. Over his shoulder I spotted Henri, slumped against the doorway with one arm raised. I expected the sound of a gunshot, but heard nothing but the whistle of wind from the flash of silver coming toward us.

Jack flinched, then paled, struggling to keep his weight from pinning me to the floor as we slid down the wall together. When I saw the knife hilt protruding from his back, I knew how much his protective measure had meant.

"Jack!"

He opened one eye. "S-sorry, Tess."

Panic coursed through me like the blood seeping through his shirt. "Don't die, Jack! Please!"

He drew in a shuddering breath. "Maybe next time..."

Silence. Dead silence.

No more next times...

JACK ROLLED FROM THE BED to the floor with a fluid movement when he heard her screams. Scanning the room from a crouch, he discovered Ellen, writhing in her sleeping bag. A sense of relief flooded through him, easing his thundering heart, but not his pounding head. She was evidently caught in the throes of a bad dream.

"Ellen, wake up." Moving closer to her, he used one hand to fend away her clawing fingers as he shook her shoulder. "C'mon, you're having a nightmare."

"No, Jack, you can't die—" her voice dropped to a whisper "—I love you."

Jack swallowed hard. "Ellen...wake up!"

She awoke with a start, wearing a look of absolute fear.

He tried to dilute her emotion with a reassuring smile. "It's all right. It was just a bad dream."

"D-dream...it was just a—" She sat up abruptly, then wrapped her arms around her knees. "But it was so real!" She moaned. "It was the same horrible dream all over again. He threw a knife in your back. I thought you were dead!" The glow from the fire highlighted her pale cheeks with a golden wash.

Jack restrained himself from touching her face, swallowing the surge of emotion that appeared from a hidden depth within him. He tried to blame his sudden shiver on the cold night air that permeated the cabin, not the fact that he was awakened from a dead sleep by a woman's screams.

After a moment she straightened and looked around, as if reassuring herself she was in a safe place. She pushed loose strands of hair out of her eyes and released a sigh. "I hate nightmares, don't you?"

He nodded, then shifted uncomfortably as a cold chill slithered down his spine.

Ellen offered him a poor imitation of a smile. "Look at us. Both shivering in the dark. We ought to get back to bed."

Together. Jack drew in a sharp breath. Where had *that* thought come from? He assumed he barely knew the woman and yet the idea of taking her to bed seemed natural. Almost a matter of the next logical step.

Maybe I do know her.

He stared at Ellen, suddenly feeling as if he was on the verge of breaking through the barriers stonewalling his memory. She acted as if she had never met him before, but somehow, deep inside, Jack began to feel as if it was a lie.

Why wasn't she telling the truth?

Every snatch of memory that filtered through his perforated mind included her: the way she moved, how she laughed, her delicate scent. It was maddening to be on the verge of remembering, then lose it all in the next moment.

The fire sputtered, and a sudden flare of light revealed the tension in her face which the darkness had hidden. The truth hit him. This wasn't a woman in love. This was a woman fighting fear—of him.

"I... I think I'll try to stay up for a while." Ellen squeezed her eyes shut and turned away from him as another violent tremor rocked her body. "Maybe I can think of something better to dream about."

Jack moved to the edge of the bed. His head pounded with more fury as he struggled to make sense of the facts as he knew them. However, the connection between memory and reality seemed oddly blurred, reducing his collection of facts to a single revelation: *I don't know a damn thing about myself. Or Ellen.*

"You don't have to stay up on my account," she whispered, shattering his train of thought.

"I can't go back to sleep."

"Your head hurts?"

"Uh...yeah." The cabin swallowed up his unspoken questions in an oppressive silence.

After a few moments Ellen's voice finally broke through the shadows. "Do you want some aspirin?"

"No. Thanks." Mere aspirin wouldn't begin to interrupt the rhythm of pain that assaulted his temples. A nameless, formless recollection flashed before him, disappearing as soon as it emerged. Perhaps the sledgehammer which pounded in his brain was loosening some of the memories and allowing them to float free from his subconscious. He waited, hoping he'd have a second chance to remember something—anything. His name, the reason why he was there, the reason why sometimes she seemed so familiar to him. Anything to fill the void which was his memory. After a long wait, the words tore loose from the back of his mind.

"Ellen, do you know me?"

She took a deep breath before answering. "No."

"Then why do I think I know you?"

"You don't."

"C'mon. I know what I feel." The huskiness of his own voice surprised him. She offered no reply and he continued. "I was in your dream, wasn't I? You called my name. You said...you said you loved me."

"It...was only a dream. A nightmare. It was someone else. Someone else named Jack."

His body tightened in response to the way she said his name. Stretching down from the bed, he grazed the material of the sleeping bag with the tip of his finger. She lay only a few tempting inches away from him. It would be so easy to reach out to her, to stroke the silk of her skin, to memorize her features by the sensation of touch alone. He wanted to wind her long braid around his hand and pull her closer.

Why couldn't he remember the sensation of being undressed by her? The feel of her hands sliding into his waistband and trailing down to his hips? The visual image sent a stab of longing through him as sharp as any blade.

Her face. It should evoke so many definite memories. Her tentative smile, her pained concern, even her tears...

The void that should be filled with memories haunted him with its emptiness. Somehow Ellen had to be part of the void. If she would only admit it.

Jack listened to the uneven rhythm of her breathing and realized belatedly that she was crying.

He slipped out from beneath the covers and knelt beside her. Even in the shadows of the night, he could see her face twist in uneasy remembrance. He hesitated only a moment before raising a hand to touch her cheek in reassurance. "It was only a nightmare."

She trembled beneath his simple gesture, her eyelids fluttering. "A n-nightmare. You're right." She sighed.

Jack pushed away the thoughts of propriety that demanded he keep her at arm's length. With little else but companionship in mind, he took her hands in his.

"Stand up," he ordered gently.

After a moment of hesitation, she complied, allowing him to lead her to the bed. She remained stiff as he coaxed her beneath the covers and slid in next to her. It evidently surprised her when he did nothing more than wrap his arms around her.

After a few moments of silence, during which Jack could sense her distrust, Ellen relaxed, nestling next to him for warmth if nothing else. She sighed and shifted even closer, her fears evidently purged, then settled into a remarkably easy sleep with her cheek against his chest. When he shifted so he could lean against the headboard, she didn't wake.

Jack studied her face from his awkward vantage point. He stroked the length of her heavy braid. Somewhere in the back of his mind he remembered someone else with a braid. A braid which he had slowly undone, slipping his fingers between the strands and slowly combing the tight ropes of hair into a loose, shimmering cascade. Hair he mussed when they began to make love.

A memory?

A dream?

Or merely wishful thinking?

The significance of her dreams worried Jack. Dreams could be a matter of a fanciful imagination, or memories of things past.

The impact of her words echoed in his mind.

A knife in your back.

An uncomfortable itch danced between his shoulders. Hoping not to disturb Ellen, he snaked a hand down the neck opening of his thermal shirt, trying to reach the irritated spot on his back. When he discovered the ridge of the thin scar above his shoulder blade, his stomach twisted in an angry knot.

Oh, hell.

TANTALIZING AROMAS penetrated the heavy fog of sleep that blanketed Jack's mind. The odor of bacon released a flash of memory that passed by too quickly for him to recognize, but the sensation finished waking him up. He stretched and rediscovered a host of aching muscles.

"Good morning." Ellen's quiet voice carried above the sizzling noise from the stove.

"Morning." His words were slurred by a sour taste in his mouth. He sat up and ran a hand through his sleep-tousled hair. His headache had subsided to a tolerable roar.

"I hope you don't mind soup for breakfast. I'm afraid I don't keep a big variety of foods around here, and I think you should stay with liquids for a while." She turned back to the stove.

"Sounds fine." *Sounds nauseating.*

Jack made a wavering beeline to the curtained bathroom, where he found a claw-footed tub, a chipped porcelain sink and an old-fashioned high-tank toilet. Once he relieved himself, he stumbled back to the bed, where he found his jeans neatly folded and waiting for him. He slid the dry, stiff pants over his legs, praying his energy level would hold out and he wouldn't relive yesterday's embarrassment of passing out in nothing but his underwear. Feeling just a bit stronger, he stood to finish the job. The sound of the grating zipper filled the cabin, and he looked up to catch Ellen as she gave him a quick, hooded glance.

"Coffee?" she asked.

"Yes, thanks." He started to get up, but she shook her head.

"No, just stay there. I'll bring it to you. How do you like it?"

He paused and stared blankly across the room. *How in the hell do I like my coffee? Black? No. Sweet? Yeah... very sweet. With lots of cream.* "Uh, two creams, three sugars."

She stiffened and pivoted to look at him. "T-two creams and..."

"Three sugars," he finished. Jack watched her face drain, then flush with sudden color. "Ellen, what's wrong?"

"N-nothing. Nothing at all." She turned her back to him, hiding her reactions.

"Ellen . . ."

"It's . . . it's just an unusual way to drink your coffee."

Jack started to speak but realized she'd shut him out. He fumbled with the buttons of his shirt, which swam in and out of focus. Ellen startled him when she shoved the mug toward him, heedless of the hot liquid that sloshed onto his leg.

"Here." She retreated to the stove.

"Thanks." As grateful as he was for a shot of caffeine to jump start his sluggish system, her change in attitude bothered him. Their fingertips brushed while he accepted the coffee, and he felt her hand tremble.

In fear?

"Ellen, did I say something wrong?"

"No." Ice edged her single word.

Jack grimaced at the taste of the pale, syrupy-sweet coffee, then glanced up over the rim of the mug to find her gaze trained on him. He lowered the cup, offered her a wan smile and tried to take another sip without gagging.

"Something wrong?" she asked, dividing her attention between him and something beyond the door.

He swallowed, allowing himself the latitude to make a face at the taste. "I'm sorry . . . I can't drink this. My memory is so full of holes I can't remember even the most basic things."

"Like what?"

He tried to grin, but the aftertaste of the coffee turned his expression into a scowl. "Like, I think I take my coffee black."

Her face lost some of its pinched look, and she released a shuddering breath. After a moment of silence, she gave him a small, relieved smile. "Let me get you another cup."

As he leaned back and waited, Jack knew he had passed some test of hers, but he had no idea how or why he was being tested in the first place. Beneath the surface of his hostess's gracious poise, he sensed a deep layer of fear. Last night he'd assumed her anxiety could be blamed on the lingering nightmares. But hadn't she overcome her doubts about him? At least in her subconscious? After all, she'd fallen asleep in his arms.

During their uneventful breakfast, he caught her staring at him with an uncomfortable look during odd moments. His headache returned halfway through the meal and he gave up, returning to bed. The pain sapped his waning strength, and he slept.

Turbulent snatches of memories tugged at the corners of his dreams, sending them off on wild tangents.

Faces without names.

Recollections without reason.

Memories of a dream lover with a single braid . . .

Chapter Four

Jack woke up in a sweat, his gaze raking across Ellen without the light of recognition. She placed a cool hand against his damp, flushed face and winced at the heat radiating from his bristled cheek. Draping a wet washcloth over his forehead, she offered him a reassuring smile to hide her panic.

"I'm hot," he complained. "And wet." He fixed a glassy stare in her general direction.

Beneath her apprehension, a small pang of sympathy arose. "I know. You were running a fever again and it just broke."

"Good. I—" Jack started to sit up but deferred to the restraining hand she placed on his shoulder. Settling back onto the pillow, he groaned and pressed the heel of his hand into his uninjured temple. "Everything hurts."

"Everything?"

He nodded then winced. "My head hurts." He flexed his neck, then rolled his shoulders. "My back hurts, my legs hurt. I feel like I tangled with a grizzly and lost."

"I think it was more like you lost against a mountain."

"Mountain?"

"The best I can figure, you injured yourself in a fall." She managed a half smile until she glanced into his eyes.

Yesterday they had appeared brown, but today they possessed a decidedly green cast. She swallowed hard. *Green like Hank's?*

Oblivious to her internal struggles, he reached up and placed a warm hand on her arm. "I know I asked this last night, but it's still bothering me. Are you sure we don't know each other?"

"What do you mean?" Her stomach tightened.

Jack stumbled over the words. "I mean, it seems like we've known each other for a long time. Not just a couple of days."

Ellen broke loose from his grip and adjusted the washcloth on his forehead. She prayed he would simply close his eyes and save her from being the object of his sharpening gaze. "Sorry." She dared her trembling hand not to reveal her fear. "I've never seen you before." *At least I'm sure that part is true.*

"Are you positive?" He probed his bandage gingerly. "I can't shake the feeling that I know you, or maybe knew you in the past."

Faced with little other choice, she relented to his insistent eye contact, trying to keep her voice low and unemotional. "You don't know me." She searched his face for a hidden glimmer of recognition, but she found his brown-green eyes to be undeniably honest. Confused but honest.

Hank had been equally good at hiding his thoughts from her. The night he tried to kill her, he had looked up with the same sort of open, uncomplicated expression plastered across his face. He knew she'd fall for the air of innocence.

One more time.

But that time she didn't, and Hank's answer to her rejection turned out to be, "If I can't have you, nobody can."

She spent the six months following the incident waiting to testify at his trial. Once Hank was found not guilty by reason of insanity and institutionalized, she lowered her guard. But she discovered he could use that same innocent-looking expression of his to fool the experts, too. He eventually won his release with the help of a slick lawyer, naive parents and some well-greased judicial palms.

Ellen parried his threats with injunctions, but his cunning, wealth and madness triumphed. It was a lethal trio from which she had little protection.

So Ellen ran and kept on running until she found her mountain hideout.

Isolated. Safe. Alone.

Until now.

Now, things had changed. She was no longer alone. No longer safe.

Ellen looked over at the dark-haired man stretched across her bed, a man with no memory other than an unshakable feeling he knew her. Was he Hank? Had Hank finally gotten to the last stage of his revenge?

If so...

Jack shot her a confused half smile, then closed his eyes.

Drawing in a shaky breath, Ellen glanced at the notebook she'd left on the arm of the chair.

Oh, Tess. What would you do if you were me?

Her strong alter ego always met danger with panache, romance with passion and life with an unflagging *joie de vivre,* succeeding in the very same world Ellen had been forced to abandon. *Tess would protect herself. That's what she'd do.*

Ellen sat on the floor beside the bed.

Unsure. Uncertain. Unprotected.

She watched him carefully, to make sure he'd really fallen asleep. Once she was positive, she stole into the kitchen area, wincing when the drawer scraped open. Inside it lay the knife—the only real weapon in the house. Holding it by the worn wooden handle, she contemplated its deadly edge.

Could I do it? Could I actually use this to defend myself?

She jumped when she heard a noise. Staring toward the bed, she watched a hand reach up and brace against the iron headboard. She caught her breath, trying to come to grips with her sudden panic. The knife tumbled from her hand and embedded itself in the floor near her shoe.

Jack jerked in reaction to the sound, turning to see its source. His bleary gaze dropped to the knife stuck in the floor. "What happened?"

Her heart lurched painfully in her throat. "I...uh...I dropped a knife. Go back to sleep. It's all right." She trained her attention on him while she bent to retrieve her weapon. When her fingers closed around the blade instead of the hilt, it bit into her hand, the painful sensation slicing through her control and her palm with equal efficiency. She released the knife with a gasp and examined the thin cut. A line of blood formed in the incision.

"Did you cut yourself?"

She waited, expecting the amount of blood to match the stinging fire of pain that creased her palm. It was easy for her to equate fear with pain, and the combination of the two made her weak in the knees. She leaned against the sink, fighting a wave of tears.

Suddenly she became aware of a presence beside her.

"Do you need a bandage?" He stood beside her, supporting himself with an elbow on the counter, straining to focus on her injury. "Jeez, you do. That's bad."

When he reached for her hand, overwhelming terror returned to replace the phantom pain. "No!" She stepped back from him. *Where's the knife? I've got to get the knife!*

Jack seemed totally oblivious to her anxiety. "Let me help you. It'll be hard to put a bandage on, one-handed. I can—" He stopped and stared at her. "Are you all right? You look as bad as I feel."

His pale smile evoked opposing emotions within her. Something akin to attraction dared to battle with what should have been an overpowering sense of dread. *Weak, Ellen. You're so weak! Don't fall for the package. You know what's inside.*

When he reached down and pulled the knife out of the floor, Ellen closed her eyes, unwilling to watch the final blow. At least there were no innocent bystanders this time.

Just a murderer and his victim.

The oppressive silence of the cabin absorbed the pounding of her heart.

"Ellen?"

She opened her eyes.

He offered the knife, handle first. "Better take this before I drop it." His pallor grew. "I think I stood up too fast."

When Jack carefully placed the weapon in her trembling hand, hilt first, her sinking feeling stopped its downward spiral. She studied the patterns of light reflecting in the blade.

She had expected death. And she'd received gentleness.

Her conscience climbed back from the numbing depths of resignation as she watched Jack sag toward the counter. He leaned against the sink and cradled his head in his hands. Ellen released some of her apprehension when she recognized his posture of pain. The desire to help him replaced the fear. She wrapped a dish towel around her hand.

The words came after a moment's hesitation. "Let me help you back to bed."

When she reached out to place a supporting arm around his waist, he waved off her help. "That's okay. You just take care of yourself." Jack turned and began to shuffle back to the bed. "I made it over here by myself," he mumbled. "So I'll take the responsibility of getting myself back." He grimaced when he reached the bed. "I just thought if I could do something to help you, then I wouldn't feel like such a damn invalid."

Ellen pushed back the curtain that formed the bathroom. She returned with the blue metal box of supplies.

If he was aware of her discomfort, he chose to ignore it and instead, tended to her cut. He unwrapped the towel and pried open her clenched fingers, revealing the bloodied slash in her palm.

He said nothing as he squeezed a blob of first-aid ointment on the wound, then covered it with gauze. After anchoring the bandage in place with strips of white tape, he turned her hand over and pressed her knuckles to his lips. "All better, now?"

His hooded gaze and devilish grin bored a hole through her reserve and her heart quickened. Fear or attraction? Ellen wasn't sure which. Indecision made her pull her hand away.

Concern replaced his smile. "Why are you frightened of me?" he asked in a hoarse whisper.

A chill brushed down both of her arms. "I'm not f-frightened."

He reached up to touch her cheek, but dropped his hand before she could flinch. "You're a bad liar. I know something's bothering you and I'm fairly sure that something is me."

Their gazes locked for a moment until Ellen turned away, unable to meet his intensity head-on. Somewhere, deep inside herself, she knew he could read her thoughts by merely looking into her eyes. Her chill developed into a full-blown case of goose bumps, which she tried to halt by wrapping her arms around herself.

"I'm c-cold," she said, stuttering. "Are you? I think I'll put more wood on the fire." After throwing another log on the healthy flames, she paused to stare out the window. "It looks like the snow's not going to let up."

"You're changing the subject," he said, over the sound of the crackling flames.

She sighed. *Caught.* "I know."

Outside, the wind kicked up, creating a mournful lament through the flue. A small cloud of smoke wafted into the room, and Jack inhaled deeply.

"That smells good. It almost reminds me of... of something."

She felt her spine stiffen. "What?"

He ran a hand through his hair, pointedly avoiding the bandage on his forehead. "That's the problem. It's so frustrating to be on the verge of remembering, then have your thoughts fade away like a puff of smoke." His face grew pensive and his words hushed. "Do you think anyone's missed me yet?"

Ellen shrugged. "I don't know. Maybe. Most people hike around here in pairs, at least."

"I wonder if they're worried."

"I'd guess so."

"What if they're still out there?"

"Looking for you? Not in this weather. They'd have to wait until the snow stopped."

"I don't mean that. What if they're out there, hurt? What if I was supposed to get help?" Pain etched his features.

Jack's depth of emotion triggered a sense of relief in Ellen which diluted her doubt. This man couldn't be Hank; Hank never cared for anyone other than himself, never concerned himself with the welfare of others. The "what ifs" in Hank's life only served to fuel his greed. What if his parents died and left him a million dollars? What if he could get even with everyone who had wronged him? What if he had a chance to gain control of everyone around him?

Hank had no compassion for others, but to her relief, Jack evidently did. They were two separate people. They had to be.

"Ellen?"

She looked up, seeing him in a newer, better light. "Yes?"

"Why do you live here... all by yourself?"

Ellen returned to the rocking chair, surprised at the way the answer flowed freely from her. "I write and I draw. I guess you can say the solitude is beneficial to one and the surroundings help with the other."

"Surroundings? What do you mean?"

"I never run out of subjects around here."

"Subjects?"

She nodded toward her work table. "Animals. I do pen-and-ink sketches."

"Pen and ink? Then you work only in black and white."

"Yes."

"Why?"

She leaned back in the chair and released her weight, creating a steady rocking motion. No one had ever asked her that question before. Not even George.

She shrugged. "I don't know. I just prefer ink."

"It must be terrible to spend fall up here and try to keep everything in a black-and-white perspective." He pointed out the window at the few yellow leaves that still clung stubbornly to the snow-covered branches. "The trees, those yellow ones, I...I don't remember what they're called...."

"Aspens."

"That's right. Aspens. How can you watch the changing of the leaves during autumn and not try to capture it, as an artist? How can you pass up a challenge like that?"

Ellen thought for a moment, then shrugged. "I guess I know my limitations. I can't do it, so why try?"

He continued to push. "But if you succeed, think of the sense of satisfaction it would bring."

She glanced around her stark cabin. "I have enough challenges in my life. When the weather gets bad, my biggest challenge is to survive."

"But is mere survival enough?"

Ellen planted her feet, stopping the motion of the rocking chair. "I'm beginning to get a good idea of just who you are. You must be a professor of philosophy—no, better yet, of psychology—who spends all his time contemplating the quirks of a modern society. But you're the one who should be the patient and lie on the couch, not me. After all, your *childhood* is the big question of the moment."

He resettled himself on the bed and laughed. "Okay, so I'll play patient. It all started when I was six and I got my...my d-dog." His laughter faded away as his expression grew thoughtful, then triumphant. "Ellen, I had a dog! He was black and tan and always wore a red collar and his name was..." He faltered and pressed back into the pillow, crestfallen. "Damn! It's gone."

She watched him grip the iron bed frame, his knuckles white. "It'll come to you," she offered in a gentle voice.

He shut his eyes, the energy draining from his face. "But it hurts so much to try."

"Then don't try so hard. Just sit back and relax. It'll come back to you in due time, I promise. Now get some rest, Jack."

He settled uncomfortably into the pillow and sighed. Ellen remained beside him, keeping watch over him until she was sure he was asleep. Only then could she allow herself time to study his features.

Staring at him, she made a mental sketch of his face—his high forehead, the shallow cleft in his chin, his full lips, chapped by the fever, the shadow of his beard darkening the feverish flush in his cheeks. The thin scar by his jawline had a slightly jagged edge, then straightened to a thin line. Certainly no plastic surgeon would be so careless as to leave such a telltale mark of his handiwork.

She mentally shook herself out of the grips of speculation. *Deal with the here and now, not the past. Certainly not the future.*

She searched for something to occupy her hands, something mindless and automatic. As she scanned the room, her gaze stopped at the rack where Jack's ripped jacket hung. After finding her sewing box, she returned to the rocking chair. Her needle flashed to the tempo of the gentle rhythm, slowly creating rough, puckered seams through the black material. She wasn't much of a seamstress, but it would hold together and keep him warm when he eventually needed his jacket. After all, he wouldn't stay there with her forever. A chill crept across the back of her neck, and she forced herself to return her attention to the jacket.

Once she completed the repairs, an irritating, itchy feeling replaced her sense of accomplishment. If left unchallenged, she knew her thoughts would go places where she didn't want to go. She sought distraction. She glanced at Jack, who shifted fitfully in her bed.

He flipped over and groaned, throwing an arm across his face.

Ellen stepped closer to the bed. "Jack?" He shifted in obvious discomfort, muttering something she didn't quite catch.

She repositioned the washcloth he'd knocked off. "Shh, you'll be all right."

He responded to her voice with a sleepy sigh. "I'm hot," he complained.

"I know . . . I'm sorry."

A half smile flitted across his face, then faded away as he pushed at the sheet that twisted around him.

Ellen talked to him in a soothing voice as she unwrapped the sheet and smoothed it out. As long as she spoke, he remained calm, but as soon as she stopped, he grew more agitated.

"Don't go." He reached out and snagged her wrist.

"I'm not going anywhere," she replied, easing out of his grasp.

"I like hearing your voice. It always makes me feel better."

Always? Her throat clogged on her response. "I'm g-glad. Jack. But you need to get some rest. What if I read to you?"

"Yeah. Read." He burrowed into the pillow, his fears evidently allayed by whatever role he'd given her to play. Ellen forgave herself for her impersonation. If the sound of her voice brought him some relief, then she'd continue talking. She eyed the bookcase of manuscripts, selecting one at random. Once she started a gentle motion in the rocker, she began to read in a soft voice.

THE LANTERN SWAYED gently back and forth, reflecting the balmy cadence of the ocean. The easy motion of the ship appealed to my exhaustion and soon I slept a deep, dreamless sleep. When I awoke, I panicked.

The lanterns! *I watched them cut wide arcs through the air, hitting the cabin walls with a thud. The shattered glass chimneys dropped in shards to the cabin floor.*

The deck rose to meet me as I stumbled from the bunk. A roar outside swallowed the voices I heard from above. The ship lurched back and forth, slamming me into furniture and bulkhead. A loud cracking sound echoed through the ship, and a wall of water poured into the cabin. I tucked the hem of my white dress into my sash and scrambled for the ladder leading to the deck. A wave of water washed me off the first rung and slammed me into a heavy trunk. The seawater turned the delicate lace of my dress a sickly brown-green, but I didn't have time to worry about a wedding gown when faced with the challenges of survival.

I made my way to the ladder again, this time wrapping an arm around the rungs to successfully meet the next wave. Climbing to the deck, I ducked in time to miss a large barrel bobbing like a cork in the water.

Jack clung to the mast, working the ropes. One sail still flapped in the ferocious winds, making an awful popping sound I could hear over the roar of the storm. I clutched a railing and called out, but the waves washed away the strength of my words.

Somehow Jack knew I was there. He turned to face me, his handsome features turned into a mask of concern and anger. He opened his mouth to yell, then looked up. The mast splintered and dropped, pulling the sail down with it. He raised his hands in a useless act of protection, then disappeared under a ton of wet, ripped canvas.

I screamed, and in my panic, let go of the railing.
The sea claimed its next victim.

JACK ROLLED OVER in bed, his mind cut loose by delirium.

The ship rolled and pitched, slamming him against the deck, which rose halfway up to meet him. He called her name, knowing she would never hear his last words. The churning green waters poured over the side rail, splintering the wooden deck and washing the remains away. He clutched at the mast to save himself from a watery death. The next wave hit with such ferocity that it snapped the mast in two and carried him over the side of the ship and into the boiling brine.

Time ceased to exist while he fought to survive. He grabbed gulps of air when the powers that be allowed him to surface. The waves pummeled his body, pushing him into debris and sweeping him away. Then, as quickly as it seemed death was inevitable, he felt sand beneath his cheek. The waves rolled him up the beach and deposited him in a shallow tidal pool. He lifted himself up and peered through the curtain of seawater that dripped into his eyes. He looked to the sea, releasing a shuddering sigh. The storm withdrew, leaving only destruction bobbing in its wake.

All was gone.

His ship. His crew.

Tess!

Why had he ordered her belowdecks? He thought it was for her safety, but that very command, retrospectively foolish, had sealed her doom. When the ship broke apart, she was below. His hand went to his chest, where he found the small cross she had given him. Somehow the thin gold chain had survived the torments of the sea. His hands shook as he fingered the only memento he had left of her. He lifted it to his lips and closed his eyes for a moment.

He staggered to the edge of the tree line and collapsed in the lush foliage.

When he opened his eyes again, two suns were rising in the east, one a reflection in a tranquil sea. He had never expected to see another sunrise. He tried to raise his hand to shade his eyes, but something weighed him down. When he turned, he felt a shock of recognition and relief course through his soul.

Tess was curled up next to him, one arm thrown across his chest and her head in the crook of his shoulder. He raised one hesitant hand to stroke her cheek, and her eyes sprang open at his touch.

"Hello," he whispered.

Tess offered him a weak smile, reaching up to place a kiss on his forehead. "Good morning."

"GOOD MORNING."

Jack opened his eyes and realized Ellen stood over him. The skin on his forehead tingled, and he wondered if perhaps she had kissed him. Or had it been Tess? *It was only a dream, you idiot.*

"Hi." His voice came out a croak, and he coughed to clear his throat. His second attempt was more successful. "Good morning." The headache had lost its cutting edge during the night, but still remained in the back of his head like a guilty memory. He glanced past her at the feeble ray of daylight streaming through the window. "Did I lose another day?"

She nodded. "I'm afraid so. How do you feel?"

"Better, I think. How's the weather?"

She shrugged. "It's snowing, what else?" She dipped a clean washcloth in the pot, wrung it out and handed it to him. "Here. Are you hungry?"

After making it to a seated position, he wiped his face, then his hands. "I guess."

"You ought to be. You've slept almost around the clock."

He pressed a damp palm to his forehead. "I don't feel as hot, as feverish."

"I woke you up several times to take aspirin and drink water." She crossed her arms. "Don't you remember?"

"No." He couldn't help but grin. "But isn't that par for the course? Par...hey, maybe I'm a diehard golfer. Anyway, thanks."

"You're welcome." Ellen came close to generating the first genuine smile Jack had seen. But as quickly as her grin appeared, it faded away with a self-conscious blush. "I'd better fix some breakfast." She moved toward the kitchen and began to busy herself with pots and pans.

"Can I do something to help?" He saw only a poor imitation of her earlier smile when she turned around.

"Don't be silly." She waved him back to the bed. "You're not that much better."

"I know, but I feel guilty about being here, taking up your time."

Ellen pointed to her bruised arm and bandaged hand. "All I have is time, right now. It's hard to hold a pencil like this."

Some unidentifiable emotion sliced through him as he stared at her swathed hand. Sympathy? Guilt? He covered his confusion by clearing his throat. "I'm really sorry about that. You wouldn't have hurt your hand if it weren't for me."

She didn't look up. "Nonsense. It was an accident."

Accident? No way. I remember the panic in your eyes when you looked up and saw me coming toward you.

But this time, when she glanced up, he saw more hesitancy than confusion. Either way, Jack decided not to push a subject she seemed so intent on dismissing. He went for the most innocuous topic he could think of. "What's for breakfast?" *Please... no more soup.*

The apprehension must have been apparent on his face. She gave him a wan smile. "Somehow, I think if I say *soup*, I'll have a full-scale insurrection on my hands."

"Hand," he said, nodding at her bandaged palm. "Let's put it this way—what are you having?"

"How about pancakes?"

He let his smile answer her. Twenty minutes later, Jack struggled with a diminished appetite easily satisfied early into the enormous meal. He pushed his nearly full plate away from him and shrugged. "Sorry."

She made a dismissing gesture. "No apology necessary. It won't go to waste. Hermitt loves pancakes."

Jack remained at the table and examined his hostess as she ate. Dark tendrils of hair escaped from her long braid and framed her face. Her clothes hung loosely on her, as if she had recently lost weight. Maybe she wore her clothes too big as some sort of camouflage. But what was she trying to hide? And from whom?

Ellen looked up and gave him another half smile. He found himself drawn to her eyes, with their range of emotions. Concern. Determination. Fear.

It was the fear that bothered him the most. It had erupted at such an odd moment, over nothing more challenging than a cup of coffee.

Coffee.

"Did you say you wanted some coffee?" Ellen paused with the fork midway to her mouth.

"Uh...no." Jack hadn't realized he'd said anything out loud. She continued to eat and he watched her closely.

Finally she noticed his less-than-polite stare. "Is something wrong? I'm...I'm not used to having someone watch me eat, much less stare a hole through me."

He blinked. "I'm sorry. I didn't realize I was doing that," he lied, turning away, then back again to meet her unemotional gaze. "Aren't you lonely up here?" he asked. "All by yourself?"

She shrugged and dug her fork into the pancakes. "Not really. I like the solitude."

"Which I've destroyed," he stated, completing the unspoken end of her thought.

"Only for the moment. You'll eventually leave and it'll be quiet again."

He scanned the cabin. "You live an...interesting life."

"It is pretty simple."

"Simple? I'd describe it as damned rustic. Antiquated, even. Living in a one-room cabin on the side of a mountain. No modern conveniences, no electricity."

She shrugged again. "I like it. It's quiet. I get a lot of work done here." Ellen pointed to the drafting table, then gave the bookcase a lingering look.

Jack got up and crossed the room to admire the sketch attached to the slanted surface of her table. "You do nice stuff." He grinned, adding, "Of course, what do I know about art? I can't remember my own name."

She covered her mouth quickly, trying to hide her response to his remark.

"Gotcha!" he said, triumphantly, pointing at her. "I knew I could make you smile."

Ellen slowly lowered her hand, and Jack could see the color that highlighted her cheeks. Her eyes lost their pained look, and her sheepish grin turned into laughter.

Jack joined her. "That sounds good. I was afraid you'd been living up here by yourself for so long you'd forgotten how to laugh."

The brief flare of amusement abruptly faded from her face, leaving her pale and drawn. "There's not much to laugh at around here."

"So I noticed."

It's not fair, he thought, watching her solemn mask of self-control slip back into place. *How can I stand to watch her be so serious, when I know how beautiful she looks when she laughs?* An awkward silence built between them, almost daring him to disturb it.

It was a dare Jack had to take. "So what's the hot entertainment around here? Solitaire?"

She turned her attention to the pile of dirty dishes.

"Go Fish?"

Ellen ignored him.

"Strip poker?"

She pivoted, clutching a plate. "What is it with you?" Her somber, ivory mask slipped, revealing a flushed anger. "I don't need anything from you. Especially not entertainment."

Her outburst caught him by surprise. Jack had expected laughter, but he got an explosion of temper instead. He bristled. "Wait a minute. I'm not trying to give you the business. I'm not that kind of guy. . . ." *I think.* "Anyway, where do you come off yelling at me? I'm just some innocent schmuck who—"

"Innocent? Don't give me this innocent crap! Some things don't change no matter what disguise you—" The plate slipped from between her fingers and shattered when it hit the wooden floor.

Jack stepped around the shards of china and grabbed her by the arms. "You do know me!"

"N-no!" She struggled, trying to pull out of his grip. "I don't... I mean, I'm not sure."

"Not sure of what?"

"I'm...I'm..." She dropped her head, then slowly looked back up at him. "For a moment...when you laughed, you sounded just like him," she whispered.

Jack released her, unwilling to add to her fear by the simple act of touching her. He took a step backward and jammed his hands into his pockets. "Him who?"

"Hank." Her voice cracked. "Hank B-Bartholomew."

Jack paused, wondering if the name would start a chain reaction in him. Would locked-up memories suddenly break loose and reveal all?

When no flood occurred, he became impatient for her explanations. "Why aren't you sure whether I'm this guy or not? Do I look like him? Do I act like him?"

"No. But..."

"But what?"

"I'm not sure what he looks like...now."

"Ellen, you're not making sense. You either know what he—"

Ellen raised a pale hand and gestured for him to stop, while she fumbled behind her for a chair.

Jack reached for her elbow, but she jerked out of his grasp. "Judging by your reactions, I don't think I want to find out I'm this Bartholomew character." When she looked up, Jack didn't like what he saw in her face. He sat down on the end of the bed. "Tell me about him, Ellen. Tell me everything."

She dropped into the rocking chair and began an immediate rhythm. Her eyes glazed as she stared into the fire.

"I was a freshman in college...."

Chapter Five

"Hank?" The empty theater magnified her voice and sent it back to her in pulsating waves. "I don't understand. There's no one here but us."

"I know." Her boyfriend squeezed her hand a bit too hard. "I can't stand the thought of sharing you with anyone else."

Ellen pulled away from him. "But you said we were going to a play. You lied to me!"

"But only for the sake of romance, Ellen." The humor in his voice died away when she tried to take a step back from him. "Don't leave, Ellen. The night and the fun has just begun." His face twisted into a steely smile which frightened her more than his initial display of anger.

"No, Hank. I want to go home. Now!" She tried to pull her hand from his grasp, but he clamped down on her fingers, causing her to flinch in pain. When she moved closer to him to relieve the pressure, he pulled her into an awkward embrace.

"You're hurting me!"

"So, now you'll listen to me?" He squeezed her fingers again for emphasis.

"Of—of course." She disguised her fear with a shaky smile, hoping to conceal the rapid calculations that filled her mind. "I'm sorry. I don't know what came over me. Of—of course, it's a romantic idea." She used her free hand to stroke his peach-fuzzed cheek, playing for time.

In the beginning of their relationship, she hadn't recognized the early signs of his instability. As his acts became less capricious and more unbalanced, she decided the relationship had been a mistake. His actions tonight merely drove the point home.

Hank released his viselike grip, but the vestiges of suspicion in his expression made her wait for the right time to make her move.

Her innocence—no, she should use the proper term—her ignorance had placed her in a delicate, perhaps potentially dangerous situation. Her only recourse was to make a well-planned, well-thought-out escape. She started with a tentative smile.

He grinned in return and seemed to relax. "Ellen, my love, I've planned a wonderful evening for us. First, dinner in a Paris café, followed by a stroll down the Champs Elysée. You do love French food, don't you?"

Her stomach churned. "Of course I do."

Keeping a firm grip on her arm, Hank pulled her down the aisle toward the stage. "I had a hard time getting the wine. I had to bribe a senior into buying it for me." He made wide theatrical gestures, playing to an unappreciative audience of one. "Why in the world does society set such an arbitrary age for drinking? Will I be any more mature at twenty-one than I am right now at twenty?" He glared at her, evidently irritated at her lack of response. "Well, will I?"

If he had said the moon was purple, she would have agreed. Ellen knew she'd do anything to keep him from hurting her again. She also realized she had to stall for time and choose the ideal moment to run. Her smile was strained. "You're very mature, Hank," she lied.

He nodded. "I know. That's why you're attracted to me. Maturity, good looks, plus an intelligence that's light-years past the other guys around here. *They* dream of scoring, cutting notches in their bedposts. Me, I consider the *romance* of making love." He paused and turned his head slightly. "We will make love, won't we?"

The curious tilt of his head, combined with the odd sound of his plaintive question, gave her the final motivation to put her plan into action.

She started with what she hoped was a seductive glance. "You're the only man for me, Hank. Close your eyes, darling."

A look of rapture crossed his face, and he followed her instructions. When he closed his eyes, she placed both hands on his chest and pushed with every ounce of strength she could muster. He lost his balance and fell backward over the theater seats, giving Ellen a chance to turn and run.

He bellowed like a wounded animal as he scrambled to his feet. Ellen ran toward the nearest door and pushed her way backstage. Scrambling through the cluster of curtains hanging in the wings, she deliberately knocked down tables and props in her wake, hoping to slow Hank down. Skirting around the rear stage wall, Ellen headed for an exit to the alley only to discover the double doors chained and padlocked. She edged along the scenery flats, trying to find the stairs that led back to the auditorium.

"Ellen, you can't run away from me!" His scream echoed through the empty building. "You can't run away from love!"

She wasted no energy with useless retorts, and, instead, clawed her way between the canvas frames, looking for either an exit or a hiding place. Stumbling against the side of a chain-link storage area, she slipped through a narrow gap between the gate and its post. She ducked into the shadows of a substantial-looking fireplace, realizing it was made of nothing more than papier-mâché and balsam.

"El-len, where are you?" He sang the words like a child playing hide-and-seek. "Olly, olly oxen free!"

Ellen covered her mouth, blocking the scream which threatened to erupt. She closed her eyes, praying her thundering heart wouldn't give her away.

His voice bounced from the shaky edge of whimsy to frenzied hostility. "I'm tired of playing this little game, Ellen. Come out here. Now!"

The room grew deathly quiet, and her fears mounted in the fatal silence. She huddled by the fireplace, interpreting every little sound as impending danger, seeing Hank in every shadow. She even believed she smelled smoke. Moments later, she heard the crackling of flames and saw the real smoke rise lazily to the ceiling.

ELLEN WIPED AWAY a tear.

"God only knows how I got out. I made it to the door and stumbled into a campus security cop, investigating the smoke."

"And what about Hank?" Jack asked in little more than a whisper.

A sudden specter haunted her, the vision of a man's face, pale beneath the soot. She remembered the fire fighter's labored struggles to breathe, the blood streaming into his face. For one long moment, two faces merged in her mind.

Not Jack and Hank, but Jack and the dying fire fighter. Ellen pushed the mental image away, daring herself to stay calm, in control. "Hank survived." She swallowed hard.

"But during the course of the fire, two fire fighters were killed and three others were injured."

Jack's face tightened.

"The next time I saw Hank, we were in court. I was prepared to testify against him, but the trial was stopped when the judge realized how sick he really was. When the prosecution recommended institutionalization, his defense team quickly agreed. After all, it meant a couple of years of therapy rather than twelve to fifteen in Leavenworth. Hank's own lawyer described him as—" Ellen shivered "—uncontrollably obsessed." While she drew in a shaky breath to calm herself, her mind raced ahead, reliving the pain and frustrations.

Obsession.

It ran in his family.

His parents were obsessed with obtaining his freedom, no matter whether he was guilty or not. Hank's fundamentalist mother had stood in the courtroom and pointed an accusing finger at Ellen, calling her a host of archaic names, the least of which were "a scheming harlot" and "that Jezebel." Hank's father kept staring at her throughout the arraignment with a mixture of disbelief and curiosity. She heard him speaking with a news reporter, saying he didn't understand his son's attraction to "a rather plain girl with little if any appeal."

Ellen still remembered Mr. Bartholomew's conspiratorial grin and his booming voice bouncing through the marble halls as he made no attempt to speak quietly.

"My boy's dated much better-looking girls than this Coster gal, ones with big—" he paused for a theatrical moment "—personalities!"

Ellen closed her eyes, hoping to erase the scene from her mind and return to the cabin. When she opened them again, she found herself clutching the rocking chair. Swallowing hard, she made herself release the worn wooden arms and try to pick up only the most essential threads of her tortuous story.

"After the fervor of the press died down, we became yesterday's news. I had almost a whole year of peace until the threats began."

Jack looked up. "Threats?"

Ellen nodded. "I started receiving roses every week. No note. After a month they came with a card. 'Thinking of you.' No signature. It continued for a couple more weeks. Then one day, I received a dozen wilted roses. I called the florist, and he told me the person who ordered the flowers specifically requested the roses be dead. When I forced the issue, the man finally admitted the order came from Dr. H. Bartholomew of the Mountain Point Hospital."

"What did you do?"

"Ignored it. What else could I do? I was supposed to be protected from his madness while he was in treatment. Some treatment. Tennis courts, gourmet food and sessions with a doctor who credited his problem to whatever was the lead story in *Psychosis Today*." She looked down and discovered her hands knotted in white-knuckled fists. "But no matter how unorthodox his treatment was, I should have been safe!"

Jack leaned forward in his seat, resting his elbows on his knees. When he looked up at her, his expression of pained sympathy seemed genuine to her.

She continued. "This went on for two more years, until I graduated from college. His parents made no effort to stop him. I don't think they ever believed he was guilty. They blamed everything on me. I was supposed to be the girl from the poor family lusting after their fortune. You see, the Bartholomews were well-off. They tried for a long time to use their wealth to buy their son's release, and I guess eventually it worked. Luckily, his court-appointed doctor stalled the paperwork long enough to warn me, before Hank left the hospital. Shortly after his release, the first bomb went off."

Jack glanced up, wearing a confused expression. "You mean *bombshell*, as in revelation?"

She shook her head. "No. I mean bomb—as in plastic explosives. When the next delivery of flowers came, I threw them out without opening the box. It was the only thing that saved my life. The bomb squad found pieces of my metal trash can over a forty-foot radius. At that point I decided it would be better if I stayed out of sight for a while. I packed my things and moved out of my apartment. That night a suspicious fire broke out near my front door and gutted the entire complex. Three people were killed and sixteen injured."

"You think Hank was behind it?"

She shrugged. "The fire inspector said it was started with the same type of incendiary device found in the box of flowers. A few weeks later Hank contacted me. I don't know how he found where I was hiding, but he did.

"It was a very strange call. He rambled on about our past and my 'betrayal' of his love. He made threats—" she swallowed the sudden wave of nausea the memories evoked "—about what he was going to do to me. I tried to put it all in context—an insane man making sick statements. Until..."

Ellen tried to continue, but her voice gave out. It usually did at that point in her memories. But this time was different. This time, she wasn't telling the story in order to wallow in self-pity, but to inform.

She tried again. "Until..." The words clogged in her throat.

Jack lifted his head and stared at her for a moment. "Until what?" he prompted. His voice was a whisper, soft, strained and sounding for a moment exactly like Hank's.

Ellen closed her eyes. *No,* she told herself. *Hank wouldn't ask me why. Hank would provide the answer, telling me all the gory details, bragging about his insight and talent.*

"Ellen?"

When she felt a light touch on her knee, she opened her eyes.

"I have to know. You must tell me."

It was the look of shock in his expression that gave Ellen the impetus she needed to continue. Pushing her feet against the floor, she began a slow, rocking rhythm. "That very night, Hank's parents died in an explosion. At first it looked like an accident, like their furnace blew up. Then the investigators started examining the scene, and they found evidence of an explosive device and a timer."

She increased the rhythm of the rocking chair to match the intensity of her story. "Nobody suspected Hank would take his anger out on them. After all, they'd helped him, supported him. Believed him. Then I realized what their death actually meant to him. All of a sudden, Hank had the financial means to make his threats come true. He had my telephone number. How long would it be until he got my address? So I ran away."

Jack reached out for her hand, but she shifted away, knowing she couldn't suffer anyone's touch at the moment.

"Ellen, how long have you been hiding here?"

She glanced up, trying to focus on him through the thin veil of tears. The rocking chair slowed to a standstill.

"About four years."

"Good God!" Jack rubbed his bristled jaw with his hand and crossed over to the window by her drawing board. After a moment of silence, he spoke in a hoarse whisper. "You mean to tell me you've lived here, all by yourself for four years, because of this one crazy guy that—" realization slowly dawned on his face "—that you think is me?"

Ellen ducked her head, unable to face him. His indignation seemed genuine, but she was still uncertain. She glanced up beneath the fringe of hair that hid her eyes and watched him.

Instead of returning to the bed, he knelt carefully beside the rocking chair, gripping the worn armrest with both hands.

"Ellen ..." His voice cracked. "Am I Hank?"

When she looked up, she found bewilderment in his gaze, but no sign of guile or deceit. No hidden agendas. If only she were positive... "I—I'm not sure." She turned away, unable to stand the sight of his confusion.

"Please, Ellen. Either I am or I'm not."

"I'm not sure," she repeated.

He stiffened. "Look!" He placed his palm under her chin and forced her to tilt her head and face him. "Look at me! I have a right to know the truth. How could you not know?"

The room spun. The blood rushed in her ears. Unwanted images flashed in her mind. She couldn't help but think the unthinkable, speak the unspeakable. "Because Hank ... he threatened to undergo plastic surgery."

Fire drained from Jack's expression. "Plastic surgery?"

"Yes." Ellen screamed the word in her mind, but aloud it came out sounding feeble and uncertain. She drew a deep breath. "He could be anybody. He could be... you."

Rocked by her confession, Jack probed the contours of his face, searching for signs of surgery. When his finger-tips discovered a thin scar near his jawline, his stomach sank. He lowered himself blindly to the bed.

"Me?" *Could it be possible?* "Plastic surgery..."

Huddled in the chair, Ellen drew her knees up and wrapped her arms around them. "He said he would return when I least expected."

The fear had drained from her eyes, leaving her face pale and expressionless. Emotionless. She remained silent for a moment, then her faint voice took up its tale. "He said betrayal had to be punished. And the next time, he'd make sure our love pact would succeed."

"Love pact?" A fist of pain slammed Jack in the chest—a pain of sympathy for her, mixed with the guilt of uncertainty.

"His love pact...till death do we part. That's what he called the fire in the auditorium." She leaned her head against her knees and sighed. "The reporters described it as a poorly executed murder-suicide attempt." She shivered. "They actually used the word *execute*."

Jack knew it was his duty to end Ellen's doubts and re-assure her of his honest intentions, but suddenly he was unsure of his motives or his principles.

Was he a jealous man, a dangerous man willing to kill his lover rather than lose her? If it was true, it would explain the unsettling, oddly familiar feelings he was having about her; he knew so much about Ellen, more than he should have learned in just a few days.

"Do you have a picture of...him?" A chilling thought made his heart lurch in guilt. *Damn...I almost said a picture of me.*

Ellen met his solemn gaze and nodded slowly. "Yes, one." She unfolded herself from the chair and shuffled to the bookcase. From behind a stack of books she withdrew a thick photo album. Leafing through the book, she peeled the plastic back on one page and pulled off a photograph. The picture of smiling coeds was folded so it didn't show one male figure on the side. She flattened down the crease and handed the photo to Jack.

"That's Hank." She pointed to a clear shot of a young man with his arm around the waist of a younger Ellen. Instead of staying beside Jack to point out the comparisons between image and reality, she returned to the chair.

Jack stared at the picture, riveted first by Ellen's youthful smile. She had been a pretty girl, lacking only a little maturity to fulfill the promise of her true beauty. Her hair was cut short, curling around her face and softening her tomboyish features. He glared at the boy touching the younger Ellen.

Could he see his own features somewhere in the earnest young man's smiling face? When Jack glanced up, Ellen was watching his reactions carefully. He turned his attention back to the picture's smirking subject. "Do I look like him?"

She merely shrugged. "From what I understand about plastic surgery..." Her voice trailed off.

He examined the youthful features, experiencing a sudden, startling revelation of his own. "I don't even know what I look like!" His voice rang though the silent cabin, and she flinched, making him regret his abrupt response.

She drew a deep breath, then rose to her feet for a second time. Reaching into the curtained bathroom, she pulled out a silver hand mirror that she shoved in his direction.

The glass oval reflected a marked difference between his weary, mature countenance and the fresh-faced college student in the picture. Jack stared at the man in the mirror, realizing he was seeing himself for the first time.

Dark hair, ambiguous-colored eyes, a relatively straight nose, an ugly bruise half-hidden by the bandage on his head. No remarkable features which would be instantly recognizable.

Hank's hair was lighter, covering his ears. What visible differences they possessed could easily have been achieved by a skilled surgeon and a bottle of hair dye.

Jack fingered the thin ridge of scar tissue on his jaw, wondering if it was a sign of an operation or merely an innocent injury. He glared at himself. The mirror served only to fuel his questions, not answer them.

"I guess a good surgeon could turn this—" he pointed to the photograph "—to this." Jack rubbed the several days' growth of stubble on his cheeks.

Ellen drew a deep breath and took the photograph from him, staring at the figures caught in a happy pose. "I knew one day someone would come. Someone who looked different, maybe even acted different on the surface. But Hank couldn't help but be the same on the inside. He could never hide the sickness inside."

Sickness...

The thought of Hank's retribution, and her terror combined with his own ignorance, coated his heart with an icy layer of regret. "I know I—" He stopped, unable to lie to her. Considering how hard she'd fought to survive, she deserved the truth, however ugly or uncertain. He rubbed the back of his neck, knowing she was probably watching him with unusual intensity.

"Ellen, I wish I could swear to you I'm not Hank, but..." He looked up to meet her disturbingly quiet expression. He couldn't speak in anything louder than a whisper. "I don't know who I am."

She remained quiet as she folded the picture and returned it to the album.

Jack knew he had to say something to reveal his new convictions, separating him from a madman. "But I *can* swear this—I promise I'll never hurt you." Pain pooled in her eyes, and he felt his heart lurch in sympathy. "I mean it, Ellen. I'm not going to become a totally different person when I get my memories back. It's not a case of being a Jekyll and Hyde, a split personality."

She drew a deep breath, then released it in a long sigh. "You can't be sure of that. Hank had two very different sides. One moment he could be loving and generous, the next moment, vindictive... malicious. After the fire he became so unbalanced, no one could guess when he would switch gears."

Loving, generous, vindictive, malicious...

Two personalities, one person.

Jack's stomach turned sour at the idea he could transform into another man with different priorities and lesser principles. And who was he to judge himself as harmless? Maybe Hank considered himself a nice guy, too.

An annoying buzz signaled the thundering return of his headache. He lay down and closed his eyes, feigning sleep until the real thing decided to rescue him from his troubled thoughts. He couldn't face Ellen, much less confront his own lingering doubts.

Jack begged for sleep. He prayed, he demanded, he pleaded...

He woke up and discovered a two-hour gap in time where neither the conscious nor subconscious world had reared its ugly head to remind him of his problems. However, his conscience returned in a rush as he grew aware of his surroundings. He was shocked to realize the groaning sound came from himself.

"How do you feel . . . Jack?" There was a deliberate pause between her question and his name. He wondered whether she was forced to make a conscientious effort not to call him Hank.

Ellen stood in a circle of soft light from a kerosene lamp placed on the kitchen table. Jack wondered if the knife was within her reach. Somehow the significance of the weapon had come to him right before he drifted off to sleep. It was her only protection from a purported madman.

"I feel tired." He ran a hand through his hair, wincing as he probed the sensitive spot.

"Does your head still hurt?"

He stretched sore muscles, testing his flexibility. "I don't think it'll ever stop feeling as if a jackhammer is drilling a hole through my skull."

"It's just like the snow—no end in sight." She nodded toward the shadowy window that reflected the glow of the lamp. "Before it got dark, it looked like another storm was coming through."

"Great."

Snow . . . suffocating, cold . . . crawling through . . . The memory faded away as quickly as it surfaced.

"Are you hungry?" She tried to cover her obvious tension with an artificial smile.

"Yes."

It didn't take a genius to know which question she really wanted to ask. He decided to save her the trouble. "And I'm still Jack, the man without a memory."

Her voice lost its false ring. "I couldn't quite figure out how to ask the question without sounding paranoid."

"Well, you know what they say—you're not paranoid if they're really out to get you." When her shoulders slumped, he sighed and leaned back against the headboard. "That was an incredibly stupid, insensitive thing to say. I'm sorry."

Ellen turned back to the stove. "At least we've established the fact I'm not paranoid. Supper will be ready in fifteen minutes."

Jack sat up, watching her move around the small kitchen. Hermitt forsook his place by the hearth and swaggered into the kitchen, nose lifted in search of a handout. As the savory aroma increased, Jack's hunger did, also.

He tried to be congenial. "What's on the menu tonight? It smells great."

"Stew and—ow!" A pan of biscuits hit the floor, and she pulled back from the stove, clutching her hand.

Jack got to her side in seconds. "What happened?"

"Burned my finger," she said through clenched teeth.

Hermitt got between them, staring at his mistress with a dog's cocked-head curiosity. She batted at the faucet handle with her elbow, but Jack reached around her and turned the water on. He pushed her hand into the numbing stream and held it there. "Just keep it there a little while, okay?"

She shivered, then nodded.

He searched for a topic to dilute the intensity of their sudden proximity. "You know, I'm surprised you still have running water, what with winter on its way."

Her bottom lip began to tremble. "W-won't last for long. Ground'll freeze. I'll have to m-melt snow."

"Let's see." Jack pulled her hand from the water, dried it off with a nearby kitchen towel and examined the burn. "It's not bad." Cradling her hand in his, he looked up in time to see an odd mixture of emotions cross her face. He understood how she felt; he had his own uneven collection of feelings to deal with, as well. Something deep inside demanded that he protect Ellen from all dangers—even if the worst threat to her well-being was himself.

"Th-thanks."

Her teeth chattered. Was it the cold water or something else just as chilling? He'd assume the best. "Don't mention it. Why don't you sit down and let me try to rescue our supper from this animal." He grabbed the towel, knelt and began to retrieve the hot biscuits from the floor, elbowing away the hungry dog. "Move, Hermitt!"

The dog backed away reluctantly.

"Not much worse for wear," Jack announced, placing the bread back on the cookie sheet. He reached for the pan and recoiled with a sharp "Damn!"

"Did you burn yourself, too?"

"Forgot the pan was still hot," he mumbled around the finger he stuck in his mouth.

"That's not how my doctor did it." Ellen led him to the sink and tugged on his elbow until his hand was plunged into the cold water.

"Jeez, it's cold!"

"Quit complaining."

"But—"

"I didn't complain when you did the same thing to me."

"I didn't know it was that cold."

"Now you know."

On the surface their bantering seemed on the good-natured side, but Jack felt a hard edge to her words. *Concern but not trust. Can I blame her? I'm not sure I trust myself.*

His enthusiasm for the meal waned halfway through, and he stirred his stew idly, hoping to disguise his lack of appetite.

When Ellen looked up from her final spoonful, she eyed his bowl critically. "Don't like the stew?"

"What?" He straightened in the ladder-back chair, feeling the wood slats dig into his spine. "The stew? It tastes fine. I just— I mean ..."

"Eyes too big for your stomach?"

He nodded, rubbing the heel of his hand over the tensed muscles at his waist. "Guilty."

"Your misfortune will be Hermitt's gain. I hope he doesn't get spoiled by it, though. It's rare he gets any leftovers with meat in it."

Jack stared at the remains of his supper and tried to hide his grimace. "I didn't think to ask what type of meat you used in this." His mind raced ahead. *Squirrel? Venison?* His stomach lurched. *Bear?*

"It's canned beef." She sighed. "From a nice mom-and-pop grocery store in Copper Springs, about thirty miles from here." She stretched over to the counter and picked up an empty can, turning it so he could see the label.

He realized she was enjoying herself in a perverse sort of way, and for some reason, he didn't mind. However, he would have been happier if he could push back the green-gill feeling that was marching through his stomach.

"You don't look so good, Jack." She pointed toward the bed. "Time to retire."

Jack stretched, finding a few more protesting muscles, including those in his stomach. He clenched his teeth together to stop his yawn. "I'm tired of sleeping. It's nothing but sleep, eat and sit around trying to figure out just who in the hell I am, and I'm bored with it!" He slammed his open palm against the table, making sharp contact between the smooth wood and the burn on his hand. "And pain!" he added with a groan. "I'm so tired of putting up with the pain!"

Ellen leaned back in her chair and crossed her arms, making him squirm beneath her solemn gaze. "Are you through?"

He stiffened, self-conscious of his tirade. "Yes." Struggling to his feet, he tried to maintain his dignity while stumbling toward the bed. "I'm going to go lie down now." A second, more urgent request surged through him. "But first, I need to..."

His hand became entangled in the curtain that concealed both the toilet and an old-fashioned footed tub from obvious view. Struggling, he freed himself in time to drop to his knees and send up a fervent prayer before being called to a more pressing need. He retched like a freshman at his first keg party.

ELLEN DECIDED her unwanted guest was capable of handling his own problems of the moment. When he finished throwing up, she offered him a drink of water, a wet washcloth and a helping hand back to the bed. He accepted all three with relative grace, evidently understanding she could give him nothing more. But it was his attempts to trivialize his health problem that really concerned her. She searched for some vague, half-buried memories of a first-aid course she completed years ago as a Scout. Concussions and vomiting...they were supposed to signify something serious, perhaps even life-threatening, but she couldn't remember exactly what.

She sat in the rocking chair until he fell asleep. With a deflated sigh, she realized she'd meant to confront him about taking his turn in the sleeping bag. After all, it was *her* bed.

Grabbing her flannel gown, she slipped behind the bathroom curtain to change. Although he was asleep, she couldn't bring herself to stand in front of the fireplace and strip off her clothes.

After she finished, she allowed herself another sigh. She was both sleepy and wired. The day had held too many surprises for her, and she needed something to help her relax. *My private stock...*

Ellen searched through the lower shelf of the pantry for her only bottle of wine. It had been a Christmas present from George, something she'd planned to save for a special occasion, like the sale of a first book. He'd even taped a corkscrew to the bottle's side. He did think of everything.

Pouring a generous amount in a glass, Ellen tasted it.

George definitely knew his wines.

She savored the flavor, wondering how long it had been since she'd had a glass of wine. It seemed like years... a lifetime ago. She finished it quickly, hoping the alcohol would hit her system hard and she could surrender to its drowsy effects. As she lowered the wick of the kerosene lamp, her thoughts shifted back to Jack.

Maybe he had a serious injury. Requiring serious attention. Maybe even a fractured skull.

Darkness draped over the cabin, releasing the harsh, rigid shadows and allowing them to join the hypnotic, flickering dance conducted by the fire.

Chapter Six

Ellen woke with a confused start in the middle of the night to find the bedroll twisted around her legs and the hearth cutting an uncomfortable ridge into her back. She listened to the silence, finding the cold stillness to be too quiet, too damning.

Standing up, she left her warm sleeping bag in order to watch her guest. He shifted and groaned in his sleep, then grew oddly quiet. Ellen watched him for a few minutes, deciding that whatever made his sleep uneasy had passed. Suddenly a single shudder convulsed his body.

Ellen's worst fears whispered their prophesies of gloom and doom. She stared at him, horrified by his look of lifelessness. Gathering all her strength, she reached out and placed a hand on his chest, expecting a deadly stillness. But she felt the deep, steady thrum of his pulse instead, which purged the worst of her fears.

He cracked open one eye. "I'm alive," he croaked. "I think."

She fumbled for his hand. "I wasn't sure—" Emotion choked off the rest of her admission.

He drew a hesitant breath, then expelled it with almost a relieved sigh. "Pain's passed for the moment. Just seems to hit out of nowhere."

"You need medical treatment, Jack. From a professional." She reached over and pushed a strand of hair out of his eyes.

"I know, but until the weather clears..." They both glanced toward the dark window. Somewhere out there the moon hid behind a curtain of snow. "I was up earlier, sick," he admitted darkly. "But at least I got some memories back."

She flinched, her nerves going on full alert. "What memories?"

"Only snatches." He closed his eyes and released a shallow sigh. "Disjointed flashes of faces, voices... I'm not sure I want to tell you much about it."

The reason was too obvious to her. *It might prove you're Hank.* Staring into the fireplace, she was mesmerized by the movement of the flames along the breadth of the largest log. The fire consumed the wood, just as fear seemed to eat away her sense of hope.

Jack cleared his throat. "I like to sail. I can remember the sensation of leaning out over the water, balancing the power of the wind in the sails. The feel of a stiff breeze, the spray of the water, the speed as you skim over the waves...."

The fire crackled.

"I remembered my dog's name. It was J.B., as in John Barrymore. That mutt was a real ham. He could make you believe he hadn't eaten in a week, even if you had just gotten through feeding him." Jack reached down and ruffled Hermitt's head. "He died when I was fourteen."

A blast of wind blew down the chimney, and the flames jumped.

"I've read *Moby Dick*. You know, 'Call me Ishmael'? With Captain Ahab and the whale?"

Ellen watched his face tighten in pain.

After a deep breath he continued. "I can remember getting in trouble when I was a little kid for stealing a pack of baseball cards from the drugstore. I can remember my mother yelling at me..." His voice broke. "But I can't remember her f-face."

Ellen touched his arm. "It's all right. You'll remember her soon."

"That's not the problem." He pushed to his elbows and shifted until he leaned back against the headboard. His voice reflected the same tension which masked his face. "Have you ever heard of Thermit?" He continued without giving her time to answer. "It's a mixture of aluminum powder and a metallic oxide like iron or chromium. Welders use it. But you can also pack it into a cylinder and add a timing device with a firing mechanism."

"So?" Her forced calmness was designed to camouflage the growing pain of fear that made her stomach clench.

Shifting to the opposite side of the bed, Jack stood on shaky legs and braced an arm against the wooden mantel over the fireplace. "It's a bomb, Ellen. A goddamn bomb and I know exactly how to make one!"

"It doesn't prove—"

"The hell it doesn't!" he thundered, pivoting to face her. "Why would I know how to make something like that if I weren't... him?"

Ellen moved next to him, a gesture she supposed she couldn't perform if she truly believed he was Hank. "Other people know how to make bombs, Jack. Chemists, police, people in the military. Knowing how to make a bomb is *not* the same as making one." She read the doubt in his eyes and touched his hand lightly. "Just because I know the principles behind making a Molotov cocktail doesn't mean I've ever made one before."

Jack pulled away and stared at her in shock. "My God! You're defending me—I mean him." He lowered his voice. "Why?"

Why? she repeated to herself. The answer was obvious. Either he was Hank or he wasn't. It was a black-or-white situation. No shades of gray. He couldn't be half-Hank. Half-guilty.

Uncertainty crept in.

Could he?

"I don't know," she admitted, voicing her doubts in the most honest way she could. She crossed over to the familiar comfort of her drawing table. In the flickering shadows, she found a soft eraser which she kneaded between nervous fingers. Things always seemed to make better sense when she was around her drawing board. That's where things *were* always a matter of black and white. No rosy-tinged futures. No bloodied pasts. Just a monochromatic present. One of fearful anticipation as she waited for eventual death.

"Ellen . . ."

"I'm desperate," she whispered. "If I believe you're Hank Bartholomew, I'm going to have to prepare myself for death." She spun around. "And I'm not ready to die."

He held on to the mantel with a white-knuckled grip. "That's a damned foolish way of looking at things."

"It's the only way I can keep my own grasp on sanity."

"By bending reality to suit your purpose?"

"I'm not doing that." The gummy eraser became soft and sticky in her fingers. She dropped it on the table, wondering if her instincts were becoming equally pliant.

Jack took an unsteady step toward her, gesturing with open palms. "Then what are you doing? Rationalizing your doubts?"

She stared at him. Hank would always cross his arms when they argued. But Jack's body language said something totally different. Could Hank's subconscious mind really be so adept at masking the intent behind the guise of another identity?

He stopped beside the drawing table. "I think you're afraid to face your fears."

She bristled. "At least I know what my fears are. You don't even know *that* much. And when it comes to facing fears, you sure as hell don't know the half of what I've faced!" Her raised voice reverberated through the small cabin, only to be overpowered by a louder noise. A heavy chunk of snow slid from the roof, and the rafters creaked in relief.

Jack glared out the window. "If we keep on yelling like this, we're going to start an avalanche."

Ellen saw a sudden element of macabre humor in his observation. She released a short, brittle laugh. "I can just see the headlines. Mountain Lovers Perish in Each Other's Arms in Deadly Avalanche. The problem is the newspaper would conveniently neglect to mention our hands were around each other's throats."

His face darkened. "Don't do this."

"Do what?"

"Try to change the subject with a sudden attempt at humor." An awkward silence followed in the wake of his observation. He was right and she knew it. A few moments later, Jack shattered the uneasy stillness with a few simple words. "Were you and Hank…lovers?"

Ellen sighed, fighting an unwelcome bout of memory: Hank's repeated attempts at seduction. "No. We never made love." Suddenly a scene of Tess's life exploded behind her eyes, becoming as realistic to Ellen as any of her bona fide memories. The past and the future blended together for a volatile moment.

Ellen lived a solitary life, experiencing vicarious thrills through the exploits of her alter ego, Tess. In the absence of her own real life, Ellen allowed herself to be entertained, perhaps even distracted, by Tess's fictitious adventures. But Ellen realized Tess was only a fictional character. Good ol' Tess, who always won her man. And that man was always Jack, the fictional Jack.

But the real Jack was slowly integrating himself into the fiction, taking over the role of the fantasy Jack, bringing a new edge of reality to what had only been harmless fantasies before.

When the dream lover spoke, Ellen and Tess both heard Jack's voice. When Tess touched her Jack's face, she discovered the same thin scar on his jaw that the real man had. Although Tess hadn't made love to Jack yet, when she eventually did, would she discover the same—

"Why didn't you two make love?"

Ellen stiffened. "Isn't that a little personal?"

"Not if I'm Hank." His flat voice spoke a truth Ellen didn't want to acknowledge.

It took her several minutes to build the nerve to speak. She'd told him so much already. Why not finish what she'd started? She took a deep breath. "I was eighteen, impressionable, inexperienced, young. Too young to deal with the emotional responsibilities of sex, of making love."

"Yet you were mature enough to realize your own limitations?"

She shrugged. "I was innocent, not stupid. Hank wanted to change my mind. He badgered me constantly, wanting me to make a sexual commitment to him, but I knew it wasn't right—not at that point in my life. Maybe somewhere deep inside I knew he wasn't the right man. But

Hank loved challenges and, because I was a challenge to both him and his manhood, he thought he loved me.''

Jack braced himself against the stone as he slowly sank down on the hearth. He picked up the fireplace poker and began to shift the logs. "Did you love him?"

"I thought I did for a little while."

"Until he tried to kill you?" Jack shot her a hardened glance, his fist tightening around the handle of the poker.

Ellen stared at him, discovering an expression of his she'd seen before. She covered her frightened response with her hand and moved back until the drawing table dug into her spine.

Jack's angry look dissolved into confusion. "What's wrong? Why are you..." He followed the trail her gaze burned to his hand. The poker fell to the stone hearth with a sharp clang. "Ellen. I didn't...I mean...when I said..."

"You're left-handed."

He looked down at his empty fingers, still curled around the nonexistent handle. Realization sank in after a few seconds. "Hank?" he whispered.

She nodded numbly, watching his face reflect a multitude of emotions.

Finally his face grew stiff with determination. "That's it. I'm getting out of here. For your sake. For your safety." He struggled to his feet and started toward the door, pausing at the coatrack where his newly repaired jacket hung.

"No! Don't leave, Jack." The words took Ellen by surprise, a blurted truth that reflected the desires of an inner woman Ellen didn't realize could exist outside of fantasy.

"Why not?" he asked, battling the sleeves of the coat. "Do you really want me to hang around here until I change back into Hank and—and kill you?"

"Jack—"

"Why don't you start calling me Hank? I need to get used to the name." He wrestled with the boot, trying to balance himself as he pulled it on.

"Jack, please." She crossed the room in a few steps and grabbed his arm. "Listen to me! I don't think you're Hank."

The boot hit the floor with a loud thud, and he caught himself just as he was about to lose balance and fall. The anguish in his face tore at her heart, releasing a flood of emotions within her: sympathy, sadness, attraction. . . .

He looked up at her with a pale face and indeterminate-colored eyes. "Are you willing to take that chance on me, Ellen? To put your life on the line?"

Ellen felt herself pulled toward him. She ached to relieve him of the responsibility of the past and the future. His only obligation should be the present.

He gripped her by the shoulders. "I said, are you willing to stake your life on me?"

Jack was touching her. She should be frightened but she wasn't. "Yes," she whispered. "Yes, I am."

He released her. "Why?"

"Why? Because if you and Hank share a single, common thought, you'd be like him—a cold-blooded bastard, self-serving, greedy, treacherous—" she swallowed before adding the final and most important description "—unbalanced." Ellen brushed the tips of her fingers across his cheek. "Do you understand what I'm trying to say to you, Jack? Hank wouldn't care. He would lie, cheat or steal to get what he wanted. The only things about you which remind me of him are physical attributes. And that's too vague a connection to worry about."

"What do you call the other things? Coincidences? I'm left-handed, I have hazel eyes—"

"I could go to Denver and find a thousand other men who are left-handed, have hazel eyes and—"

"And who can build a bomb from scratch?"

"Yes," she lied. "And build a bomb from scratch!"

Another sudden sound interrupted them. They both listened to the rafters groan as a layer of snow slid down the fire-warmed roof. Their gazes locked for a moment and stayed that way until Jack broke away, tearing off his jacket. "Why are you willing to put so much faith in me, Ellen?"

She waited for divine inspiration, having no real logic to back her reasoning. Where was the thunderbolt that would arrive from the heavens with a message of revelation pinned to its side?

All Ellen could see was the reflection of the fire in Jack's eyes. Warm, honest, caring eyes. Eyes that were more brown than green. At the moment.

The thunder was no louder than an extra heartbeat. "Because I like you, Jack. Whoever you are...I like you."

Ellen returned to the cold sleeping bag, pointedly turning her back to him. By deliberately placing herself in a vulnerable position, she hoped to prove her faith in her decision.

To Jack.

And herself.

She closed her eyes and listened to every sound. Jack made little noise as he shuffled across the wooden floor to the bed. The box springs made a metallic protest as he lay down. He shifted several times, releasing one hushed sigh before he grew quiet.

Ellen fell asleep listening for the next sound.

A VAGUE, BUT INTERESTING, aroma filled the air. Groggy, Ellen sat up in the bedroll, trying to focus both her brain and her eyes.

"Good morning." Jack stood by the stove, gesturing with a spatula. "I hope you don't mind that I made myself at home. I looked through your supply area and found a new toothbrush, which I stole. And then I got hungry. Want some breakfast?"

"Uh…yeah. Sure." She tugged at the zipper of the bag, trying to free herself. Sliding her feet into the slippers warming by the fire, she adjusted the red flannel gown and joined him at the table. Before, she hadn't thought once about her mode of dress. But now, in the faint morning light, she felt self-conscious.

He grinned. "Hope you don't mind. You tossed and turned so much last night, I decided not to wake you. I figured it wouldn't bother you if I got my own breakfast. I made plenty," he offered between mouthfuls.

"Plenty…" She surveyed the mess on the counter: three mixing bowls, two skillets, four wooden spoons, a spatula and a measuring cup, all of it splattered with batter and dusted liberally with flour. Ellen sighed, then joined him at the table, sitting at the chair he held out for her.

"May I suggest the specialty of the house? Pancakes?" He brought his fingers to his lips like a proper French maître d'. "They are *très magnifique.*" He paused to lick a bit of batter from his forefinger. "Very *très*. And unusually *magnifique*. Right, Monsieur Hermitt?"

Ellen looked down at her dog, who had a streak of flour across his black snout.

Jack heaped a daunting amount of food onto her plate. "Hermitt was my official taste tester. Right, boy?" The dog wagged his tail and looked ready to volunteer for more duty.

Ellen dribbled maple syrup over her stack, mindful that half her month's rations of butter, flour and syrup had likely disappeared into that morning's meal. If the snow kept up, they'd have to plan their food consumption more carefully. She watched Jack resist one of Hermitt's finer begging ploys. "Looks like you got your appetite back. I'm glad you're doing better."

He stabbed his fork at a pancake, his expression growing a bit more solemn. "I'd feel better if I could get back more memories. Only new thing I remembered was how to cook."

"It's a start." She didn't mind savoring his newfound talent; he was, indeed, a good cook. Yet she couldn't help but wonder if his memories about cooking included a few basic instructions on how to clean up.

He gave her a grin over his next forkload. "And before you say anything, I'll admit I do remember something vaguely about placing dirty dishes in a sink full of soapy water."

"And scrubbing, rinsing and drying them, too, I hope." She wondered if his good humor and returning appetite signaled some physical recovery. "Has your headache gone away?"

He nodded. "For the most part. Oh, by the way, you're almost out of firewood. I can go out and chop some, after I finish breakfast."

"That's not necessary. There's plenty of wood out there, already cut. All I have to do is carry it in."

He swabbed the final morsel of pancake around his plate, soaking up the last drops of syrup. "I can handle it."

Ellen pushed back her chair and stood. "No."

A flash of disappointment crossed his face. "Why not? I'm feeling much better now."

"And you're going to stay that way. You can play doorman for me if you like, but I'm getting the wood." She reached up to the coatrack, grabbed her jacket and started putting it on.

"In your nightgown?"

Ellen looked down at the red flannel material that extended beyond the end of the jacket and sighed. She grabbed the clothes from the back of the rocking chair and slipped through the bathroom curtain. Emerging minutes later, she made a point of ignoring the glint of amusement in his eyes, as he held out her gloves and hat.

The wind had blown a heavy drift against the side of the house, and she struggled to shoulder the storm door open. The lean-to shed sheltered the wood from the worst of the snow, allowing the split logs to stay relatively dry. After four trips, the inside bin was nearly full, and she headed out for one last load. Jack held the door open for her, giving her a stiff doorman's salute every time she passed by.

Ellen tried to pick up one particular log, but found it frozen to several other pieces of wood. Wedging her hands between the two largest pieces, she attempted to pry them apart. When the ice finally broke, it took her by surprise, and she lost her balance. Her arm hit the house with a dull thud. Making a face, she rubbed her smarting wrist, then bent to retrieve the fallen wood. Suddenly she heard a scraping noise and looked up in time to receive a faceful of snow falling from the eaves.

Jack laughed when she turned toward the window, her face covered in snow. Wiping it away like a character in a silent movie, she collected a chunk of snow from her shoulder and formed a good-size snowball. He read her lips. "Laugh, will you?"

The snowball splattered against the glass pane of the door. Jack smiled. "Missed me," he taunted. She was bending down, probably arming herself for a second strike, when he heard a creaking noise. A huge sheet of snow and ice slid down the roof, slamming into her back and burying her under a cold, white blanket.

One moment she was there.

The next, she had disappeared.

Jack waited, expecting her to rise from her icy prison. When she didn't appear, he acknowledged his worst fears by rushing outside. Ignoring the biting cold, he scrambled to the pile and pawed through the snow, searching for her. He found the broad plane of her back and dug her out. Fear clogged his throat as he rolled her over. A layer of ice and dirt clung to her slack face. "Ellen!"

She opened one eye and squinted at him before she spoke. "Don't say a word. Not one d-damn word."

Jack gave her a quick nod, trying to suppress his relieved laughter. "I understand." He strained admirably to keep a straight face.

Ellen declined his offer of help and struggled to her feet. She stubbornly insisted on walking into the cabin under her own power. Once she stepped inside, she stripped off her jacket, displaying a layer of snow that covered her shirt. She shivered as she began to brush off the wet slush.

"You're cold."

She glared at him. "H-how obs-servant of y-you." The chattering of her teeth blunted her attempt at sarcasm. Her fingers shook as she began to unbutton her shirt.

A gentleman's code of honor should have told him to turn around. Watching her slip out of the shirt, Jack wondered whether he was a gentleman or not. Just when he decided he might possess a degree of propriety, she revealed a light cotton undershirt that provided her with a modest level of coverage.

Without the camouflage of the heavy sweater, she seemed overly thin. The ruffles of her long flannel gown had hidden the sharply defined bone structure to which the thin undershirt now clung. He covered his surprise by shoving the quilt in her direction.

"Th-thanks" she said, pulling it around her shoulders.

"Here." Jack steered her toward the fire, sympathetic to the uncontrollable tremors that continued to rock her. He remembered how cold a person could feel. He waited, fighting the urge to take the next step in their indecisive relationship.

Don't rush it. For God's sake, don't rush it.

Ellen stood on the hearth, hunching toward the fire. Hermitt wandered up and tried to nudge his way closer to the warmth by pushing his cold nose within the folds of her wrap.

Jack swatted the animal's rump. "Move it, dog." Hermitt growled, then moved away, giving Jack a tilted glare.

The quilt shook as Ellen held her trembling hands toward the fire. "C-can't get warm," she complained.

Jack moved behind her and unbuttoned his shirt. The blood roared in his ears, yet his voice remained low and even. "Come here." He reached around Ellen, removed the quilt and pulled her next to his bare chest. He wrapped his arms across her body, and for a brief moment she remained stiff and unbending. Then she molded to him, absorbing the warmth he was so willing to share. Her tremors eventually subsided, and he felt his own body begin to react to her nearness.

But somewhere in the back of his mind the ghost of Hank still lurked. Jack knew her... from somewhere. He knew her strengths, her weaknesses, but just as a familiar thought came within reach, it slithered away, mocking him.

She shivered again, and he knew it wasn't because she was cold. A delicate feminine perfume rose up, riding the waves of sudden heat that passed between them. Glancing at him for one quick, veiled moment, she managed a small smile which cut through his reservations like a razor—neat, exact and with surprisingly little pain.

"Warmer?" A flame began to burn in the center of his body, matching the intensity of the real fire before them. The allure of the heat captivated his imagination and transformed half-formed thoughts into full-fledged desires.

"Yes. Thank you," she whispered, turning in his arms.

Her bottom lip quivered, and he could feel the racing rhythm of her heart. Erotic images danced through his head, moving to an age-old tempo. Pulse became impulse, and he acted on the desires of the heart.

Jack bent toward her, aware of how her lips trembled beneath his. Slowly, gently, he searched for a sense of recognizable intimacy in her response. He brushed her cheek gently with his fingertips in an unassuming gesture of familiarity. Pulling her closer, he touched his lips to hers again, generating an electricity between them that took him by surprise. His initial reaction was to pull away and hide his hardened response to thoughts of passion.

Jack couldn't remember ever feeling like this before. The newness of the sensation ripped through him, exposing a sense of desire he didn't know himself capable of feeling.

But he was a man, and there had to be things a man couldn't forget....

He kissed her.

Ellen accepted his initial passion, magnified it and returned it. Encouraged, he allowed himself the freedom to act and react. Like a young man experiencing his manhood for the first time, Jack explored. He discovered warm flesh that reacted to his touch, the sensation thrilling him as much as it seemed to please her. Her simple actions elicited complicated responses in him, and his desire mounted.

They ascended to the next level of sensuality, searching for ways to please each other. Then, using his instinctive skills in the basics of lovemaking, Jack proceeded to the next plateau. He led her to the bed, where they fell back on the quilt. He pulled at the neck of her undershirt to reveal one smooth shoulder. When his lips brushed her exposed skin, she arched toward him. Her hands seared his bare chest, teasing him with both their innocence and their experience. She tugged at his shirt and he obliged, removing and tossing it to the floor.

Growing bolder, she used both hands to draw a broad trail down the hard muscles of his chest to his waist. Her fingers taunted him, tracing a path around the waistband of his jeans. When he reached to unfasten the brass stud at his waist, Ellen captured his hand, twining her fingers in his.

"No...not yet."

He groaned in spite of himself, allowing self-doubt to surface for a minute. But instinct used an erotic flood of sensations to wash away his momentary flare of guilty ignorance.

Ellen lifted his hand to her lips for a gentle kiss on each fingertip. Then she leaned forward and whispered in his ear. "That's my job...."

Slowly, provocatively, she worked down his zipper. He closed his eyes and rested against the pillow, waiting with trembling anticipation for her to finish. She pulled at the denim, sliding it from his hips. "This is the second time I've undressed you."

He open his eyes and stared at her. Overwhelming desire robbed him of any response.

She positioned herself on her knees at the end of the bed, dressed in her jeans and the thin undershirt. "Now it's your turn." She beckoned him with a gesture and seductive glance.

He moved to his knees in front of her, then lowered his head to kiss her. The taste was intoxicating. Caught up in a sudden surge of emotion, he began to remove her clothes. At the same time, he succeeded in stripping himself of all doubts, releasing himself to act on the pent-up urges that were fighting to control him. His body shook when he discovered the tantalizing sensation of flesh against flesh.

Instinct.

Insight.

Intuition.

He didn't know what to call the inner force that guided him in a way his conscious mind couldn't. He had no memories to direct him. No comparisons to make. No guidelines to meet. No limits to his imagination. No end to his desire.

The ferocity of his newfound feelings made his heart thunder and his blood roar. Ellen responded with an intensity of her own, taking him by surprise with the strength of her fervor.

She became everything to him.

Unquenchable and wanton, demure and yielding.

Seduction became a joint effort, a matter of action and reaction. He gave, she received. She offered, he accepted. Enraptured pleasure and ecstatic pain built like a fever, growing hotter until the moment when he could suffer no more.

He had to speak. He had to call out her name. To make her his, forever. The first love. The best love. The only love. His body and soul screamed simultaneously.

Ellen moaned, then shuddered in his arms, her body quaking with the same involuntary tremors that rocked him. Consumed by the effort, his fever broke. Yet absolute consumption merely turned his fiery passion into glowing embers, less intense than a flame but just as hot.

He realized the act of making love had become the ultimate demonstration of Ellen's trust and acceptance of the man named Jack. It relieved him, freeing him from the burden of proof. He knew he wasn't Hank, if merely for the fact Ellen wouldn't make love to Hank. He knew his name was Jack because that's what she called him in the throes of their climax.

Simple, solid reasoning.

She stretched against him, and he could feel the reassuring beat of her heart. In the warmth of her arms, pain faded to no more than a bad memory, relegated to a forgotten corner of Jack's mind. Spent, exhausted and experiencing a sense of total surrender and triumph, he was content to hold her and let his mind wander.

Images flashed behind his eyes, fleeting glimpses of faces and snatches of voices.

"I love you."

"I can't live without you."

"I won't live without you."

"You won't live without me."

And the last, an undeniable threat . . .

"You won't live . . ."

Chapter Seven

The cabin looked different to Ellen.

She forgot all about the days when the walls closed in on her, overlooked the austerity of the simple furnishings. She failed to remember the chilling cold that seeped through the cracks in the floor during the long, harsh winters. She dismissed the periods of soul-crushing loneliness.

All because of Jack.

The heady success of passion had overcome all obstacles, giving her a new rose-colored perspective on life and love. Jack offered her a chance to replace bad memories with new ones. Memories of tenderness, of desire, of a level of fulfillment she had always assumed would be beyond her reach.

Safely immersed in a newfound cloud of satisfaction, she released a sigh of contentment. Jack reacted by tightening his arm around her, an act that quickly fanned her spark of interest into another flame of desire.

Embarrassed by her insatiability, she was nonetheless ready to join with him in intimacy again. She ran a hand through the hair on his chest, toying with muscles that flexed beneath her touch. Just as she thought he was about to respond to her invitation, he shuddered, released her and turned his head away.

After years of emotional and physical sterility, Ellen felt
herself plunge from the dizzying height of triumph to the
depths of despair in the space of one heartbeat. All of a
sudden, she was forced to relive a young girl's insecurity
when it came to love, real or perceived.

Not love, she corrected herself.

Passion.

Sexual attraction.

Her heart sank lower. *Lust.*

Fear threatened to fill the space where her sense of contentment had resided only moments before.

Jack gave her a pained smile as he leaned over and
placed a chaste kiss on her forehead. Ellen wasn't sure she
was ready to hear the answer, but she asked the question
anyway.

"Is something wrong, Jack?"

"Nothing, really." He seemed distant and distracted. "It
was just a bad dream."

"But you weren't asleep."

He shrugged. "A bad daydream, then."

She, of all people, understood how the subconscious
could overrule someone's thoughts, even when awake.
She'd suffered the same problem on more than one occasion. An unchained imagination accounted for several of
the misadventures of Tess and Jack.

He ran a hand over his bristled cheek, then gave her a
more assured smile. A moment later it deepened, as if he'd
banished the thoughts that had interrupted his concentration. When he pulled her closer, she tried to match him,
curve for curve.

"Hmm...you feel good." Jack toyed with her braid,
holding it beneath his nose. "You smell good." He played
with the rubber band that bound the end of her hair, tugging it from the braid and shooting it across the room. "I

should have done this earlier." Combing his fingers through the unraveling braid, Jack turned the tightly woven strands into shimmering, crimped waves of hair. "Sit up for a minute."

When the quilt slipped and uncovered her, she felt no shame. The absence of embarrassment surprised her.

Jack arranged her hair so it fanned out over her shoulders. He moved back to admire his handiwork. "Beautiful." His voice was little more than a whisper. "I could live in a place like this forever if it weren't for one little thing."

"What?"

His provocative smile bordered on the wicked. "You need a hot tub up here."

She grinned, feeling the heat begin to grow between them again. "I came to that conclusion a couple of years ago."

"How often do you have to pull yourself out of a snowbank and warm your chilled toes by the fire?" He reached under the quilt and gave her foot a quick tickle.

She motioned for him to come closer, then splayed her hand against his chest. "As I recall, sir, my toes weren't the only things that were cold." She fingered the muscles flexing beneath her palm. "But I thought your way of handling my problem was... sufficient."

"*Just* sufficient?" He brushed the hair from her shoulders and began to trail kisses across the back of her neck. He spoke, sandwiching each word between kisses. "But think about combining the two—you and me—in a hot tub...."

When she groaned, she had no idea whether it was in response to the mental picture she had of making love to Jack in a hot tub, or to the captivating sensation of his lips warming her.

"I have a tub." Ellen managed a strangled whisper. She leaned back as a wave of overpowering desire made her gasp for air. "We can . . . heat the water. . . ."

He gently pushed her against the metal bed frame, imprisoning her against the headboard. "How long does it take?" He didn't wait for an answer. His lips captured her total attention, melting her control.

"Too long . . ." she whispered.

ELLEN WOULD HAVE STAYED in bed with Jack all day if Hermitt hadn't whined to be let out. She got up and waited at the door impatiently, hopping from one foot to the other until he bounded back into the cabin, leaving messy tracks across the floor. Forgetting about their guest, Hermitt jumped onto the bed and shook the snow off into Jack's face.

Jack ruffled the dog's fur. "You sure do know how to bust up a guy's good time, dog-breath. If you think you're protecting her virtue, let me clue you in." He dragged the big animal closer and spoke in a stage whisper. "You're too late!"

She shifted her robe to cover her bare legs as she sat on the bed, scratching Hermitt under the chin. "You're no protection, are you, boy?" The dog buried his nose in her hand, and his tail started a new tempo.

Jack shook his head. "Don't be too sure about that. He became more than a bit territorial with me this morning. I thought he might decide to bite first and ask questions later."

"Hermitt? Bite you?" She giggled at the mental image. "He might lick you to death or asphyxiate you with his terrible doggitosis, but I really doubt he'd bite."

"Oh, c'mon, Ellen. Cut my buddy here a little slack." Jack gave the dog a resounding thump on his solid flank, resulting in a series of enthusiastic wags. "You might be surprised what a guy could do if properly aroused."

Ellen's eyebrows went up at the word *aroused*. She waggled her finger in Jack's grinning face. "Oh, no, you don't! We've been in bed all day, and I still have chores to do!"

"Chores? Like what?"

She stood and placed one hand on her hip and used the other to stab in Hermitt's direction. "Chores, like cleaning up after this beast." She turned and pointed to Jack. "And after you, too!"

"Me?"

Ellen nodded toward the kitchen table. "Don't you remember the big mess you made in my kitchen with your Julia Child impression?"

He threw back the quilt to reveal a bare torso. "I'll help—"

"No." She gestured for him to remain in bed. One look at his nude body would prevent her from concentrating on absolutely anything else. "Even here, the regular rules still stand. You cooked. I'll clean."

Jack draped the quilt over his lap, leaned back against the iron bed frame and laced his fingers behind his head. "Nice rule."

She forced herself to ignore him as she cleaned up the breakfast dishes and planned for their evening meal. Somehow lunch had been lost in the shuffle, forgotten as other appetites were being satisfied.

Ellen's sense of contentment manifested itself in music, and she started humming as she plunged her hands into the cold, soapy water. She heard the bedsprings creak as Jack stood. Sneaking a glance over her shoulder, she admired the view as he dressed. She kept humming, hoping her uninterrupted tune might camouflage her growing interest.

Watching him dress was nearly as provocative as watching him undress. But neither was nearly as much fun as undressing him herself.

Jack looked up after snapping his jeans. "Ellen, what's the name of that song?"

"The song? I don't remember." She turned back to the dishes, wondering if her curiosity had been too terribly obvious.

"I'm sure I know it." He began to hum the same tune, eventually breaking out in song. Ellen stopped to listen to his clear tenor voice as he completed the verse. When he reached the chorus, he crossed the room, doing his best imitation of a leading man in a Broadway musical. At the end of his performance, Ellen applauded, trying to blame the soap for the tears in her eyes.

"Ta-da!" Jack stretched out his arms. "Hey...a standing ovation? For me? I wasn't *that* good, was I? Or is it my reward for remembering the words?" He moved closer, reaching around her for a dish towel.

"Yes. And here's your reward for staying in key." Ellen took the towel from him, tossed it to the countertop and pulled him into her arms. She put all the passion and warmth she could into the kiss they shared. Jack responded with equal conviction. When she broke away from him and returned to the sink, she could feel his gaze centered on her back.

"I can get a kiss like that just for singing?" Awe filled his hushed words. "In key?"

Ellen glanced back over her shoulder and grinned. "Hank couldn't carry a tune in a bucket!"

Jack watched renewed animation light her eyes, and the truth hit him: it was over. The ghost called Hank Bartholomew had been banished forever by nothing more than a simple melody.

No more wondering, no more worrying.

Jack no longer had to prove who he wasn't, but could now devote his time and energy to discovering who he *was*. He reached to kiss her again, but Ellen pushed him away, giving him a good-natured smile. She thrust her hands into the bubbles. "If I stop now, I'll never get back here to finish the dishes."

He leaned over and placed his lips dangerously near her ear. "Would that be so bad?" he whispered.

"You." Ellen poked him in the chest with a soapy finger. "Over there." She pointed to the fireplace. "Make yourself useful. The fire could use some attention."

After he tucked in his shirttail, adding a couple of grumbles for emphasis, he crossed to the fireplace. Tossing a log in the fire, he warmed his hands in the heat of the flames. "So, who do we think I am? Jack...who?"

Ellen laughed. "I have absolutely no idea. There's Jack Sprat, Jack Knife and of course, a jack-of-all-trades."

He thought for a moment. "You mean like Mac-Guyver?"

"Ooh, I loved that show. Is it still on?"

"No. They ended it, but on the final episode they finally revealed his first name—hey!" Jack felt a weight lift from his mind. "Listen to me! Current events! I'm getting some memories back." He closed his eyes, hoping to be rewarded with another event which would signify the return of memories.

A few moments later he opened his eyes, sighing at the emptiness. "And what do I remember? Details about a defunct TV show."

She shrugged. "That's okay. It'll come back to you soon. Maybe you'll find out you're involved in the entertainment world or something like that."

"Actually, it's the investigating portion that sounds familiar to me."

She stacked the dishes on the drain board. "If you're some sort of investigator or troubleshooter, it might explain your memory about the explosives."

"You're right. I hadn't thought about that." He scratched his chin, then ran a finger down his bristled cheek. "I wonder if I've ever tried to grow a beard before."

Ellen struck a theatrical pose, gesturing with the dish towel. "A handsome, bearded stranger lurks in the shadows. He tails the criminals through their own element, the streets of an impersonal city."

Jack snorted in laughter. "Probably more like Mr. A hires me to follow Mrs. B because he thinks she's having an affair with Mr. C."

"Aha!" She wiped her hands on the towel as she approached the fireplace. "The famous Alphabet Divorce Case."

Jack pulled her into the circle of his arms. "You know what, lady? You have a helluva imagination."

Her heated smile made the blazing fire seem redundant. She snapped the towel at him. "Of course I do. It's been honed by four years of solitude." An impish light grew in her eyes. "Of course, you could ease my mind with one small piece of information."

"What?"

"What *is* MacGuyver's first name?"

Jack paused, closed his eyes and waited for the answer to pop into his head.

"Well?"

He grimaced. "I don't remember."

Ellen threw the towel at him. "Yes, you do! You just want to keep me in suspense, to keep me a prisoner of your ignorance!"

"Well, what about me?" he countered. "I'm a prisoner of the weather." *And love.*

The thought stopped him cold.

Where did that *come from?*

If he loved her, how could he expect her to invest herself in a relationship with a man who didn't even know who he was? In a blinding flash his world changed; it became absolutely imperative for him to discover his identity. Ellen deserved to love a complete man, one with a background and memories.

Oblivious of his new mandate, she stirred the fireplace ashes with a poker. "Well, Prisoner Number 4726420...I *have* to get some work done. Someone around here has to earn a living to afford all this luxury."

Jack gestured toward the drawing board. "You work. I'll take care of my own entertainment for a while." As tempted as he was to stand over her shoulder and watch her sketch, he decided to find some reading material to pass the time.

Her bookshelf was packed with book club volumes, paperbacks, and an entire shelf devoted to nothing but reams of paper, bounded by rubber bands, and wire-bound notebooks. The mystery of the notebooks beckoned to him. Sneaking a look over his shoulder, he was relieved to see that Ellen appeared totally absorbed by her work. Sure that he was unobserved, Jack chose a volume at random and settled in the rocking chair.

Her schoolgirl-style handwriting was easy to read.

How could I tell him what I felt for him? He didn't even know I was alive. All he could do was moon over

Patricia, like she was the only girl in the world. It makes me want to puke.

Jack stared at the page. *What is this junk?*

He examined the inside of the notebook cover. "My Diary— Volume 4: September 1, 1974, to April 26, 1976." Feeling a twinge of embarrassment, he shoved the notebook back into its gap. But curiosity returned, fought and won the battle it raged for his attention. Jack skipped down several notebooks and pulled out another, marked Volume 7.

November 12. If I have to conjugate another verb in French, I think I'll blow my lid. I've demonstrated repeatedly I have no aptitude whatsoever for foreign languages, so why continue to make both me and Madame Randolph miserable?

A few notebooks down he found Volume 10.

October 23. College has always represented so many hopes for me, but now that I'm here, I find it strangely lacking. I guess I expected everything to change once I became a coed. In some ways, it has. No one knows about Mom and Dad, so there's no stigma about being an orphan. I hate that word. It sounds so Dickensian.

Jack turned to a dog-eared page.

December 6. It's midnight and I'm much too excited to sleep. Phyllis talked me into attending a smoker at the Theta house and, of course, it was smoky, noisy and totally boring. That is, until one of the jocks tried to make a move on me. I thought I could handle him, but he was big and drunk and started getting rough. Then my knight came and rescued me.

It was just like a dream. He rushed up and got me away from the slob. My rescuer and I spent all evening talking on the quad. He's funny, cute, smart—and a great kisser. He wants to go out Saturday night to a really nice restaurant. I think I'll always remember this date—the night I met Hank Bartholomew.

Jack felt his stomach grind in protest. *You're not kidding.* He skipped a few entries.

January 9. We've been going out for a month now, and Hank surprised me with an elaborate picnic to celebrate. He was real understanding when I refused to make love to him. I know I'm a prude. I can't help it. It just doesn't feel right . . . yet.

March 26. Something's wrong and I can't put my finger on it. When Hank came back from spring break, he seemed different. When we go out, sometimes he won't even talk. I wonder if I should think about breaking up with him. He's too moody.

April 13. Damn Hank! He out-and-out lied to me. I don't mind if we change our plans—but this! Tomorrow, I'm telling him to take a hike.

May 5. I'm so tired of being the celebrity on campus. If it weren't so close to the end of the semester, I'd quit. I can't take much more of this. I have to go down to the courthouse tomorrow and make yet another statement to the prosecution. How many different ways can I tell the same stupid story?

July 6. Trial postponed.

August 14. Another postponement. Got to make a

decision about registering for fall semester.

September 23. First day of testimony. God help me, I have to be in the same room with him.

December 2. It's been almost a year since I met him and I'm finally free. I just wish Mountain Point Hospital weren't so close to campus.

December 23. Other girls get nice presents for Christmas. I get a four-page spread in the Sunday supplement. Newsmen are such vultures.

Jack closed the book. *Poor kid. No parents, crazy boyfriend. It's a wonder she's not totally screwed up.*

Ellen shifted in her seat, and Jack fought his guilt as he hid the notebook at his side, hoping she wouldn't see it. How could he explain his voyeurism? How could he justify snooping in her diaries and reading remarks she'd probably never meant for anyone else to see? He'd violated her privacy. He was no better than the news reporters she called vultures.

Jack replaced the notebook and pulled out a novel at random. The words he read had no meaning to him, and he began to get a twitchy feeling as he closed the book.

You shouldn't be just sitting here, boredom whispered.

You don't have time for a vacation, guilt reminded.

You have a job and responsibilities, duty chided.

Jack ran a hand through his hair. *What job? What do I do? Who am I?*

The words began to whirl in his mind, circling, blending...

Job. Responsibility. Snooping. Vultures.

I'm a reporter. A goddamn reporter. Looking for material for another Sunday supplement. "Where Are They Now?" An investigative reporter...

Investigating...

Investigator...

Just like MacGuyver. Looking for clues, evidence, information, locations—hidden locations, hard-to-find places and hard-to-find people. Like Ellen.

Why would I be looking for Ellen? No, I'd have a client. Someone who would hire me to look for Ellen. Who would want to find her?

The questions were vague and rambling but the answer was singular and clear-cut: *Hank.*

Jack swallowed hard. "Ellen . . . ?"

"Uh-huh?"

"Do you think Hank would go so far as to hire someone to find you?"

She thought for a moment before answering. "No. All during the trial, he kept arguing he could do a better job than his lawyers. He always believed he was the best at everything. Better than his doctors, better than any expert. Hank would never hire a detective. He'd be sure he could do the job himself."

He'd do the job himself. That should make me feel better—but it doesn't.

Jack found the photo album and carried it back to the bed. His heart and his feet both felt like lead. Propped up against the headboard, he started at the front of the book.

She was all freckles and teeth. A tomboy in jeans and a young heartbreaker in ruffles. School photos gave a year-by-year report on her transition through puberty. Her chubby face grew angular, turning from a pretty little girl to a classic beauty. Ellen in the school play, Ellen dressed for the prom, Ellen in cap and gown.

Then he found the picture of Hank that Ellen had shown him earlier. The camera had captured a split second of innocence on the young man's face. Hank Bartholomew looked like any other average college student, convinced of his own immortality and out for a good time. But somewhere along the line the convictions became corrupt, and Hank's overly fertile imagination emerged as a liability.

Jack stared at the picture until his eyes refused to focus. The colors swirled together like paints mixed on a palette. His eyes closed and he drifted off to sleep.

SHE WORE PINK.

Pale pink taffeta that rustled when she walked. With her hair pulled up and the neckline sufficiently low, it was the stuff to fuel a boy's dreams for nights to come.

For one special night, however, it was a dream come true. The hall was crowded, full of laughter and music, but we had eyes for only each other. Every song was played for us. Every star shone for us.

When the dance was over, we sat out in the quad. Talking, laughing, kissing and making plans for a wonderful future. Only a dorm curfew could put an end to our heaven on earth.

I stood on the steps, holding her hand until the last minute when she had to go inside. Only a thin piece of glass separated us, and she placed her hand against the pane. I matched her gesture, then watched her fade into the darkness. Racing around the side of the building, I kept a close watch on her window, waiting for a light to flare.

Her silhouette on the curtain...

Patience would persevere, and one day it would pay off. There would be two silhouettes on the curtain for someone else to watch. Then the intertwined shadows would slowly sink out of view....

SHE WORE RED.

I laughed about how she matched the tablecloth and she pouted until she saw the contents of the picnic basket. Then, she forgave me.

Bread, cheese, grapes... The dining hall cook had reassured me this was standard make-out fare. "You stick with the simple foods, son," he'd lectured. "A woman 'preciates the classic things in life, like roses. Now, you don't forget the roses if you want to impress her. Act like a man and treat her like a woman. Then you'll learn why we call it a make-out basket."

SHE WORE BLACK.

A serious, sympathetic color. I didn't like how it made her look pale and drawn. It was the sort of dress she might wear to a funeral. But this wasn't a funeral. Or was it? Instead of burying a body, we were there to bury a relationship. To make it official. Splitsville.

She'd said she loved me.... Lies. All lies.

And I hated her for making me believe in myself. Our love had given me a reason for existence, and without her what good was I? Without love there was no justification for life. I wanted to die. Right then and there. That would show her.

Death was the ultimate lesson, they said....

AS SHE GREW DROWSY, Ellen fought the sensation until it began affecting her work. Shifting the drawing out of the way, she decided she could afford a few moments to rest her eyes. Folding her arms, she rested her head in the crook of her elbow and closed her eyes. Immediately a dream caught her in its clawing grasp.

I WORE WHITE.

It was tradition, and I was never one to flaunt an established practice in society, even if this wasn't a conventional wedding.

I wore all the obligatory accessories. "Something old"—my great-aunt's antique brooch. "Something new"—my dress. The minister's wife lent me a yellowed veil for "something borrowed." For "something blue"...

The ring felt heavy on my hand, knocking my entire balance off. Maybe it was the weight of the commitment it signified that actually threw me off kilter. After all, it wasn't a rock, just a simple, microscopic sapphire buried in a cheap setting. But to me it was the Hope diamond for what it represented in love and commitment. And since the stone was blue, it fulfilled the last duty of tradition.

The minister began. "Do you take this woman to be your lawfully wedded wife? To have and to hold, for richer or poorer, in good times and bad, until death do you part?"

Jack squeezed my hand. "I do."

I answered with equal conviction when it became my turn.

"With the power vested in me by the state, I hereby pronounce you man and wife. You may now kiss the bride."

After a long, soul-searching kiss, we broke apart, still holding hands. I stared at Jack, mesmerized by the love I felt.

The minister cleared his throat. "Let me be the first to congratulate you—" he glanced down at the marriage license "—Mr. and Mrs. Hank Bartholomew."

Wearing an icy smile, the man I had called Jack tightened his grip on my hand. "Didn't I tell you, sweetheart? I got my memory back. I know exactly who I am."

ELLEN JERKED AWAKE, propelled by some hidden self-defense mechanism that wouldn't let the nightmare go on any longer. After a few moments of blind confusion, she realized she'd fallen asleep at her drawing board. She stretched, then smoothed out the paper she'd crumpled in her sleep. Glancing toward the rocker, she discovered Jack had fallen asleep, as well. He flipped restlessly on top of the covers.

"Jack?"

He didn't answer, at least not with words. Before she could cross the cold floor to the bed, she could see the fine sheen of perspiration coating his face. Evidently caught in the throes of a dream, he muttered something incomprehensible.

I hope your fantasies are better than mine. She touched his cheek. The fever was back with a vengeance, setting up a spiral of fear within her. *What's wrong with you? Why do you seem to be fine, then get sick again?* She pushed a stubborn curl of hair off his forehead.

"Oh, Jack . . ."

HE OPENED HIS EYES, instantly aware of the knife of pain that split the two hemispheres of his brain. Ellen sat beside him on the bed, dabbing at his forehead with a washcloth.

"Welcome back."

He rubbed the sleep from his eyes. "I've been gone?"

"In a manner of speaking. You've been delirious for almost twenty-four hours. You were awake part of the time, but I wasn't sure you knew where you were." She stopped to run the tips of her fingers along his fledgling beard. "Jack, I've been so worried about you."

"It's over now." He tried to get up, but the fireworks display which exploded behind his eyes convinced him to lie back again.

Ellen reached over and tucked the quilt around his chest. "No, you're not well at all. The weather's gotten much better, and I think I ought to go for help. You need medical attention."

He grabbed her wrist, then released it, wondering how many times he'd grabbed her in the past. How many times he'd left bruises. The thought of having actually hurt her made his stomach turn. "Don't leave me, Ellen. Please..."

How many times had he pleaded with her? How many times had his needs turned into demands, then threats?

"But, Jack, you need a doctor." She smoothed a damp curl from his forehead. Rising, she started toward the coatrack. "It won't take long for me to hike to the ranger station."

He could hardly catch his breath, and his heart hammered in his chest. Adrenaline flooded through him, buzzing through his veins and making his muscles vibrate like taut strings. "No, that's not what I mean. Come here and sit down. I have something to tell you."

Chapter Eight

Jack ran his finger along the quilt binding.

"This piece—" he pointed to a square of plaid material "—is from a dress you wore on the first day of school." He gently traced the square of red gingham. "And this one is part of a tablecloth from a very special picnic we had."

His voice broke as he pulled the quilt to reach another piece. "Your p-prom dress. You looked so pretty in pink. This shade..."

The pale rose-colored material shimmered in the light from the kerosene lamp. Jack heard her gasp, but he refused to watch the light cast a honey gold halo on her dark hair. If he did look at her, the expression of shock and fear on her face would be more than he could stand. "We were wrong, Ellen. So damn wrong. I am Hank." The name left a bitter taste in his mouth.

"N-no. You're not him. You can't be." She placed a shaky hand on the quilt, and he looked up to see her weak smile of reassurance. "It was just a dream, Jack."

His words were cold and flat. "My name isn't Jack."

Tears began to form in her eyes. "Maybe it isn't. But it doesn't mean you're Hank Bartholomew. You're different from him. Hank was selfish, greedy. He was sneaky and vindictive—"

"Exactly. How much more vindictive can I be? I've exploited your compassion and made you take pity on me. I know so much about you, yet you say we've never met before. Damn it, Ellen, I wormed my way into your cabin and eventually into your bed. Isn't that exactly how Hank would do it? Wait until you're off guard, then strike?"

"But you haven't tried to hurt me."

"Not yet. But don't you see? My memories are coming back, and at some point, I *will* become dangerous to you."

"I'll never believe you'd hurt me, Jack." She shifted to touch him, but he knocked her hand away.

"Don't be so damned sure. Your life depends on it."

The tears washed the last traces of hope from her face, and her sobs tore into his heart. Jack found himself consumed with a desire to comfort her, a desire he had to deny. "I want you to go for help. Tell the ranger everything, and make sure he comes back armed."

"No!"

"It has to be done, Ellen."

She lifted her head, letting the crimped waves of unbound hair fall back and reveal her ashen cheeks. "It's too dark to go now. I'll have to wait until morning."

He grabbed her by the arms, digging his fingers into her soft flesh. "Ellen, you're stalling. You were willing to go when you thought I needed a doctor."

Determination began to fill some of the emptiness in her eyes. "Maybe I was. But since I'm the one who has to face the weather out there, I'll decide when to go. And I say tomorrow."

He released her, suddenly aware of how tightly he had been holding her. He couldn't touch her again; he had no right. Jack drew a deep breath and spoke slowly. "What if tomorrow's too late?"

She ignored his question and turned to the quilt, stroking the edge of the material. "Do you know what this piece is from?" She pointed to a triangle of black fabric.

He stared at it, finding no image, no occasion in his mind associated with it. "I . . . I don't know."

"It's the dress I wore at my parents' funeral. They died on my sixteenth birthday. You see, Jack—" she pronounced his name with unusual clarity "—this is a memory quilt, and not all memories are good ones. My grandmother always told me you have to recognize the bad memories as well as the good. 'How can you know what sweet tastes like if you don't understand a little bitterness?' she used to say. She taught me you can't learn from your mistakes if you don't remember them. I've been able to deal with both the positive and negative sides of my past because I let myself remember the sad times and the glad times. The quilt documents my life as accurately as a photo album or a diary. That's what makes this quilt so important to me."

He stared at the intricate stitches that had turned a collection of scraps into a prized treasure. "Did your grandmother make this for you?"

"She finished it two days before she died. I came here a month later. She said she wanted me to remember everything—the triumphs and the tribulations. The three pieces of material you recognized were from good memories, and that's not like Hank. He always remembered the bad." Her gaze became unfocused. "Hank took great joy in reciting the list of wrongs he thought people had committed against him."

She dragged her attention back to Jack. "Now, you lie still." She retrieved the fallen washcloth and draped it across his forehead. "I'll bring you some aspirin for your headache and make you some tea."

"Ellen, I—"

"Jack . . . shut up."

The cool, soothing sensation of the cloth did nothing to ease the storm of thoughts that whirled in his head. Snatches of memories blended with each other until the mere effort of thought made his head ache even more. Early evening darkened into night, and for the first time he could see stars beyond the window.

Moonlight created a tableau of silver snow and pewter shadows with glitter-flocked branches hanging low and still. With no trace of a breeze, the only sounds he heard came from the contented crackle of the fire that hypnotized him and offered him peace.

He lost the fleeting sensation of tranquillity when Ellen lifted the quilt and slid in next to him. Before he could make any protest, she placed one finger on his lips.

"It's our last night. I just want to be next to you."

She wore red flannel. Simple, practical, prim. Yet the sensation of flannel against his skin was more intoxicating than any lingerie made of silk and lace. Jack fought against his body's betrayal, trying to push away the attraction he felt.

An attraction he had no right to experience.

But proximity succeeded in destroying the painful act of concentration. Each contact, inadvertent or deliberate, burned through his resolve. As a primal urge mounted in intensity, his physical woes diminished.

He was raging a war against himself.

And losing.

When Ellen shifted in his arms, he could smell the light perfume of her hair that made him stiffen in desire.

"Jack?"

"Uh-huh?" He couldn't trust himself to speak other than a noncommittal grunt.

"Make love to me."

Every muscle in his body contracted. "No."

"We may never have another—"

"No. Don't say it." He couldn't let her finish. He couldn't let her tell him they might never have another chance to make love as Jack and Ellen.

She lifted wet lashes and looked at him. "I'm convinced—"

He placed his hand over her mouth, unwilling to let her finish her words of misguided support. "I'm not."

As soon as he touched her, he knew the gesture was a mistake. When he pulled his hand away, his fingertips trailed over her lips, slowly, deliberately. She closed her eyes and arched toward him, sending another wave of desire to flood over his dammed-up emotions. His fingers traced a languid path down her chin and throat, then stopped at the ruffled neck of her nightgown.

The world swam before his eyes. A relentless need replaced the buzzing pain in his head. He eyed her with a renewed sense of hunger, knowing nothing short of death would prevent him from joining with her one last time....

Ellen reached down to the hem of the gown and began to work it up, but he stopped her. The quilt slid to the floor as he moved to his knees beside her. He cupped his palm around her ankle, then began to slowly, torturously push the nightgown up. A deeper form of desire seemed to knife him in the heart when he discovered the lace beneath the flannel. His hands shook, his heart raced, and his mind grew blank. Instinct overtook reason.

Silk and lace.

Fire consumed the last of his control.

Jack straddled her, his hands dancing over the edge of the material, finding warm flesh beneath. She moved with a rhythm that matched the driving tempo of his heart. He untied the thin ribbons that held the two sides of the lacy top together. He pushed away the silk to reveal her breasts, small, firm and responsive to his circling touch. He abandoned her lips and began to concentrate on the soft peaks of flesh beneath his fingers. She moaned, her hands fluttering against him. He realized she was trying to remove the last silk barrier between them.

"Not yet." He nudged her hands away, gently pushing her arms up, until they were over her head. She grabbed the iron bars of the headboard and gasped in pleasure as he used one finger to draw a path from her wrist, down one breast and to her lace panties. He pulled them slowly, provocatively down her hips. A lone cloud muted the penetrating rays of the moon.

"Please, Jack." Her husky demand made the room swirl in darkness. "Please..."

He ran his hand through the thick brush of curls, and she twisted in delight. She released the bars, and her bold hands elicited a gasp of pleasure from him.

At first their actions were orchestrated like a chess game. Move. Countermove...

But soon, strategies gave way to intuitive abilities. Love by instinct and instinct alone.

Lost in the ecstasy, he forgot everything. The pain, the anxieties, the guilt. She was sweet escape. Escape from the threat of memories he didn't want to recall, much less relive. Shuddering sensations drove away the fears, replacing them with a stronger memory to carry in his heart for the rest of his life: a mental image of his Ellen, caught in the throes of ultimate pleasure.

His Ellen.

My Ellen.

Hank's Ellen...

Imperfect images returned as swiftly as they had been banished. Accusing thoughts invaded his mind, blotting out the glow of satisfaction.

Exhausted, he struggled to breathe, knowing he'd used his meager energy reserve for a good cause. If he suddenly woke up with the rest of Hank's memories, perhaps the side of his personality that concocted Jack would remember and even claim the act of making love as his own. It might keep Ellen safe for a little while longer. He prayed it would.

Jack fell asleep, savoring the memory of their last passion.

Ellen stayed awake, haunted by the task she would have to perform in the morning.

She couldn't sit by and watch the ranger bundle his suspect back to civilization. *I'll go with them. If Jack is really Hank, the cabin will never be safe again. If he isn't, then maybe we can come back and live here together.*

Ellen ignored the voice that suggested Jack might have another life to return to. She glanced around the room, grateful for the bright moonlight that returned to disarm the shadows. *If I leave, what do I take with me?*

The shelves of the bookcase were sagging under the heavy load, half of which was her diaries. *I can live without my journals,* she told herself. Her gaze dropped to the quilt that rose and fell with Jack's even rhythm of breathing.

The quilt. If I take nothing else, I have to take the quilt. It has all the memories I need. I can leave the diaries and the stories. Tess and Jack will always live in my imagination, and I can always write their stories down again.

Ellen thought of her possible return to civilization, and panic rose in her throat. The idea of leaving the tranquillity of her mountain for the jungle of steel and glass made her shiver.

A jungle of sounds—honking horns, irate drivers, impersonal faces. Loneliness within the vast sea of people.

A jungle where the most dangerous animal was man.

THE SOUNDS OF THE JUNGLE *faded in my ears as my concentration turned to survival. I ducked into the supply tent seconds before the sentry rounded the corner. Swallowing a tide of revulsion, I removed the heavy Luger from the holster strapped to my waist. Should the situation arise, I doubted I could fire the gun. I wouldn't even have known how to load the weapon if Jack hadn't shown me.*

Jack.

I swallowed once more when sorrow unseated fear. He was gone and there wasn't a damn thing I could do about it.

A sudden noise caught my attention. It came from behind me. I wasn't alone.

Circling through the maze of boxes, I spotted a dark form leaning against one of the tent poles. At first I thought it was a sack. But it wasn't; it was a man, sitting on the dirt floor and leaning against the post. Thick ropes were knotted around his wrists and another around his chest, pinning him to the upright support.

I walked around the body, keeping my distance. A shadow covered the man's face. In the pale light I noticed a golden object dangling from a leather thong in the open neck of his soiled shirt.

Jack's cross! I almost shouted the words. The dirty S.O.B. must have stolen it from Jack after he died. I reached into my boot top and grabbed the knife.

I want to see the face of the man who killed my Jack. I slipped the broad side of the blade beneath his chin and lifted his head. He met my anger with what little life he had in his eyes.

Brown eyes with gold flecks...

Jack! My heart accepted what my mind couldn't fathom; Jack was alive!

"Jack," I whispered hoarsely. "It's Tess. Can you hear me?"

He groaned in response.

"Wake up, Jack. We've got to get out of here!" I touched his face, expecting him to feel deathly cold. Instead, his skin was hot and feverish. Too hot.

"T-Tess..." The blank stare faded and a small gleam of recognition grew in its place. "Tess?" he croaked.

"Yes, Jack. It's me." I lowered my voice, remembering the dangers beyond the tent. "We've got to get out of here," I repeated.

He looked up, and I began to see the cunning Jack Benton reappear before me. His flecked eyes came to life. "Yeah...get out of here." He looked around the tent, then returned his bronzed gaze to me. "Where are the others? Standing guard?"

"No. It's just me."

"What?" He drew a shaky breath and pushed himself into a straighter position against the pole. "You came into the compound by yourself? Are you crazy? You could have gotten killed!" His voice grew uncomfortably loud.

I raised a finger to my lips. "Shh...our compatriots are gone."

Shock flooded his face. "D-dead?" he stuttered.

I nodded. "It's just you and me, and we're getting out of here—now!" I picked up the knife, wiped the dirt from its blade and started to saw through the ropes.

"Tess..." He squirmed around to peer at me from over his shoulder. "Stop. Don't cut them. I can't...can't make *it back to the village."* He sagged against the strap that pinned him to the support post. *"Hell, I couldn't even make it to the edge of the compound. All I would do is slow you up and get you caught."*

"So..." My voice cracked along with my heart. *"You expect me just to leave you here?"*

"You have to," he pleaded. *"C'mon, Contessa. I know you've wanted to see me strung up once or twice since we've met."* His attempt to laugh came out as a cough. *"Remember the lizard in your sleeping bag? You mentioned something then about a rope and my neck."* He shot me a puffy, insolent wink.

"Jack..." Choking back another sob of emotion, I found I couldn't continue.

"Shh, kiddo. It's okay. Nothing will happen to me."

I caressed an unbruised spot on his cheek. *"I don't want to leave you here."*

"I know."

"Damn it, Jack! Are you just going to sit there? Can't you get angry? I know I'd feel better if you were mad about all this. Jack? Jack?"

His eyes flickered, then closed, and his head slumped to his chest. I stared at him for a moment, then leaned forward and kissed him. *"I love you, Jack."* I sheathed the knife and slipped it into the top of my boot, then moved cautiously to the tent flap. Before I could melt into the quiet darkness of the jungle, I heard his whisper.

"I love you, too, Tess."

"I LOVE YOU, JACK."

She rested on her elbow as she addressed the man who slept beside her. *I hope you're still Jack.*

He shifted in his sleep, rolling over toward her. A patch of sunlight brought out hidden highlights in his dark hair.

One eyelid opened, and a lazy smile filtered across his face. "Good morning. Do you know you snore?"

His grin scattered her fears to the winds before they had time to completely form. She crossed her arms and pretended to pout. "Hermitt's never complained."

"Hermitt's practically deaf."

She shrugged. "How did you sleep?"

"Better than the last couple of nights. I almost feel back to normal. Whatever my normal might be." He reached over and ran the pad of his thumb over her lips. "Thank you for last night. It was quite a last hurrah."

Last? "It . . . it doesn't have to be."

His smile faded as sweet turned to sad. "Yes, it does. You made me a promise last night, and I'm holding you to it."

"But—"

"But nothing. After breakfast you'll bundle up and take that hike."

"Then I won't eat breakfast."

"Childish semantics won't change the situation. Do you really want to hike on an empty stomach? Don't fight me on this, Ellen. Both of our futures depend on it."

"Jack . . ." Overwhelmed by a sudden desperation, she decided to make one last effort to change his mind. She shifted closer to him, capturing his mouth with hers.

He pulled away from her and shook his head. "It won't work. You have to go get help. You agreed and, if I've learned anything about you, I know you're a woman of principle. Go fix yourself something to eat. I'll feed the fire." A cold rush of air destroyed her brief cocoon of warmth as he slid out from beneath the quilt.

Logic survived the onslaught of emotion.

He was right. She could neither prevent nor even delay his transformation into Hank Bartholemew, if it was inevitable. They were trapped somewhere in the nether-world between the power of knowledge and the bliss of ignorance.

Ellen got out of bed, pulled on a robe and shuffled toward the kitchen area while Jack stood by the fireplace. She stirred the coals in the oven, hoping to warm her end of the room, and tried to make her sluggish brain choose a breakfast menu. Sweet memories captured her thoughts, and as her mind sought refuge in their nocturnal adventures, the cast-iron skillet slipped out of her hand. It struck the stove with an earsplitting clang.

"Wha—ow!"

At the sound of Jack's anguished voice, Ellen turned and watched him fall to his knees. He was holding his head between both hands, muttering his pain in four-letter words. She realized he must have stood suddenly and hit his head on the solid wood mantel of the fireplace.

Her heart pounded, but her body refused to move. There was something in his tone of voice, in his bellow of pain, that frightened her. She had to swallow a sudden surge of panic before she could speak. "Are y-you okay?"

There was no answer.

"Jack?"

"No, damn it! I'm not." Anger filled his rough voice.

A fist of fear pressed down on her lungs, and she struggled to draw a full breath. She watched him stumble to the bed, still holding his head.

He rocked back and forth. "Damn, damn, damn..." His voice grew louder with each repetition.

She stood still, oblivious to the cold which had surrendered to the open flame of terror.

"Ellen." The single word was strained, spoken between clenched teeth.

Was it his voice? Hank's? "Y-yes?"

He spoke as if he was wedging each word between waves of pain. "How long will it take you to get to the station?"

Her mind went blank.

"How long?" he raged.

She jumped at the harshness of his tone. "W-with this much snow... two hours, maybe a little more."

"Get ready." He stood, then sagged against the headboard. "Take water, food, all the stuff you'll need."

"But..."

"Get it now!" He lurched toward the bathroom, ricocheting off furniture and walls. The fear that had riveted her to the floor now screamed for her to move.

"Jack! Wait!"

Pushing away her attempts to restrain him, he pawed through her small collection of medicines. "There must be something stronger here. Something..." He whirled around, grabbing her by the shoulders.

In one hideous moment her oldest and worst fear blossomed to life. Hank was exacting the ultimate revenge; he'd taken her heart and now he was going to take her life.

But to her greatest surprise, Jack released her. He slumped toward the mirror, resting his head and forearm on the glass. His voice dropped to a near whisper. "Don't you have some sort of medicine that'll knock me out?"

"Knock you... I don't understand, Jack. Why are you doing this?"

His face darkened and he dropped to the bed. "When I hit my head, it—it loosened all sorts of memories. And what I saw..." He closed his eyes and swallowed hard. "Ellen, you've got to get out of here. Now!"

She stood in front of him, reaching out to touch him. "Jack, I'm not scared," she lied.

He tipped an anguished face down to meet hers. "I am, though. I'm scared to death." He released a shuddering sigh. "Get your stuff. Gloves, hat... Just get ready."

Ellen responded to the steel-edged urgency in his voice. She gathered her emergency pack, which contained the essentials for a winter hike, then laid out the rest of her gear.

Jack shuffled toward the bed. His quiet words cut through her concentration. "Find me some rope."

"What?"

"Rope. Get me some rope. If you don't have any medicine to keep me sedated, then you're going to have to tie me up."

A flash of pain traced a path down the muscles of her back. "No, Jack. Don't make me do that."

He bent down, cradling his head between his palms. "You have to. I know it's all going to come flooding back—any minute now. And I don't want Hank following you on the path. Just get the—" he swallowed an expletive "—rope!"

She fumbled with the clasp on a footlocker where she kept her tools and repair supplies. When the lid swung open, she immediately saw the neat coil. Her stomach soured when her mind stumbled over the proper description for it—a "hank" of rope.

"Bring a knife over here, too."

When she turned around, he was tugging on the iron rail of the foot board, testing its strength. Taking the rope from her, he cut it into two long pieces and handed back the knife.

"Make sure you put this where I can't reach it."

By the time she numbly stuck the knife back in the drawer and returned, he had knotted the rope around his ankles, lashing them to the rail. He held the second length out to her.

"N-no..." she whispered. "I can't."

"You have to." He pushed the rope into her palm. "You *have* to, Ellen."

She saw a different emotion trying to break through his forced stoicism. She watched the battle rage in his eyes. "Please don't ask me to do it, Jack."

He crossed his wrists and stretched them out in front of him. "I told you—my name isn't Jack." His voice broke. "Hurry."

She looped the rope around his wrists, following his terse commands to pull and knot.

"No, tighter."

She winced as the strands dug into his flesh.

"Now feed the rope through the headboard...around the top rail—through two. Wrap it around twice and tie it. No, with two knots." He tested his bonds. "Good."

When their gazes met, Jack turned his head. "Go."

"Jack..."

"Hurry. If I change..." He swallowed. "I might forget how I feel about you."

She jammed the stocking hat on her head and tugged on her gloves, heedless of the tears that spilled down her cheeks. She didn't like the formality of the word *good-bye,* yet she had to say it.

Aloud.

Just in case...

Ellen stood by the bed and looked down, then she bent over and kissed his unresponsive lips. Her teardrop left a glistening trail down his cheek, and she thumbed the moisture away with her glove.

"Goodbye, Jack. You'll always be my Jack, no matter who—" Her voice broke as the words spilled freely from

1er honesty. "How can I love a man who may or may not 3e the worst enemy I have in this world?" she whispered. "I don't understand how it could have happened."

Ellen paused for a moment, then turned away from him, :hooing Hermitt from the hearth. She banked the fire with ogs, hoping to fix a blaze that would continue for hours 1nd keep the cabin warm until she could hike back.

Returning to the bed, she kissed her lover one more ime. This time a tear lingered in the corner of his eye, ;pilling down to make a wet track across the bandage on 1is temple.

She gently touched the tape, allowing her glove to ab-sorb the droplet. "I love you, Jack."

Ellen swung the pack into place and headed out.

After the door closed, Jack released the breath he held. He had clung to consciousness, fighting his dizziness so he :ould say aloud the words he had held for so long.

"And I love you, Tess."

Chapter Nine

Ellen respected the treacherous nature of snow, which camouflaged the dangers lurking on and off the path. After her first winter on the mountain, she'd learned not to rely on a compass and map as much as she did her own instincts and a strong walking stick.

It was the same instinct that protested the need for the trip. She found it disturbingly easy to ignore the evidence that supported Jack's theory: Hank had been sidetracked from his vendetta only by a temporary memory loss.

Vendetta.

She had never thought of using the word in describing Hank's threat. A vendetta meant a payback, and she had never done anything to Hank to demand a payback. She usually used the word *revenge.* It had a suitably unbalanced ring to it. *Revenge, retribution, retaliation—*

A sudden misstep plunged her into snow up to her knees. *Watch what you're doing.* She stopped and probed around in the snow with her stick, using it for balance as she stepped over a hidden tree trunk. Her success was fleeting, and she tripped over a second branch and fell face first into a deep drift.

The sudden darkness frightened her, and she flailed for a minute before figuring out how to extract herself. She backed out of the suffocating snowbank, spewed out a mouthful of snow and brushed away the clumps that clung to her coat and pants.

White. Her mind latched on to the word as she fell back in step.

White gloves. Grandma Clara and her wonderful tea parties. With white gloves, dainty pink cakes and a miniature china tea set.

White shoes. Trying to cover the scuff marks on my good white shoes after Mother caught me climbing the tree on Sunday morning.

White paint. Learning the chemistry of the paints from Daddy.

White coats. The color of the coats the doctors wore who treated me for smoke inhalation after the auditorium fire.

Each step broke through an undisturbed expanse of snow, and the rhythm turned into a chant. "White... white... white..." Instinct took over when her conscious mind shut down. She lost all sense of time and distance, measuring her world only in steps.

Step. *White.*

"ELLEN?"

Step. *White.*

"Ellen, can you hear me? Ellen? Honey, what in the hell are you doing here?" George grabbed her by the elbow and led her inside the warm cabin. He propped her up by the fireplace and began to strip off her gloves and hat. "C'mon, sweetheart. Let's try to thaw you out. That's the way."

She began to grow aware of the inviting fire that crackled its welcome to her by returning some of the life to her frozen fingers. Savoring the familiarity of the rangers' station, she allowed herself a few minutes to collect her thoughts. She knew George would wait patiently for her explanation.

Finally she drew a deep breath and plunged into her story. "There's a man in my cabin," she began.

George gripped the edge of the hearth. "Are you all right? Did he hurt you?"

Ellen shook her head. "It's nothing like that. At least, not quite. He's hurt and needs medical attention."

"How did this happen?"

"He fell from one of the trails. I found him a couple of hours before the storm started."

The result of his rapid calculations stunned her. "That was almost a week ago. How's he doing?"

It's been a week? "I don't know, George." She tried to gloss over Jack's memory loss. "He doesn't remember much. One moment he seems healthy, but the next, he's running a fever and throwing up."

"Sounds serious. Can he walk, or do we need to get him out on a litter?"

"He can walk... I guess."

"You stay here by the fire, and I'll get on the radio and contact the Mountain Rescue Squad. If we can get this guy to the clearing, the pilot can bring the chopper in and airlift him to the hospital." George disappeared into his radio room, and she could hear the static turn into vague voices. A few minutes later he reappeared and shoved a glass in her hands. "Drink this."

"What is it?"

"Brandy."

Ellen had only tasted brandy once. Hank had given it to her during one of his moments of planned seduction, but she had refused to finish it after one sip. It had tasted odd, nothing like the liquid she sipped now. In a belated flash of wisdom, she realized Hank's drink might have tasted peculiar because it was drugged. Had he hoped her inhibitions could be loosened by one of his mother's many tranquilizers?

Ellen tasted the brandy once more, then drank deeply, almost wishing the drink did contain some drug to make her forget.

"Hey, go easy on that stuff. It's potent." George crossed his arms and glared at her. "What's going on, Ellen? There's something else you're not telling me."

Do I have to tell him? Yes. "I think...he...the man in my cabin is Hank."

George's face paled to an ugly shade of gray. "Good God! Did he do anything? Say anything? Threaten you?"

"No." She stood, flexing stiff fingers toward the fire. "He didn't hurt me at all. In fact, the only reason we think he may be Hank is because he knows so much about me. Things only Hank would know."

"We? You mean you talked to him about it? I don't understand."

"He has amnesia. He thinks his name is Jack."

"This is crazy! You actually told him about Hank?"

She shrugged. "It seemed the right thing to do at the time. Jack's memory started to come back in bits and pieces, and he insisted I go for help. He was afraid he might revert and become Hank again."

George planted his fists on his hips. "This is weird. You're saying this guy isn't Hank right now, but he's afraid he will turn into Hank? And he wants to protect you... from himself?"

She nodded.

"So he's just waiting for you to come back with help?"

"Yes," she whispered. "And he said for you to bring a gun."

A red flush flooded George's grayed features. "Good God."

"Please, George. We've got to get back there and help him."

"Yeah—rush back and find out he's waiting to attack both of us? No way, missy. Harlin went to town this morning on a supply run. We'll wait for him to return, then you'll stay here while the two of us check out the cabin for any traps this guy may have set. You told me yourself he was a tricky, vindictive son of a bitch." George paused and scratched his chin. "Then again, he might even decide to ambush us here. I better—"

"He can't." Ellen wrapped her arms around herself, suddenly flashing on an image of Jack, tied to the bed. She shivered. "He c-can't ambush us. He's…he's tied up. He insisted I do it before I hiked here, because he was afraid he'd revert and follow me."

George stared at her for a moment before he finally released a long sigh. "I hate to call him sensible, but it was a bright suggestion." He rubbed his hands together. "Tell you what—I'm going to hike to your cabin and check this out. When Harlin comes back, you can—"

"No!" She gripped his arm, pleating the material of his sleeve between her stiff fingers. "I'm going back with you. I can't stay here and wait. Don't ask me to, George."

He sighed. "Can you manage another hike, or do you want to wait a little while and recover?"

"I'm fine. Let's go now." She scrambled for her gloves and hat.

"Let me get my pack." When George returned, he had his coat on, his backpack in one hand and a shotgun in the other. He pulled on his gear, then slung the weapon onto his shoulder.

"I called back and put a hold on that Mountain Air Rescue chopper. Let's go." George held the door open for her and ushered her back into a sunlit world of stark white.

HE COULD HEAR NOISES, small insignificant sounds the silence amplified and distorted. With his eyes still closed, he imagined how the sound waves entered his head and bounced around the interior of his brain. Judging by the way he felt, something certainly had been bounced off his skull.

Two or three times, at least.

And I'm so damn stiff I can barely move.

A shock of adrenaline flashed through him. He was right; he couldn't move. He tested his arms, realizing they were pulled awkwardly above his head. *Ropes? Oh, hell...*

Alexander Brody opened his eyes and strained his neck to see the ropes knotted around his wrists.

A bed. I'm tied to a damn bed.

Alec twisted and pulled at the bonds, ignoring the pain in his head. Panic flooded him with new strength, but when brawn failed, cunning took over. He eyed the glass sitting on the bedside table.

It was a calculated chain reaction; he bounced against the mattress as hard as he could, which bumped the bedside table, which caused the water glass to rock slowly back and forth. When it fell to the bed, Alec shifted his weight to make the tumbler roll next to his shoulder.

Clenching the rim of the glass between his teeth, he strained backward until he could wrap his fingers around the smooth cylinder. After the third attempt, the glass shattered as it hit the iron railing.

Using a jagged shard, he laboriously sawed through the individual strands of the rope. After fifteen minutes, the final filament separated and Alec pulled his arms away from the headboard and worked the ropes off. He sat up, rubbed his wrists and scanned his prison.

A simple one-room cabin.

How long had he been there, trussed like the fatted calf?

He turned his attention to the ropes around his ankles, untying the knots. When he tried to stand, his muscles revolted and his head screamed in agony. Alec touched his throbbing temple, discovering a bandage.

"What the hell happened to me?" His words roared through the quiet cabin, and he winced at the sound, half expecting a burly mountain man to burst out of the shadows.

Alec heard a sudden noise behind him, and he pivoted, dropping into defense mode before the next heartbeat rocked his chest. His fierce gaze dropped to the hearth.

The big black dog let out a rattling snore, stretched his paws toward the fire, then opened one dark eye to glare at Alec.

Although he knew the rudiments of protecting himself from an attack dog, Alec had never used his training. Nonetheless, he prepared for the animal's next move, which turned out to be nothing more than a yawn and a sleepy but enthusiastic tail wag. Alec sighed in relief. "Good dog…er, Blackie, Midnight, whatever your name is. Where's your master, boy?" The dog snorted, wagged again, then stretched out across the hearth, ignoring his inquisitor.

A brief search proved that, other than the dog, Alec was alone in the one-room cabin. Through the window in the door, he saw fresh tracks in the sunlit snow. They led from the front porch and disappeared between the trees. Alec assumed his "host" was out doing whatever it was mountain men do in the great outdoors—hunt, trap, shanghai hapless victims. . . .

Chilled by the mere sight of the snow, Alec returned to the fire to warm himself. His attention was drawn to a drafting table, filled with sketches in various stages of completion. They were mostly of dewy-eyed fawns and fluffy rabbits, reminding him of Bambi and Thumper... the sentimental stuff women always seemed to like. He glanced at the signature on one of the completed drawings: Tess.

An explanation began to form in his mind, and its implication left a sour taste in his mouth.

Not a mountain man. A mountain woman.

Isolated, alone... love starved? The sort of thing you expected to read about in the screaming tabloid headlines found in the supermarket checkout lanes. Nothing like that could happen to him... could it? Alec struggled with his incomplete memories, remembering the fall but not the landing.

Closing his eyes, he strained to remember why he was on the mountain in the first place. A case? A client? An irritating buzz filled his head.

He ran his fingers over the edges of the bandage. What about the woman who found him? His nurse turned warden? She must have found him, carried him back to her cabin and decided to keep him. The sex-slave angle seemed a little severe, but it fit the evidence at hand. After all, hadn't he just woken up and discovered himself tied to some woman's bed?

In his mind's eye, he conjured a picture of a woman capable of dragging him to the cabin, strong enough to withstand the ravages of winter in such a rustic setting. A tough old crone with an eye for captive entertainment.

Alec swallowed hard, deciding to clear out, and leave no trail behind for her to follow. When he found a pair of familiar-looking briefs on a chair beside the bed, he ran his finger around the waistband of his jeans, and discovered a conspicuous absence.

With the sex-slave idea gaining more credence, he hurried through the cabin, trying to erase any signs of his presence. His jacket hung on a peg near the door. Fingering the puckered seams that crisscrossed his jacket, Alec glanced down and saw only one boot. *Did I lose the other one when I fell? Or did she take it in order to keep me a prisoner here?*

Desperation guided inspiration; he rummaged through the kitchen, forming a makeshift snow boot out of a plastic bag, a dish towel and the same ropes that had imprisoned him earlier. Alec took one last look around at the cabin, then struggled into his coat, praying she wouldn't come back soon.

He followed the tracks in the snow, matching them step by step. The cold crept into his stopgap boot after only a few steps, but he trudged on, thankful for the numbing qualities of the pain. Following the trail, he walked for about a half hour until he rounded a curve and suddenly heard voices ahead.

Stand or run?

Alec ducked behind a snow-flocked scrub oak and waited. Two figures came from the opposite direction, both well bundled against the cold. They shuffled up the slight incline, making clouds as they puffed in wordless exertion. After they topped the rise and disappeared completely from view, Alec returned to the trail. He began to run, paying little attention to the tracks, as a sense of panic rose from his gut.

One of the figures was a woman.

And the other one had a gun.

GEORGE PAUSED on the porch, pulling Ellen back from the door. "Honey, let me go in first and check this guy out. You stay here. I won't be long." He pumped a shell into his shotgun, then entered the cabin.

Ellen waited impatiently, wondering whether she shook from the cold or from a case of nerves. She could hear the floorboards creak under George's heavy step. *What can be taking so long?* She refused to speculate on Jack's possible transformation.

George appeared in the doorway and beckoned for her to enter. Ellen drew a deep breath and stepped inside. Her gaze settled immediately on the bed.

Empty.

The quilt had been neatly folded at the foot, and the spread turned back to reveal the worn white sheets. "Where is he?" She took a step to the side, trying to peer around George.

The ranger's face reflected a mixture of concern and disbelief. "There's no one here."

"But he *was* here."

George raised one eyebrow in a wordless comment, then made a sweeping gesture. "Well, he's not now. In fact, I don't see any signs anyone was ever here, except for you. And that worthless mutt of yours over there." He stared down at the dog and shook his head. "For God's sake, Hermitt, would you please wake up? You don't even know I'm here!" Hermitt remained asleep, oblivious to the raised voice.

Ellen twisted her gloves off, wadding them in a small ball. "I don't understand. He was here. He insisted that I—" George's condescending smile interrupted her train of thought, filling her with irritation. "Damn it, George Pembroke. Don't give me that look. You've known me for almost my entire life. I'm not one of those crazy people who make up invisible companions."

"Of course not, El." His voice was soft. "I know you have your head screwed on right. But after what you went through with that psychopath, is it any wonder you might have a bad dream every now and then?"

"He was no nightmare, George. And I can prove it!" Ellen glanced around the room, desperate to find her proof. She knew it had to be there. Somewhere.

Crossing to the kitchen, she peered into the sink, finding one set of dirty dishes there and a clean set on the drain board. She glanced at the empty peg where his coat had hung. The single boot was gone, as well.

She tore back the curtain, exposing the bathroom. Her own articles were lined up as usual on the back of the small chipped enamel sink. A single set of towels hung neatly on the racks.

"The ropes." She squatted down by the foot of the bed, looking for the ropes she'd used to lash his ankles to the rail. "The rope has to be here," she stated, her voice and her resolve wavering on the edge of breaking.

"Ellen?"

When she turned around, George held up the empty wine bottle he'd found by the sink.

"Sit down, honey. I think we have our explanation."

She refused to budge. "I didn't drink that by myself. And I didn't get drunk. This was no alcohol-induced hallucination. I know there's proof."

"Sweetheart, who are you trying to convince, you or me?" George reached out and took her hands, pulling her closer to the fire. "Ellen, you've been living by yourself for a long time, living in fear of discovery. It's got to have taken a toll on you. And no—" he raised his hands to stop her interruption "—it doesn't mean you're crazy. It means you're tired of being lonely and of being scared."

The past few days began to swim in her mind, the edges and the facts blurring together until it became hard to separate them. "Tired..." she repeated, sinking to the bed. "I *am* tired. Tired of talking to a dog that can't hear me. Tired of wondering what's happening in the world. So tired of feeling afraid and empty..." Her mind sobbed the words but her hot, dry eyes refused to cooperate.

George placed a fatherly arm around her shoulders and pulled her into his embrace. "Sometimes I wish that son of a bitch Bartholomew *would* show up here. Then I'd use that shotgun to put him out of his misery."

When she dissolved into tears, George didn't try to stop her flow of emotion with useless platitudes. As they sat on the bed together, he allowed her to cry without guilt or reprimand. She had no idea how long they sat there; misery knew no time limitations.

Finally Ellen straightened up and wiped her face on her sleeve. "Thank you," she whispered. "I needed to get some of it out of my system."

He hugged her. "Are you going to be all right?"

She nodded. "I guess so."

"You want me to stay in case your visitor comes back?"

She searched his face, wondering if he was being patronizing or sincere. "No, it won't be necessary. Go on home. I'll be okay."

"Sure?"

"Yes. You'd better go on before it gets dark."

"Okay, but I'll be back in a couple of days to check up on you." He leaned forward and placed a kiss on her forehead. "Don't get up. I'll let myself out." He paused, then gave her a tight-lipped grin. "You going to be okay?"

She nodded, unable to speak, to lie to him. She wasn't going to be okay; she was going to be miserable.

He swung the weapon into place on his shoulder, gave her a snappy salute and slipped outside.

Ellen stayed on the bed, watching the blaze die down until she grew cold. Instead of throwing more wood on the fire, she pulled the quilt up around her shoulders and lost herself in the choreography of the flames. Their hypnotic dance captivated her mind, allowing her to forget the pain, the delusions, the fears....

As the flames died, Hermitt inched closer to the fading source of heat. With a sigh of reluctance Ellen got up from her cozy berth and banked the fire with several large logs. Still wrapped in the quilt, she turned around and faced the bed.

A slash of rusty red was smeared across the pristine white chenille.

A bloody handprint.

She stared at her proof, gingerly measuring her hand against the mark. The outlined fingers extended well beyond her own. Ellen remembered how Jack had fallen against her bed when she'd first discovered him in her cabin.

"Please, don't be scared," he'd said.

She recalled how his eyes had rolled up and how he'd bounced against her bed before hitting the floor.

Don't be scared...

For the first time in five years Ellen locked the cabin door.

Chapter Ten

By the time he reached the rangers' cabin, Alec had forgotten about his narrow escape from the wild mountain woman and her gun-toting cohort. Fearing the permanent effects of frostbite, he would have been glad to take refuge in hell itself. In fact, the fires of hell sounded damn comfortable to him at the moment.

Alec eyed the snowmobile parked outside the door. If no one was home, he'd leave a note, hot-wire the thing and head back to civilization.

A ranger answered the door and immediately ushered Alec in, allowing him to sufficiently thaw out by the fire before peppering him with questions. Rather than admit to his probable role as a sex slave, Alec gave the man a vague story about spending the week with a friend, which the ranger accepted without question. The man merely offered Alec shelter, food and a telephone.

Alec's hands were still numb with cold when he clutched the receiver and dialed his partner's home number.

"Hi, this is Reid Hardy," intoned the tinny voice. "I can't come to the phone right now, so leave your name and number and I'll get back to you as soon as possible."

"Damn it." Alec slammed the receiver into the cradle, then picked it up to dial again. "I hope to hell someone's hanging around the office—"

His secretary sniffed several times before responding, "Brohard Investigation and Security."

"Caroline?"

"Can you speak up? I can hardly hear you. We have a bad connection."

"Caro, it's Alec."

"No, we haven't heard from him yet. The rescue squad says—"

"Damn it, Caroline. It's me!" he shouted.

"Alec? Alec!" Her voice turned from its usual dulcet tone to a high shrill as she addressed someone in the office with her. "It's Alec. No, not *about* Alec. It *is* Alec I'm talking to!"

Another voice came on the line. "Brody, that you?"

"Yeah, Reid, it's me." Alec felt his energy level suddenly dip. He found a chair, which he fell into. "How about getting me out of here? Sometime today, okay?"

"You got it, buddy! Where exactly is *here?*"

Alec turned to the ranger. "Just where in the hell am I?"

"Ranger Station Eight. Thirty miles out from Copper Springs on County Road 26. Bancroft Trail."

"Some ranger station on Bancroft Trail," Alec repeated.

"You went to the mountain? I thought you said it could wait."

It? What? A case?

Reid continued. "We were worried when you didn't show up Monday for work. By Tuesday noon, Caroline was ready to call out the national guard."

"I wish she had. Just get somebody up here."

"Now where's this ranger station?"

Alec handed the phone to the ranger, who dutifully repeated the directions. The man listened to Reid, then nodded. "Yeah, there's one right out back. We use it for the Mountain Air Rescue Squad. We've got lights and everything."

Alec grabbed the phone. "What's going on?"

Reid spoke to someone off the phone, then returned to the line. "It's settled. We'll have someone there to pick you up in about forty minutes."

The noise in Alec's ears started to fade. "Good. The sooner the better."

An hour later he watched a helicopter raise a hazy white cloud of snow as it landed. The helicopter itself bore the same fire-breathing logo as the pilot's jacket and hat: Dragon Electronics.

Dragon? After a few moments of furious mental searching, he remembered this was their newest client, a company that was evidently prosperous enough to own its own air fleet. It irritated Alec that he couldn't remember much in the way of details concerning the company's security needs. It wasn't like him to forget those types of things.

Shaking the pilot's hand with little enthusiasm, Alec climbed on board. They'd been in the air about fifteen minutes when the sun slipped behind the tallest peak. He didn't know whether he should be thankful he could no longer see the gut-wrenching panoramic view of the mountains or be frightened about the pilot's diminished line of sight.

But through the miracle of sheer exhaustion, Alec settled back and soon fell asleep. Time surrendered to fatigue, passing without note. He was startled awake by the pilot's voice.

"We're here."

Alec shook the sleep from his mind and squinted through the bubble windshield at the well-lit helipad. Moments later he limped into a warm office and into waiting arms. Reid Hardy pounced on him, alternately pounding him on the back, then shaking his hand. Caroline Laird, the company's secretary, merely stood in the corner and dabbed at her eyes. When his partner backed away, she stepped forward and pulled Alec into a tight embrace.

He shot Reid a lukewarm grin from over her shoulder. "Listen, partner, next time I decide to take some vacation time, make me go somewhere warm and flat. Okay?"

"Vacation? C'mon, Brody." Reid punched him in the shoulder. "Tell us another one!"

He tried to grin. "I got . . . lost while I was hiking. Then the storm came up, and I found a place to stay."

"By yourself for a whole week?"

"Uh . . . no. Not by myself."

Reid gave him a calculating stare, then grew animated. "A woman! That's where you've been. You've been in some woman's cabin for almost a week. Right?" He didn't wait for an answer. "Here we thought you were working on a case for your mystery client and you turn it into the perfect vacation!"

Alec's stomach began to turn. "What are you talking about?"

"Oh, I get it. 'Yeah . . . what mystery client?' Good one, Brody! You're really good at this cloak-and-dagger stuff."

Cloak-and-dagger? His mind flashed to the sight of a knife, held in a trembling hand. A woman's hand. His brained burned with the effort of remembering.

"So did you get lucky?"

"Drop it, Reid." Caroline's voice took on a hard edge. "Something's not right."

"No way! I want to hear all the details."

Alec stared at his friend's eager face. Unable to master the finer points of reading someone else's expression, Reid Hardy was a good friend and a great partner, but sometimes a real pain in the ass.

Caroline came to the rescue with a diversionary tactic. "Alec, you don't look so well. Are you feeling all right?"

"I'm okay," Alec lied, fighting the black spot that threatened his vision.

"No, you're not." Caroline tugged off his stocking cap, revealing the bandaged cut and bruise on her boss's forehead. "Good Lord, Alec. How did this happen?"

"I—I fell." Alec tried to ignore the disapproving look his secretary wore. "When I woke up, I found myself in the cabin."

"You were unconscious?" Caroline's face grew sober. "That's all I need to hear. We're heading for the hospital."

"C'mon." Reid placed a hand on Alec's shoulder, but Alec shook off the gesture.

"No way. No hospital. I'm headed home, to TV and a beer." For some strange reason, he couldn't deal with the sympathy, concern and confusion that blanketed his partner's face.

"Jeez, Brody, you look like death warmed over. I really think you ought to listen to us and have a doctor check you out."

Alec pushed between his two colleagues, knowing if he didn't stand his ground, they'd march step him into some emergency room, where the paperwork would keep them tied up for hours.

Tied up... He flashed back to his unorthodox awakening. How would he ever explain that?

"If you're not going to take me home, then I'll call a cab. Where's the damn phone?" He stumbled toward the desk, hitting his shin. A blinding pain stopped him for a moment, and he held on to the back of the chair for support.

"This isn't like you, Alec. You can barely stand up and—" Caroline glanced down at Alec's feet. "Where's your boot?"

"I lost it," Alec mumbled, feeling like a guilty child confessing to his mother.

"Before or after you walked to the rangers' cabin?"

"Before."

"Get in the car. Now!" When he tried to object, she gave him a look that would bring a strong man to his knees.

He faded in and out during the drive to the hospital. Suffering through the indignity of a physical exam, Alec tried to argue with the attending physician, who insisted his patient should be admitted for tests. Alec relented only when the doctor outlined the worst-case scenario, involving a fractured skull and the amputation of severely frostbitten toes.

Neither projection came true. The doctor later admitted Alec had survived the worst of the side effects from his concussion while at the cabin, and his toes would remain firmly attached to his foot until the next time he tried to hike in snow without a boot. With his friends in alliance with the doctor, Alec resigned himself to a brief hospital stay for observation.

Finding himself once more in unfamiliar surroundings, he glanced around at the stark hospital room. Something about its austerity seemed vaguely familiar to him, but he couldn't place the feeling. He tried to relax, but what little tranquillity he could muster was shattered each hour as a nurse entered the room to check on him. When she came in for the fourth collection of questions designed to verify his state of mind, he was ready to take a stand.

"Mr. Brody, how are we feeling?"

"*We* were asleep. And if *we* are woken up one more time, *we* are going to pick up this chair and throw it through that window."

A pink flush colored the woman's cheeks as she nervously twisted the stethoscope in her hand. "Now Mr. Brody, we don't—"

"You don't know what the hell *we* want. Just get the—just get out!"

Residual tension kept him awake until the next scheduled interruption. When the time passed without a visit from a single member of the medical profession, Alec reveled in his triumph. Despite the stiff sheets, flat pillow and penetrating odor of antiseptic, he surrendered to a deep sleep. Disjointed images filtered through his mind, and he woke frequently, remembering he had dreamed but not recalling the content of those dreams.

Until the last one.

I MADE LOVE TO HER AGAIN.

It was more than the usual meaning of the word. Sure, it was great sex. Deep, satisfying, knock-your-socks-off sex, the sort of thing young men brag about in lockerrooms but no one takes seriously or really believes.

It was more. It was love. It is love.

But the kicker is, I can't remember her name or what she looks like. I know a few things about her. She's no love-starved mountain woman. I did her a great dishonor when I made that assumption. Strength with grace, humor and a sense of compassion. A rare combination of characteristics for someone who'd deliberately isolated herself from civilization.

The sound of her voice made my heart soar. "Jack, I love you."

My heart did a nosedive. "Great," I thought. "She loves someone named Jack. Not me." Then, comprehension exploded.

I'm Jack. At least, I was her Jack, for a while.

"Jack, I love you."

How could I have forgotten love? How could I have forgotten...

Tess! She's everything I could ever want in a woman, a stunning combination of beauty and brains. She's a survivor. I can appreciate her strength, ingenuity and sense of adventure. I remember the determination in her eyes when I dragged her to the storeroom behind the bar....

"No!" Alec sat up in bed as his consciousness fought to break into his dreams. *You've got it all wrong. You never left the cabin to go to a bar. It was a story, a fiction she created to pass the time of day. Can't you tell the difference between reality and fantasy?*

He fell back onto the pillow, his hands still clutching the cold rails on either side of the bed. Although he wanted to resist the urge to sleep, fatigue overwhelmed him.

His eyes closed.

Tess. I remembered the pale pink dress, her prom dress. She looked so young and innocent, completely out of her element in that group of social barracudas. I watched her across the ballroom...

Ballroom? I was in a cabin in the middle of the Rocky Mountains. There were no dancers, no orchestra...

A soft hand touched his forehead. "His temperature's spiking again. Do you think we need to call..." The voice faded from his consciousness.

I can feel the sensation radiating between my shoulder blades. It isn't really a pain, more of a warm energy spill-

ing down my back. Suddenly I can't stand. I'm falling to my knees, trying to reach for the knife's handle. Why can't I reach the damned thing?

"What's wrong, Mr. Brody?"

My vision is beginning to blur. "H-help me..." *I croak, gasping for breath.* "The kn-knife..."

"What did he say?"

"Something about a knife. Please, can you hear me, Mr. Brody?"

"Whoa—hold him down! He's got my hair! Can you give me a hand, Jenny? He's all twisted up—"

I ran my fingers through the single braid, turning it into a shimmering waterfall of hair covering her bare shoulders. "I should have done this to begin with...."

It was deep, satisfying, knock-your-socks-off sex....

"Ellen!"

Alec sat straight up in bed and listened to the dying echo of his voice. His cold sweat didn't even have a chance to dry by the time a nurse burst through the door.

"Mr. Brody? What is it?"

He gripped the rails on either side of the bed. "Nothing. It's nothing."

After the door swung shut behind the woman, his mind shifted to Ellen. Everything had come back to him in a flash, but some of the memories didn't make sense. How could he have been with her at a dance when they were stranded in an isolated mountain cabin?

And the bar. Alec remembered being with her at the bar, a dirty, smelly hole-in-the-wall joint. A place he wouldn't be caught dead patronizing.

What about when they made love? When they kissed, when he ran his hands through her hair, when she touched him....

Was it real or merely wishful thinking? Confusion and fatigue reigned to make a mess of the memories. He tried to sort out his jumbled recollections, to separate fact from fiction, dreams from reality.

The hospital was real.

The nurse was real.

But what about Ellen? Reality or fantasy? He wasn't sure.

He closed his eyes, hoping to find the answers in the same place where the questions originated.

Please... let me dream....

But dreams as well as sleep eluded him. He rolled over and punched the thin pillow. *I'll wake up in the morning and I'll remember everything. It'll be as simple as that.* His eyelids grew heavy, his mind swimming in murky mental waters.

I'll remember the real Ellen.

I'll remember...

SHE DREAMED OF FLOWERS that burst into fire. Of papier-mâché fireplaces that smoldered and turned into ash. Of smoke. Thick, heavy and—

Smoke? Ellen, roused from her nightmares, was unable to distinguish the real from the mundane in that split second of coexistence between wakefulness and sleep. She drew in a deep breath of air, expecting its cold freshness to dispel her fiery dreams.

Real smoke clogged her throat.

The cabin's on fire!

Struggling out of the clinging embrace of her blanket, she fell to her hands and knees, knowing where the freshest air would be. "Hermitt!" She heard him howl in response. "Here, boy!" Ellen saw a moving shadow obscured by the thickening smoke. *Smoke, but no fire.*

Maybe the damper had merely fallen closed. She turned around, crawling toward the fireplace.

Hermitt howled again.

Ellen heard a small pop and swiveled around in time to see, through the harsh curtain of smoke, the fire filling the doorway. After a second pop, flames jumped through the kitchen window.

She anticipated the third muted explosion, realizing it represented strategy rather than dumb luck. Her exits were being methodically eliminated. Another window erupted in flames.

She had one window left.

Pulling the quilt over her head, she made a desperate dive toward the glass, hitting it with her shoulder and back. She bounced off it, having neither the weight nor the momentum to break it. Desperate, she reached over and grabbed the fireplace poker, swinging it with one hand toward the window.

The glass shattered.

She jumped.

A plume of fire shot into the air as the last firebomb of the series detonated. Yet it made no sound other than the crackle of fire consuming wood.

And papers.

And dreams.

Chapter Eleven

Morning came with a vengeance—harsh sunlight, loud noises and a pounding headache. Alec scanned the aseptic room and slowly realized where he was. A soft knock heralded a visitor, and he managed to croak "Come in" with what sounded like reasonable clarity. A pot of tulips entered the room first, then a face peeped out from behind it.

"Morning, boss." Caroline's dimples brightened the room more than the red blooms ever could. She placed the cheerful pot of flowers on the bedside table and reached for his hand. "This is a heckuva way to end your vacation."

Alec tried to smile. "Tell me about it. I feel like I've been on a three-day bender that lasted three weeks."

"You had us worried." She beamed down at him. "I'm glad you're safe and sound."

Alec sighed. "Safe, maybe. Sound? I'm not so sure."

Caroline dragged a chair over to the side of the bed and sat down, propping her arms on the rail. "So tell me what happened."

He ran a cautious hand through his hair, dodging the new bandage. "Have you ever had a dream that was so powerful you knew it had to be real?"

She nodded. "Sure. Who hasn't?"

"I'm having a hard time distinguishing between what really happened up there and what I dreamed. I remember falling, but not landing. The next thing I knew, I was in a cabin. Someone had undressed me, cleaned me up and bandaged my head. It turned out to be a woman named Ellen."

Caroline crossed her arms. "Last night you muttered something about some misanthropic mountain woman who kidnapped you."

"She did nothing of the sort." Alec drew a deep breath, trying to find a comfortable position in the hospital bed. "In fact, she saved my life. I was . . . in and out of it for a while, not quite sure who or where I was. I even thought I was a guy named Jack."

"Jack? How odd."

"When the weather finally cleared, Ellen went to get help. While she was gone, my own memories started coming back, but unfortunately, I didn't retain much of 'Jack's' memories, so I left before she could get back."

"You didn't wait for her to return with help?"

"No. And that's bothering me. She saved my life and took care of me for almost a week, and I left without so much as a thank-you."

Caroline sat back in the chair, crossed her arms in maternal disapproval and gazed into his eyes. "There's more to this story than you're telling me . . . right?"

Alec released the deep breath he suddenly realized he was holding. "Is it that obvious?"

"It's painfully apparent this Ellen is more important to you than you're willing to admit."

"As Jack . . . I mean, the feeling was so strong that . . ." He closed his eyes, suddenly assaulted by the memory of a crackling fire and crimped waves of softly scented hair.

Caroline drew a deep breath, and reduced what Alec considered to be a complicated emotional situation, fraught with undefined variables and intangible elements, into a simple observation. "You fell in love with her."

Try as he could, Alec couldn't speak louder than a whisper. "Jack did." After few moments he forced himself to complete what he considered to be the crux of his dilemma. "I'm not so sure whether Alexander Brody loves her." When he opened his eyes and stared at her, Caroline's sad, sweet smile made his sudden thoughts of regret even harder to deal with.

"Then go back and find out."

"But it's not that easy—"

"It can be. As soon as the doctor releases you, go back to the mountain and find her. Talk to her. Thank her. She evidently cared enough about you to make sure you survived. You may discover you and this guy named Jack have a lot in common." Caroline stood up, leaned over the bed rail and kissed his cheek. "And before you go, boss man, find a razor and use it. You look terrible with a beard. It makes you look grungy."

"Yes, ma'am."

Concern flooded back, pushing away the momentary glimmer of mischief in her eyes. "You go back to that mountain, Alec. You'll find your answer there, one way or the other." She started toward the door.

"Caro, before you go, would you answer one question for me?"

"Sure."

"How do you drink your coffee?"

She gave him a puzzled look.

"I know it sounds crazy but I still have a few irritating glitches in my brain circuits. Please . . . just tell me."

She shrugged. "Considering how often you get coffee for me, I'm surprised you could forget. Two creams and three sugars. Any more questions?"

"No—thanks." Alec slipped into the hazy grip of memory even before the door closed behind her. His mind jumped ahead to a day in the very near future, the day he would return to Ellen.

He would knock on the door, and she would open it despite all her misgivings. The fear would dissolve from her face when he pulled out the proof of his identity. He knew IDs could be forged, but what about a photo album?

He could chronicle his life practically from conception through the present with photographs. For once he thanked God that his mother had been such a nuisance with her Instamatic camera. He'd spent a better portion of his life believing any great moment of parental pride had to be coupled with a blinding flash in the face, along with a residual burst of radiance to block his vision for minutes afterward.

When he showed Ellen his Kodacolor history, she wouldn't be able to deny or ignore how much he looked like his father. It would prove his face was a matter of genetics rather than plastic surgery. As a kid he'd grown tired of the constant comparisons, but now it would finally pay off. If that didn't work, he'd get a signed note from his father . . . hell, he'd get an affidavit from the governor of Colorado if he thought it would help.

Alec would make sure there would be no doubt in Ellen's mind that he wasn't a man named Hank Bartholomew. Then Alexander Brody would begin his courtship. Roses, champagne, caviar, the works. He'd pull her quilt to the floor in front of the fireplace, where he'd begin a seduction of her heart as well as her body. The next morning he would persuade her to leave behind her isolation and rejoin the world, knowing he had the means to protect her. After all, who understood security better than a trained expert who made his living protecting as well as investigating people, places and things?

Alec drifted to sleep, experiencing the afterglow of satisfaction from nothing more than a fantasy.

A fantasy he prayed he could turn into reality.

Three torturous days later, after surviving every test known to medical science, Alec suffered one last indignity by being taken to the entrance in a wheelchair. Reid managed to replace his smirk with an innocent smile as he held open the car door.

Once they pulled into traffic, he pointed to a bulging folder on the seat between them. "Things have been backing up since you've been out of the office. I brought an overview of our current caseload, 'cause I figured some of the details might have leaked out when you clobbered your head."

Alec stared out the passenger window, his eyes focused on a more distant goal than his surroundings. "Listen, Reid, I'm not ready to come back to work yet."

"I know."

Alec turned around and gaped at his partner. Reid always seemed to ignore the finer points of reading between the lines. Reid's sudden sense of conscience had to be evidence of their secretary's machinations. "What did Caroline tell you?"

Reid rubbed the back of his neck and shot him a rueful grin. "Nothing much. Just threatened to quit if I didn't give you a few days' rest...without questions. She had the helicopter pilot mark a map with the location of the rangers' station. She also said something about you wanting to borrow my four-wheeler?"

NEXT MORNING, after a fitful night's sleep, Alec filled Reid's truck with an array of winter survival gear. He added his family photo album and his birth certificate.

Several hours into the Saturday-morning drive, he abandoned the main mountain highway, stopping to gulp down a tasteless sandwich from a convenience store before he turned onto an old mining road. Up to that point the roads had been plowed, but the next stretch would offer him an unwanted chance to test his winter driving skills and the truck's capabilities over snow and ice.

Dexterity and good luck accompanied him along the road, and he reached the parking lot at the trail head without major problems. After a four-hour trip in a heated vehicle, the cold mountain air shocked him back to life, as he stepped out of the truck and drew in a deep, cleansing breath. The next portion of the trip was by foot, and his last experience, unpleasant as it was, only served to reinforce his growing dislike for the sport of hiking. With a shrug of resignation, he oriented himself, shouldered his pack and headed north.

Alec knew he was close to the cabin when he saw a lazy curl of smoke hovering in the nearby treetops. He remembered how the path had narrowed, shortly past the cabin clearing. Negotiating the last curve, he glanced up expectantly, surprised by the sense of anticipation that filled him.

A wisp of smoke rose from the chimney. Its blackened stones stood erect in a circle of charred wood and ashes. His stomach reacted to the sudden revelation with a queasy lurch. Some of the scorched embers were still smoking, but the fire was long over, its destruction now a thing of the past.

His mouth hung slack.

Oh, my God... He repeated the phrase under his breath, taking what solace he could from the words. Bits and pieces of debris littered the ground around the ruins. His hands shook when he bent down to touch the few remains he could recognize. A darkened metal hairbrush with the bristles burned away lay on the ground where the bathroom had been. Alec picked up the object and turned it slowly over in his hands. He scraped away enough soot to read the initials engraved into its tarnished silver handle: E.M.C. Under another piece of debris, he found the remains of the matching hand mirror.

Alec stood in shock, devastated by the enormity and totality of the destruction. He stared blankly at the surviving chimney, until a movement in the woods quickened his heartbeat.

"Ellen!" he called to the flash of red that hid behind a bushy evergreen. The barrel of a shotgun appeared from around the tree trunk before its owner came into view.

"She's dead." The voice hung like heavy smoke in the air.

A stern set of eyes and the gun's dark double bores glared unblinkingly at Alec. The voice was as uninviting as the weapon aimed at him. "Who are you and what are you doing here?"

Alec raised his hands, hoping his gesture would keep the man's finger from tightening on the trigger. "My name is Alexander Brody. I came to—I mean, I had no idea—" Lost in a moment of overwhelming pain, he ignored the deadly threat trained on his chest and allowed his hands to drift back down to his sides. "How? Wh-when did it happen?" Emotion crept into his voice.

The shotgun barrel wavered, then lowered, pointing to the ground. "My partner and I saw the smoke in the wee hours, yesterday morning. By the time we got here, the cabin was completely involved. God knows I tried to get to her, but the fire . . . the heat. I couldn't reach her." He choked back his own regrets, giving Alec a steely once-over. "You're the guy she found out on the trail a week or so ago, aren't you?"

Alec nodded.

"I thought your name was Jack . . . something."

"It was. I mean . . . I was suffering from amnesia. I didn't know who I was."

"You know, I didn't believe her at first." The man's voice dropped to a low growl. "She told me she'd found a man and nursed him back to health. She hiked to my cabin to get help, but when we got here, there was no injured man. There were no signs anyone had *ever* been here but her. I simply thought the years of isolation, of fear, had taken their toll on her. But I was wrong."

He shifted his stance, eyeing Alec with obvious suspicion. "When she came to see me, she told me how both of you were worried about your identity, how your injury had screwed up your memory. That night my partner told me how you'd appeared at the station and about the helicopter that came to pick you up. I find it damned convenient that your memory came back while she was gone."

The shotgun lifted again, and the man's face became a mask of hatred. "You bastard. What did you come back for? To check on the results of your firebombs and make sure you killed her?"

Alec stared down the endless black hole pointed at him and kept his voice even and calm. "In my pack I brought the proof. I was going to show Ellen . . . the proof I wasn't Hank." He slipped the pack off, dropped it carefully to the ground, then took a few steps backward. "It's all there. My birth certificate, photographs of me growing up, birthday parties, graduations, everything."

"Sit. Put your hands on your head." The ranger kept a wary watch as Alec followed instructions. Then the man pawed through the pack, flipping through the album and comparing the pictures of youth against the figure in front of him.

Alec understood the man's caution. "Sir, this *is* my face, not something carved from a plastic surgeon's imagination. There—that picture." He nodded toward a picture of a bandaged boy sitting by the twisted remains of a bicycle. "That's how I got this scar." Alec turned his head so the man could see the thin ridge of scar tissue along the jawline. "My bike and I tangled with a chain-link fence and the fence won.

"And the next page. That's my father. You can see the family resemblance. My grandfather says I'm the spitting image of my dad when he was young."

The ranger thumbed through the album, dividing his attention between Alec and the photographs. The shotgun began to lower to the ground. Finally the man slung the weapon onto his back and held out his hand to help Alec up. "George Pembroke."

"Pleased to meet you, sir. Like I said, I'm Alec Brody." Alec glanced around at the ruins, battling the sickness it evoked. "You sure Hank did this?"

The man pushed his hat to the back of his head and ran a gloved hand over his face. "Before I became a ranger, I used to be an insurance investigator. I know arson when I see it. There was an intense fire in the kitchen area and smaller ones at each window and door. If he wired his fuses in parallel, then they all went off at once." His voice lowered. "She never had a chance."

Alec stared at the area that had once been her kitchen. The stove was a twisted lump of melted metal. "Is there a ... I mean, did you find a ... a body?"

The big man shrugged. Sorrow weakened his impressive posture, etching years into his face. "Didn't really expect to. It was an inferno that incinerated the entire structure in minutes. It was so hot I had to wait until it stopped smoldering before I could examine the ruins. By that time there wasn't much I could identify."

"But surely you could tell..." Alec couldn't finish when a mental image suddenly swelled up, stopping him cold.

The ranger drew in a deep breath. "Mr. Brody, judging by the mountain-lion tracks I saw in the snow, we won't find any remains." Pembroke's face turned an ugly shade of gray and he ground one fist into the palm of the other hand. "Damn it! This is why I retired and came out here. I couldn't stand it any longer, summing up a person's life or death in a few lines on an insurance report. And I sure as hell can't do it again now." The man cast a weary glance at the remains of the holocaust. "You know what a special lady she was."

Alec stared at the charred beams and blackened stones. "She was special, all right. Very special."

Pembroke reached into his jacket and pulled out a folded piece of paper. "Yesterday she got this. A day late and a dollar short." He held it out.

Alec unfolded it and began to read aloud, "'Dear Miss Pembroke...'" Alec looked up. "Pembroke?"

"We couldn't take any chances. She used my name, pretended to be my daughter."

Alec continued. "'I am pleased to make an offer on your manuscript, *Once upon a Mountain*. We believe the adventures of Tess and Jack are exactly...'"

Alec looked up. "An offer? They wanted to buy her book?"

The ranger nodded. "She made just enough on her artwork to keep her here. But she always said if she sold a book, she might be able to move somewhere else. Somewhere safer but less isolated. This place..." he gestured weakly at the remains "...just proved that isolation wasn't enough." Pembroke turned away, ineffectively hiding his tears.

Watching the big man's display of sorrow, Alec began to recognize his own intense emotions and regrets. Ellen was gone, and he never thanked her or even said goodbye. He never had a chance to really love her as himself.

Both men stood motionless, paying their silent respects. The ranger finally broke the silence. "Why did you leave, Brody?"

The words threatened to choke him. "When I woke up, I...I didn't remember her. I thought I'd been held against my will, so I got out of there as fast as I could."

"Then why did you come back?"

Alec couldn't turn away from the chimney, which stood as a hulking black monument to Ellen. "While I was in the hospital, the rest of the memories came back. All of a sudden I knew who Ellen was. I realized I felt something for her...I'm not sure what. I guess I came back to find out and to see what she felt for me." He couldn't bring himself to express the hopes he'd once entertained. Unable to stomach the sight any longer, he pivoted without a word and headed back to the trail, stopping only when the ranger's words rang out clear.

"He did this, you know. That bastard Bartholomew got his revenge at last."

Alec kept walking. During the long hike back to the truck, he tried to prevent himself from thinking about anything.

Anything or anybody.

Like Ellen.

He struggled through the snow, unable to keep himself from comparing this trip with the one he'd taken an hour ago. Anticipation and hope had died so quickly it was hard to believe they'd ever existed in the first place. He tried to blame the chill in his heart on the plummeting temperatures, but he knew the truth. Ellen was dead and it was his fault.

Once he arrived at Reid's truck, he stripped off the backpack and tossed it onto the passenger's seat. At the moment, he didn't care about the photo album or the happy childhood memories it reflected. Regret, grief and overwhelming guilt all combined to numb his mind. He operated on sheer instinct as he drove down the snow-packed road.

A couple of miles from the station, a dark blur darted in front of the truck. Alec slammed on the brakes, discovering that four-wheel drive didn't necessarily mean four-wheel stop. He controlled the skid, keeping the vehicle out of the snowbanks on either side of the road. Once he came to a stop, he climbed out of the cab and stood on the running board. Staring back, he spotted an object squatting in the middle of the road. His stomach turned in recognition. "Hermitt?"

The black lump moved.

"Here, boy!"

The dog limped over the snowy ruts cut by the truck and squatted by Alec's feet, shivering.

"She's gone, boy." He ruffled the dog's ears. "And you were left behind. I'm so sorry, Hermitt."

The dog whimpered, cutting through the last barrier Alec had erected around his emotions. He buried his face in the dog's smoky-smelling fur and allowed the tears to express his grief. After a few gut-wrenching minutes, Alec wiped his frozen tears on the back of his sleeve, pulled himself to his feet and opened the truck door. "C'mon, boy. Get in."

The dog slowly obeyed. Alec drove back toward the city with Hermitt cowering on the floorboards. When he returned the truck to Reid, Alec thanked the cover of darkness for disguising his grim expression. He pleaded fatigue to forestall his friend's questions and led the dog into his own car without offering any explanation.

Alec drove straight home, stripped and took a scalding shower to wash away the guilt and the regret. Before he collapsed in bed, he lit the gas fireplace for Hermitt, but the dog refused to get anywhere near the brick hearth.

"C'mon, buddy. Don't let the fire scare you."

Hermitt cringed in the opposite corner of the living room until Alec turned off the gas flames.

"Come here, boy. It's all right."

The old dog shook as he crawled toward Alec. Alec sat on the floor and cradled the animal in his arms. Once the dog calmed down, Alec brought him into the bedroom, where Hermitt took his station at the foot of the bed. Soon the dog settled into a twitchy sleep.

Alec leaned back in the bed with his fingers clasped behind his head. Hermitt still reeked of smoke, and the odor bothered Alec, an uncomfortable reminder of the tragedy. He wanted to sleep, but he feared the dreams that might come to his unprotected, unprepared mind. As he battled sleep, he almost wished he were back in the hospital, where the nurse would come in and wake him, freeing him from any unwanted nightmares.

He stared at the ceiling. If only he'd gone back earlier, maybe he could have saved Ellen from the fire. If only he could have stopped Hank. If only...

Damn it—why don't I wish for the moon while I'm at it? If I could go back, I wouldn't go back to the fire . . . I'd go back to when they met. Think of all the grief she would've avoided if she had never met him . . . if I could go back. . . .

THE BEER FLOWED FREELY, marijuana smoke filled the air and the jokes were raunchy. Ah—college life. At first I didn't know where I was.

Then I saw her. She was younger than I remembered. Pretty but not quite put together yet. I knew how age would mature Ellen's features and turn coed cute to grown-up gorgeous. She was in deep conversation with a guy who looked as if he made up the entire defensive line of the varsity team. I knew he was about to get fresh with her. I had no idea how, but I simply knew it was going to happen.

I tried to force my way through the crowd toward them, but a tipsy nymphet grabbed me. "Aren't you a little old to be a frat? I bet you're a professor here. Right?"

"Right," I lied.

The blonde molded herself to my thigh. "I'd take your class just to watch that wonderful, tight little tush of yours! What do you teach?"

"Self-defense. Excuse me." I escaped from the cloud of alcoholic fumes hanging around her.

The football bruiser had his hand around Ellen's upper arm, pulling her toward him. When she gave him a good jab in the stomach with her free elbow, it was like the flea trying to beat up the dog. The big guy held up a threatening hand as if he was going to slap her.

I pushed through the last remaining barrier of people and wedged myself between Ellen and her attacker. "Is this *guy bothering you?'' She gave me a strained but grateful smile.*

He grabbed her arm and jerked her closer. ''Butt out, creep!'' He smirked at me, evidently displaying the extent of his expansive, collegiate vocabulary. Then, without waiting for my pithy retort, he swung out one meaty fist aimed at my nose.

I intercepted his hand, applied pressure against his fingers, then twisted his arm behind his back. Mr. Football Jock bounced between screaming obscenities and pleading for leniency. I maneuvered him to the front porch and tossed him into a handy pile of leaves.

When I returned to the party, another guy was standing near her, evidently offering his condolences. Something about him seemed both familiar and disturbing to me, as if he reminded me of someone I didn't like. I decided to intrude, cutting her new companion right out of the conversation. ''You okay?''

Her smile was warm and honest. ''Thanks.''

''You're welcome. I don't usually interfere, but he had no right to hit you. No one does.''

She nodded. ''I agree with you. My name's Ellen.'' She held out her hand.

I reached out to shake it but someone jostled me from behind, nearly pushing me into her. I suspected the culprit was the guy whom I had out-jockeyed for her attention. He certainly didn't mean for her to end up in my arms like she did. ''It's getting crowded in here. Not to mention smoky. Would you like to go sit on the porch?''

She was hesitant without being coy. ''Okay.''

I blazed a trail to the front door. Outside we found an empty porch swing.

She gave me a penetrating glance. "You're not a stu-dent here, are you?"

I blanked out. Was I a student? I didn't think so. Nor a professor, despite my lie to Lolita. All of a sudden, I knew why I was there, what I was supposed to do. Then I real-ized I'd already achieved my goal. "I came for a friend."

"You mean with a friend?"

"Uh...yeah."

"What's wrong? Are you feeling all right?"

An icy wave passed over me, making me shake. "Not really."

She put a hand on my forehead, then touched my fin-gers. "You're freezing. Let's go inside."

"No. That won't help." My teeth started chattering, and I began to lose the feeling in my legs.

"C'mon. I'll help you."

"You c-can't. You're n-not there anym-more."

Her hands gripped mine, but I couldn't feel the warmth as I did before. "You're not making any sense. Let me go get help."

"No. D-don't leave." Her compassion touched me, but it could no longer save my life. "N-no one can help me now."

I knew I didn't have much time left. How could I ex-plain it to her? How could I tell her I was freezing to death? How could I tell her that by saving her from a fated liaison, I'd destroyed my only chance for survival? Since I prevented her from meeting her knight-in-tarnished-ar-mor named Hank, she never had to run away from him.

She never had to isolate herself in a cabin in the middle of nowhere.

And because she never lived there, no one helped the hiker who fell on the trail.

Instead of surviving his injuries, the hiker slowly froze to death. Me.

"El-len..."

She bent closer. "Yes?"

"It was w-worth it."

Chapter Twelve

Ellen died in a blaze of despair, and in her ashes Tess appeared.

When the landlady had asked her name, Ellen had given in to a flight of literary fantasy and muttered her name was Tess... Tess Phoenix. The mythological bird had become her personal symbol, a reminder that life could spring from the ashes of death.

After paying the room deposit, Ellen counted her dollars carefully. When George had first opened the account for her, he had provided the bank with all her personal identification. She'd now provided them the coded answers to the prearranged questions, then walked out of the bank with a grubstake for her new life in the big city.

Ellen was bright enough to know the money wouldn't last very long in the high-priced city. A secondhand life was the best she could manage at the moment. So her next step was to locate the nearest flea market.

Once there, she discovered a few of the concessionaires attempting to draw a crowd by hawking their wares in loud, carnival-barker voices. She shied away from the noise and took refuge in the quieter areas, where she bought a pair of scissors.

There was just enough light in the dingy bathroom to see the singed braid as it fell to the floor. People had been staring at her blackened stub of hair, one of the fire's lesser legacies. Trimming the ends as carefully as possible, she emerged, feeling marginally better.

Continuing down the next aisle, she discovered a portrait artist of dubious talent, who commanded a substantial fee for barely adequate likenesses of children and adults. The line of customers waiting for such minor talent was impressive as well as inspiring. Ellen knew she had, at last, found the solution to her monetary problems.

The next weekend, she invested twenty dollars in materials and rented a stall on the opposite side of the market from the other artist. Her first subject was a four-year-old girl who couldn't keep still in the folding metal chair.

"C'mon, Tracy. Look at me for a minute." Ellen reached up and dabbed a smudge of charcoal on her own nose. "Is my nose dirty?"

The child laughed. "It's real dirty. If I got that dirty, my momma would get mad at me."

"Do you want to know how it got so dirty?"

The girl screwed up her face in thought, then nodded. "Yeah."

Ellen drew a deep breath. It was a lesson she'd learned years ago; the key to survival was desensitization. "Well, it all started when the dragon tried to set my castle on fire. I'm a princess, you know...."

"A real princess?"

"Absolutely. You see, where I live, the dragons are pretty dumb. Are the dragons in your neighborhood dumb, too?"

The child shook her head. "We don't have any dragons where I live."

Ellen affected a look of shock. "You don't? That's too bad. Let me tell you about the dragon who used to live near us. His name was Hermitt and..."

Ellen spun a tale which so mesmerized Tracy that the child listened with rapt attention, resulting in a stationary pose and an enchanting portrait that thrilled her mother.

When Ellen showed Tracy the sketch, the little girl pointed to the signature in the bottom corner. "What's that say?"

"It says Tess. That's my name."

"I can't read," Tracy stated in a matter-of-fact voice.

"Well, what if I do this..." Ellen turned the *T* in Tess into a hieroglyph of a phoenix rising from a flame with wings outstretched.

Tracy smiled and clapped her hands. "Ooh, a bird! It's pretty. Thank you for the picture." She ducked her head and smiled shyly. "And for my story, too."

The phoenix became Ellen's signature and the smartest marketing tool she could have ever dreamed up. The next weekend, she hung a large cutout of a bird rising from a flame over her stall. Soon she had her own line of customers waiting for a unique portrait and entertaining story from "The Phoenix."

Unfortunately, Ellen had forgotten one of the great disadvantages of civilization was the transmission of germs. With an immunity system that hadn't been put to a serious test in four years, she found herself susceptible to every cold and flu virus that came down the pike. Her nosy landlady, Mrs. Pritchard, took great delight in chronicling Ellen's frequent bouts of illness.

Mrs. Pritchard stopped her in the hallway. "You poor thing. Again?"

"When the little boy sneezed in my face, I knew I was doomed." Ellen sniffed, then blew her nose.

"Would you like some soup, dear?"

"Thanks, Mrs. P, but I had some at the flea market. I'm just going to try to sleep it off."

"All right, Tess. Sweet dreams."

"Good night."

Once upstairs, Ellen burrowed her head in the cool pillow and pushed the quilt away. Beads of perspiration collected on her face and body as the fever spiked. Waves of heat rolled across her body, and she searched for an oasis of comfort to relieve the inferno that built inside her. Imaginary hot sands blew into her eyes, burning her and making her thirst unbearable. Ellen fished a piece of ice from her water glass and rubbed it over her forehead and down the valley between her breasts. The soothing sensation eased the heat but fanned the flames of fantasy that sat at the edge of her delirium.

Not flames. Heat. The heat rising from the floor of the desert and clinging to her heart.

She dreamed of hot sand, ancient walled cities and tented bazaars. She dreamed of missing jewels and robed men with knives. Any minute, she knew a hero would gallop to her rescue on an Arabian stallion.

The assassins approached.

Any minute he would arrive. He would reach down, swoop her into his arms and then—

Ellen sat up in bed. *Damn!* The hero in her dream was a caricature, a mere shadow of a real man. She knew she could fall back asleep and return to the second-rate fantasy to make her two-dimensional cover-model lover perform in any way she wished. He had no real personality, no inner strength. He was nothing more than a mediocre actor in the little drama she'd created, a stage player who took direction and recited stilted sophomoric speeches about beauty and goodness and...

Jack—the real Jack—had destroyed everything.

First he'd invaded her dreams, taking over the role of her dream lover. Then he'd brought reality to life, making love to her in a way that surpassed even her most erotic dreams. Finally he'd stolen her trust and run away, leaving her nothing but the ashes of memory.

The fire. She knew it had been started by human hands. By Jack's hands? Was he an emissary of Hank—or Hank, himself? How could she have fallen in love with a man who could turn around and do such a thing?

And how could she still love him?

HE AWOKE out of a sound sleep, his mind burning with new memories. Staggering into the living room, he sat down on the brick hearth, watching the flames pretend to consume a ceramic log. It all had come back to him in his sleep. Every sordid detail, every snatch of conversation. He'd been manipulated by a master, someone who knew just how much information to give him in order to sound authentic.

And Alec had fallen for the oldest trick in the book.

He stood, his head throbbing in guilt. The memories were too much to bear. He lurched into the kitchen and found three longnecks in the refrigerator door and a forgotten six-pack hiding near the sprouting potatoes. Carrying the beer into his office, he slapped on the lamp and scattered the contents of his In Progress file across his desk.

There the file sat, nestled between legitimate business. He stared at the words, written in ignorance. Written in blood.

Ellen's.

He carried the file into the living room and dropped to the hearth.

Burn it, his guilt whispered.

Get rid of it, his sense of justice commanded.

He looked at the first page: Missing Persons Report. Subject: Coster, Ellen.

IT WAS MORNING. He didn't care. He didn't care if the sun rose, set or tumbled from the sky. He didn't care about going to work. He certainly didn't care about the knock at his door or the figure entering unbidden.

"Alec?"

He squinted at the woman silhouetted in the too-bright doorway. "Yeah, Caroline?"

"Are you okay? I got concerned when you didn't come to work." His secretary stepped into his apartment, took one look at the carnage and sighed. "Rough night, eh?"

"Even rougher morning." He picked up a beer bottle, hoping to find one last drop he'd overlooked. Unfortunately the beer fairy hadn't refilled it during the night.

"I take it your trip back to the mountain didn't go well."

His stomach soured. "You could say that."

She shifted the papers off one end of the couch and perched on its arm. "What happened? Did she refuse to forgive you for running away?"

Alec would have shaken his head if it didn't hurt so much. "She couldn't forgive me... because she wasn't there."

Caroline's face creased in a frown. "She was gone?"

"She was dead."

"Oh, Alec..."

Her sympathy was more than he could take. He felt like throwing something. Or at least throwing up. *That's the problem with guilt,* he thought. *It makes you feel even lousier.* He struggled to sit up. The room tilted on an odd axis, and he pressed his palms against his temples to steady his head.

"What happened? How did she... die?" she asked.

"Fire." The word burned his mouth. "Gutted her cabin. She never had a chance."

"I'm so sorry."

"Not half as sorry as I am." He leaned back against the couch, staring into the fireplace. "I'm the sorry son of a bitch who got her killed."

To her credit, Caroline didn't flinch. Good little mother-confessors were supposed to sit back and listen without remonstration. But they also had a way of making the silence so damned unbearable.

He groped along the floor beside the couch and found the case file he couldn't bring himself to burn. He shoved it in her direction. "It's all in here. The whole filthy story. From the first time he contacted me, up to the report I made right before I headed to the mountain."

Caroline opened the manila folder and scanned its contents.

Alec's stomach did a three-sixty revolution. "He said his name was Dr. Henry Barton from Mountain Point Hospital, and he was concerned about a patient of his."

Caroline looked up from her perusal. "I didn't think you took any cases outside of the company anymore."

Alec drew a deep breath. "I don't...usually. I only took it to repay a friend of mine. Turns out even *that* connection was bogus." The numbing alcoholic haze waned as the memories swelled. "There is no Dr. Henry Barton at Mountain Point Hospital. However, I've learned there was a Henry Bartholomew admitted there as a *patient* a couple of years ago."

"And he posed as a doctor? Why?"

"He was siccing me onto the trail of a woman who had disappeared. According to him, he was concerned because she didn't finish her treatment."

Caroline raised an eyebrow. "But she was—"

"An innocent women he'd been stalking for years." Alec stared into the fire, trying to prevent the tears from forming. "And like a good little private investigator, I led him right to her."

Caroline shifted so she sat beside him. "Alec, don't do this. Don't blame yourself."

"Why not? I did it. Simple as that."

She leveled him a sharp glance. "Then why did you go to the mountain? If you knew she was there, why didn't you just give him the location and wash your hands of it?"

Alec probed his hesitant memories. *Why?* "Because I wanted to make sure for myself she was the right woman. That she was the same misguided person he'd described to me in so much detail. I knew vague details about her role as a stalking victim, and I guess I wanted to be positive..."

"Then somewhere in the back of your mind, you doubted him."

Alec shrugged. "I guess I did."

"And if he hadn't hired you, he might have hired someone else who would have merely located her, then walked away." She placed a hand on his shoulder. "Alec, you didn't walk away. You went to the mountain to verify his information. And if you hadn't been injured, you would have discovered the truth. You would have warned her—"

"I would have saved her? Probably not." Alec shifted away from the comforting gestures he didn't deserve.

Caroline stood as well, reaching up to place her hands on his shoulders. "You can't be sure about that. If this man was thorough enough to penetrate *your* guard—" she paused to narrow her eyes " —then she stood *no* chance at all. You gave her some time, Alec. That was the best you could have done."

The best I could have done...

It would never be good enough.

SOMETIME AROUND MIDNIGHT, his exhaustion got the best of him. He'd half convinced himself to believe Caroline, to believe he'd acted out of some subliminal sense of precaution. Maybe he'd read something into "Dr. Barton's" telephone calls or read something into the back-slanted handwriting. Too bad they'd never met face-to-face. Maybe he would have recognized the picture Ellen had shown him. Maybe that could have broken through his blocked memories. Maybe that could have saved Ellen.

Maybe— He stopped.

Too many maybes. He needed to believe in something concrete, to do something concrete. He stared at the file folder, then glanced toward the fire.

No, it's too easy to simply chuck the whole thing into the fireplace and be done with it. He knew this sort of absolution required a sense of ceremony.

Stalking into his office, file in hand, he sat down at his desk. Reaching into a bottom drawer, he pulled out a humidor and a large glass ashtray. He extracted an expensive cigar, which had been a gift from a client celebrating a successful case.

But this was no celebration. This time he was performing a liturgy. An elegy. A wake.

He rolled the tobacco-filled cylinder between his palms, lifting it to his nose and inhaling deeply. He inhaled a second time after he lit the cigar, appreciating the rich tobacco smoke, soothing, reassuring.

Touching the tip of the cigar to the first page of his ill-fated report, he tossed the burning paper into the ashtray. The ink flared green, moments before the paper blackened, curled, then disintegrated.

Green... the color of envy, greed, obsession.

He lit a second sheet, watching the paper turn to ash.

And black... the color of death.

If you could only burn away the guilt as efficiently....

He reached into his drawer and pulled out a bottle of scotch and his lucky shot glass. Another gift, another client.

Pouring out a couple of fingers, he raised his glass in salute. "Here's to Ellen and Tess." He drank the scotch, then turned the glass upside down on his desk. Savoring the smoke from his cigar, he blew it out in a lazy ring and closed his eyes.

I DREW IN a lungful of smoke. It was a good Havana, but I couldn't stop to enjoy it. I touched the tip to the fuse, which sputtered, then caught fire. After stubbing out the cigar, I tugged the gas mask into place, then tossed the bomb through the open window. Once the initial confusion died away, I entered the room with my gun ready. The gas had done its job. The sentries slept peacefully on the floor.

I removed the gas mask, hid it, then entered the banquet hall, pleased that the gun fit neatly into the underarm holster without disturbing the lines of my tux. I crossed the room, ignoring the smiles of the lovelies who gave me the eye. What I do in the line of duty....

I barely glanced at the man behind the bar. "Tonic." I scanned the crowded dance floor. "Have you ID'd her yet?"

The bartender nodded. "The one in pink, by the punch bowl."

I spotted her. Her simple style made her stand out in the crowd of unimaginative, overdressed glamorettes. I threaded my way across the dance floor as she retreated behind a potted palm. Moments before I reached her, she'd spilled her punch on her dress. The old handkerchief-and-knight-in-shining-armor ploy worked perfectly, and soon she was paying little attention to the party. My impeccable charm had again worked its usual magic.

I held her elbow. "You're shaking. Are you cold? Why don't we step outside?" I escorted her to the balcony doors. When we stepped out, the heat hit us like a furnace blast.

She didn't seem to mind the temperature as she drew a deep breath of fresh air. I kept up the friendly banter, amazed at the realism she poured into her act. If she ever decided to go straight, she'd make a helluva actress. I was just about to throw out the recognition code when a voice interrupted us.

"Mr. Glascow!" She greeted him like a long-lost relative.

My instincts went on alert and I pivoted, fighting a strong reaction to go for my gun. His name wasn't Glascow. It was Barton. Henry Barton. And behind the angelic face of Dr. Henry Barton lay the heart of the devil incarnate himself.

"Thank you so much for inviting me," Tess gushed. I was surprised she was keeping up the charade of innocence.

"It's the least I could do." Barton faced me with a leer. "Did you know this charming child saved my life today, Mr. Alexander?"

I stared at him. All I wanted was one good shot at the guy. Fist or gun, it didn't matter.

She looked surprised. "You two know each other?"

"Jack Alexander and I go way back. Way back indeed." Barton faced her. "Would you join me in the next dance, my dear?" As he wrapped his pudgy hand around her arm, I took a step forward. "That is," Barton added darkly, "if your young man doesn't mind."

"I mind, all right." I pulled my gun from my jacket and leveled it at Barton's chest, ignoring Tess's theatrical gasp.

The man grabbed her, holding her as a shield. "Now, Mr. Alexander, let's not air our differences here in public."

The woman tried to speak. "I don't know what's going—"

"Shut up!" Barton glared at me. "I thought it was against your outdated code of chivalry to bring civilians into our governments' disputes."

"Cut the crap. I know she's with you." I took a step closer, and he tightened his grip around her waist.

Suddenly he had a knife at her throat. "Give me credit, sir. If I'd wanted to trap you, I'd have used more tantalizing bait."

I moved toward him, but he pressed the sharp blade into her skin. "Get back or I'll..."

"Do what, Barton?" I kept my voice low , trying to ignore the fear that flashed across her face.

"Kill her, of course."

"Not with a knife." I nodded toward the big man's designer tuxedo. "Too messy."

Barton nodded. "How true."

"Hey, wait a minute!" The woman began to struggle. "I don't know what's going on, but I'd appreciate it if you left me out of it."

"Silence!" Barton roared.

I watched her eyes widen as a trickle of blood dripped down her neck and stained the front of her dress.

She was a flurry of action. She used one hand to push his arm away, shoved her other elbow into his stomach and dug her spiked heel into his instep. As he recoiled in pain, she finished him off by slamming a potted plant across the back of his head. He landed in a limp, dirtied heap, felled by a person half his size. I almost laughed. Her technique was crude but efficient.

She glared at me. "Are you next?"

After I returned my weapon to its holster, I offered two open palms to gesture my compliance. "See? No gun." I took a step closer. "We need to—"

"You stay away from me!"

I gave her my most disarming smile. "You don't understand."

She took a step backward. "I said stay back. I'll scream. I swear, I'll scream!"

I saw it in her eyes. She was just the type of broad to produce an eighty-decibel shriek that could wake the dead. It sure as hell would alert the other agents waiting for Barton's triumphant return.

I did what my fictional mentor, James Bond, would have done. I pulled her into my arms....

And kissed her.

Chapter Thirteen

When an unexpected spring storm started dumping snow on Denver, the stream of bargain-seeking customers at the flea market slowed to a trickle. Ellen soon discovered commerce bowed to the pressure of the elements.

While she waited for a nonexistent customer, she pulled out a fresh sheet of paper and idly began to sketch. When a familiar face began to appear on the paper, morbid curiosity forced her to complete the picture of Jack.

In a moment of uncontrolled thought, she wondered if he had a scar on his head, a legacy of his misadventures on the mountain. To mask her ignorance, she added one unruly curl to fall conveniently over his forehead. His eyes seemed to stare right through her, mocking her, making a promise she knew a paper image couldn't keep.

Ellen jumped when an intrusive voice purred in her ear.

"Hey, Tess, who's the hunk?" Vanessa leaned over her table of wares, and her seashell necklace dangled loosely, hitting Ellen in the shoulder.

Ellen's hand trembled, adding an extraneous line to his collar. "J-just someone I knew." She scrubbed the line out, begging herself to stop shaking.

Vanessa emitted a shrill wolf whistle that hurt Ellen's ears. "Someone you knew? I wish I 'knew' a guy like that. Ver-ry nice!"

"Who's nice?" Jerry, the concessionaire next door, leaned over the other side of Ellen's minuscule stall. "Besides you, that is...."

Ellen winced. Jerry was always a little too eager to enter her conversations, whether invited or not. She'd tried to be pleasant, but her kindness had only served to encourage him.

Vanessa moved to block his view. "Leave the girl alone, Jerry. You know diddly squat about good art and can't appreciate something this fine." She turned to the portrait again. "And this guy *is* fine."

"C'mon, Van," Jerry pleaded. "Move over and let me see."

The woman shrugged, then moved aside.

He squinted at the portrait from across the way, then smirked. "Don't know crap, do I? What would you say if I told you I know that guy?"

Ellen felt her heart lodge in her throat. The charcoal snapped in two in her hand.

Vanessa scowled. "Sur-r-re you do, Jerry."

"Oh, yeah?" Jerry began to finger Vanessa's display of shell earrings, an act designed specifically to irritate her. "This guy just happens to live in my apartment complex. He drives a gray Mercedes."

"What's his name?" Ellen felt the words slip out before she could stop them. *What name is he using now? Hank or Jack or something else?*

He reddened perceptibly. "Actually, I don't know his name. We sorta pass in the parking lot. A nodding acquaintance, if you know what I mean."

Vanessa pointedly ignored Jerry and turned her attention toward Ellen. "I thought you said you knew this guy. So how come you don't know his name?"

Jerry shook his finger in Vanessa's face. "Leave the girl alone," he said, mimicking her. "You don't have to give her the fourth degree."

"That's *third degree,* you idiot. And you just stay on your side of the partition, you hear me? I'm getting so tired of finding you leering at my customers."

While Jerry and Vanessa waged the latest installment of their ongoing battle, Ellen took advantage of the distraction to pack her easel and supplies. Neither combatant heard Ellen mutter a hasty goodbye. She slipped through the throng, leaving behind the portrait of Jack. It was a self-inflicted pain she didn't need.

The malevolent wind cut through her coat, flash freezing her before she could get to the edge of the parking lot. By the time she reached the boardinghouse, she realized she'd lost the feeling in her fingers and toes.

Mrs. Pritchard took one look at Ellen and hustled her into the sitting room, a hallowed place where tenants were seldom invited. "Stay here by the fire," the woman ordered, "and I'll bring you something to warm you up." She disappeared, then returned moments later, shoving a cup of hot cocoa into Ellen's trembling hands.

The warmth of the mug felt like fire to her frostbitten fingers. She sipped the scalding liquid, painfully aware of the searing heat that poured down her throat.

"What's gotten into you, girl?" Tight-lipped disapproval passed briefly over the landlady's face. "With the windchill factor, it's almost twenty below zero out there! Something's wrong, isn't it? Somebody at the flea market bothering you?"

Ellen shook her head. "No... that's not it."

The woman shrugged. "If you want to talk about it, I'm willing. If not, that's okay, too." The woman patted her on the shoulder.

Ellen tried not to flinch. Personal contact was one aspect of society she hadn't gotten used to again. "Th-thanks."

Mrs. Pritchard cocked her head and crossed her arms. "Look, sweetheart. I don't care why you're hiding. I'm going to assume it's for all the right reasons." She paused, then smiled. "I know you're a nice girl. Don't ask me how I know...I just do. I also know Tess Phoenix isn't your real name."

My real... Ellen took a minute to contemplate all her options, but decided to rely on fact rather than fiction. "You're right. I'm hiding and it *is* for the right reasons." After a second thought she added, "And my real name's Ellen. Ellen Coster."

Mrs. Pritchard nodded. "You know, that name fits you. I never thought you looked like a Tess." Her thoughtful expression turned into a beatific smile. "Now you get upstairs, Miss Ellen Coster, and get into a warm tub. I'll bring you up a little supper in an hour or so."

"But—" A sneeze interrupted Ellen's protests.

"Bath, supper, then bed." She wagged a finger at Ellen's red nose. "Unless you want to be sick for the next three days."

"Yes, ma'am," Ellen muttered meekly. The prospect of a hot soak in bubbles enticed her stumbling feet up the long staircase to her room.

Ellen sat on the edge of the tub, watching the uneven foam cover the water as the tub filled. Compared to life on the mountain, this was pure decadence. Instant hot water, perfumed bubbles...

If only it were a hot tub....

Anticipation faded as Jack stepped out of the shadows of the past. She still couldn't get used to equating the face with the name Hank. The Hank in her memories wore the same features he did while in court. Belligerent, unhinged, frightening.

Jack was none of those things.

She envisioned him in his black tuxedo.

He was dashing. At ease. A threat to her heart but not to her existence.

He clutched two fluted glasses in one hand and a bottle of dark red wine in the other. Stepping over the rim of the tub, he sat on the edge and dangled his feet in the bubbles.

For a brief moment, her imagination zeroed in on the unexpected inconsistency: bare feet and a tuxedo. Then she found herself looking for similarities between his manner and Hank's.

His deadly grin was like a cold hand touching her heart. His brilliant smile failed to thaw the ice that clogged her throat. "Go away," she demanded between clenched teeth. "Quit haunting me."

"I'm not haunting you, Tess. I'm not a ghost, I'm real. I'm flesh and blood, and I live in this city."

"Leave me alone." She removed her robe and slid beneath the blanket of bubbles, trying to drive away the mental images that haunted her. She prayed for the fragrant warmth to relax her, to allow her to regain control.

He poured himself a glass of wine and savored its bouquet. *"You know I can't leave you alone, Tess."*

A tear trickled down her cheek. "You know my name's not Tess. It's Ellen."

"Oh, no." He reached out to touch her cheek, to wipe away the tear. *"You'll always be my—"*

"Tess?" Mrs. Pritchard's voice cut through the haze of fantasy. "I mean . . . Ellen, is everything all right?"

Jack dared to offer her a glass of wine, giving her a devilish smile.

Ellen shook her head, trying to bring herself back to reality. "Yes, ma'am, I'm fine. I'm just in the tub." She could hear the clank of glass and silverware in the bedroom.

"I thought I heard you talking to someone," the woman called through the door.

"I was . . . just thinking out loud."

"See you later, love." Jack waved at her, then slowly faded out of sight.

The landlady's voice cut through the steam which filled the bathroom. "Well, I brought you some soup and crackers. The tray's here by your bed, but don't worry about the soup getting cold. I've put it in a thermos. Now, enjoy your bath, dear."

"Thanks, Mrs. P."

"You're welcome. Have a good long soak."

Ellen remained in the water until her fingers started to wrinkle. Wrapping herself in her threadbare robe, she hopped across the chilled bedroom and tried to create a pocket of warmth between the cold sheets. Ellen uncapped the thermos, finding the savory smell to be strangely unappetizing to her. Even hunger failed to permeate the depression that settled around her.

How can I separate the two sides of his personality like this? How can I hate Hank so much, yet miss Jack so badly? God . . . I think I'm going crazy.

Eventually despair surrendered to sleep: a deep, dreamless sleep from which she awoke feeling tired and even more depressed. As gray threads of light began to fill her room, she glanced through the window. Night had passed to morning, bringing with it a blizzard to block the sun and cover the world with white. Outside, cars skidded down the slushy streets, narrowly missing each other.

Ellen took little time to make her decision to forego a day of hanging around the flea market and watching the diehard Sunday shoppers straggle past her portrait booth without stopping. She rolled over in bed and slept, praying once again for some sort of new dream to help her escape from her prison in the midst of freedom.

STARING OUT the bedroom window, Alec watched cars slide uncontrollably down the tree-lined road below him. Nursing a scalding cup of black coffee, he was thankful it was Sunday and he had no plans to go anywhere or do anything. In an effort to regain the remnants of his life before the mountain, he'd made up for his inactivity and ill temper by playing racquetball with Reid almost all Saturday afternoon.

Alec's sore muscles screamed their protest, complaining about the sudden overexertion after weeks of near stagnation. Now, all he wanted to do was prop himself up inside the shower stall and let the stream of water knead his body until he could stand no more.

With the massage-unit dial turned up to heavy pummel, he soaped himself, then remained in the daunting spray, dazed by the euphoria of relief. In his opinion the only thing that could exceed the soothing sensations of a shower would be a long soak in a hot tub.

A hot tub...

A shiver crawled up his spine despite the clouds of steam that enveloped him. The mental picture became almost too much to take.

Ellen, a hot tub, a bottle of champagne... and him.

FROM BEHIND all I could see was a topknot of dark hair, held with a wide white ribbon. Bubbles popped gently, dancing to their own exotic, erotic choreography, revealing an occasional enticing glimpse. Catching my breath, I took a moment to appreciate the light fragrance filling the air. The scent had no name, no description, other than the fact it was uniquely hers.

Her perfume.

Just the thought of it made me stiffen in desire. I glanced down at my tuxedo. A wild idea filled my mind and my heart, my body already consumed by a greater need. I moved closer to the tub.

Her eyes were closed and her lips slightly parted. Beads of perspiration dotted her forehead, and tiny curls of dark hair plastered her cheeks. Before I could say a word, she opened her eyes and looked up at me.

Her face reflected surprise, but not fear.

My heart soared. I held out my offerings: a bottle of champagne and two stemmed glasses. "Thirsty?"

She nodded.

I popped the bottle's cork with one hand, then poured two drinks. Sitting on the edge of the tub, I held a glass to her lips.

Her gaze held mine for a brief moment, then she took a tentative sip. "It's good."

Her smile betrayed a thousand thoughts. "I'd ask you to join me but..." She fingered the lapel of my jacket, leaving behind a trail of bubbles. "You're not dressed for it."

I returned her hooded look with my own hungry anticipation. "You mean, not undressed for it?" I placed the bottle and glasses on the edge of the hot tub. "I do believe in being flexible, don't you?" I slipped out of the black shoes and stepped into the tub, tuxedo and all.

I started to take off my jacket, but found two foamy hands pressed against my shoulders. "Not so fast. Don't deny me my pleasure."

I smiled. "What is your pleasure, my dear?"

"Turn around."

I hated to turn away, but I followed my instructions. Damp hands helped me out of the jacket, and it landed on the floor. When I turned around, she smiled, her delicately scented fingers pulling at my tie. After she loosened it, she playfully tugged my suspenders, threatening to snap them.

"It's always been my fantasy—" she reached below the surface of the water and found the metal fastener at my waist "—to undress you."

"You've done that before."

"But not in a hot tub."

Who was I to deny a beautiful woman her fondest fantasy? I remained still, wondering if the furious rhythm of my heart would be plainly evident to her. Surely she could feel the reverberations that rocked through my chest each time she touched me. I reached up to unfasten the silver studs on the shirt, but she pushed my hands away.

"Oh, no," she whispered in a husky voice that made my heart miss a beat. "That's my job." Sure fingers plucked at the studs, pushing their way into my open shirt, caressing the muscles that tightened at her lightest touch.

I groaned in pleasure as she slid her hand down the length of my body, unfastening my pants and pushing them out of her way. My desire was hard to contain, much less disguise.

Before I could move, she shifted to the opposite side of the large tub and draped her arms along the rim. She rewarded me with a wicked smile.

"Your turn."

I decided to imitate the slow deliberation she took in undressing me. Running a hand over the top of her shoulder, I discovered a thin strap hiding beneath a layer of bubbles. My hands didn't shake as I peeled the lacy lavender band from her pale shoulder. Beneath the foamy surface of the water, I could see the thin material mold to her bare breasts. When my hand brushed against her, she closed her eyes and leaned forward.

Running a hand down her lace-clad legs, I returned to her thigh to discover the garter that held the stocking in such exquisite place. Slowly peeling the hose down and over her toes, I allowed the fabric to slide against her body as I drew it up, pausing at the valley between her breasts. Then I draped the lace stocking over the edge of the tub.

She released a raspy gasp and reached for me.

"Not yet, darlin'." I kissed her hands and replaced them along the rim.

Instead of closing her eyes to savor the sensation, she riveted her attention on me, demanding, coaxing, pleading with the silent words I could hear in my heart.

I removed the second lace stocking slowly, allowing myself time to enjoy the softness of her submerged skin. The lace floated free, riding a crest of bubbles. Our gazes locked in desire. Patience disappeared. My lips discovered the sweet sensations of her breasts. My hands traced a path beneath the surface of the water. Her hands kneaded my back, digging in when waves of passion became overwhelming. I shifted in order to look at her, seeking agreement in my intent to possess her.

All of her.

She responded to my passionate request with a nod. Her lips formed a silent yes.

Bubbles, steam, perfume, hot water... all combined to become an overpowering aphrodisiac to heighten the pleasure we created. Passion rode rhythmic waves, bringing us to a pinnacle of sexual frenzy amid a froth of bubbles. Words were unimportant, giving precedence to a tactile understanding of the ultimate act of sensuality and love.

I knew it was love and I intended to tell her so.

She spoke first. "I love you, Jack."

I ran my fingers along her cheek and traced a path down her neck. "I love you, too... Tess."

ALEC LOST HIS BALANCE and stumbled in the shower, knocking the faucet with his elbow. Ice-cold water poured down, chilling his body as well as his heart. He slapped at the control to shut off the water, then reached blindly for a towel. Goose bumps danced along his flesh and unwelcome ideas flooded his mind.

Did you love Ellen?

Or Tess?

Why does it matter? She's dead.

Alec sagged against the bathroom doorframe.

She's dead.

He tightened the belt of his bathrobe and stared out the window at the snow-capped mountains outlined against the western sky. "And I never said thank you... or goodbye." His spoken words drove the ghosts and their stage settings from his mind, leaving him with nothing but his thoughts. His guilt.

"Why?" He slammed his fist into the window frame, dangerously close to the glass pane. "Why is this bothering me so much? Why can't I get her out of my mind?"

He heard the rattle of a dog tag behind him and turned to face Hermitt. The animal stretched, yawned and glared at his master, evidently blaming him for the rude awakening. Alec gave him a quick scratch behind the ears, then followed the limping dog back to the hearth in the living room. At some point in the intervening months, Hermitt had regained his love for fire.

Survival in the face of holocaust.

Hermitt had done what Alec couldn't: forget the past and live for the present and the future.

"If she's dead, Hermitt, then why does she continue to live in here?" Alec tapped his finger against his temple. "And here." He balled his fist and placed it against his chest.

The dog thumped his tail against the hearth at the mention of his own name.

Alec suddenly realized he'd erroneously credited the dog with attributes that only a human could have. Hermitt was loyal to the hand that fed him and kept the gas fire turned on. He was nothing more than a dumb animal, as faithful as a good-natured dog could be.

"You don't even realize she's gone, do you, boy?"

Hermitt sighed noisily and closed his dark eyes.

Alec glanced toward the mountains again.

"But I never had a chance to say goodbye."

Chapter Fourteen

Blinded by a watery curtain of tears, Ellen punched savagely at the telephone buttons, praying her fingers hit the right numbers. Her mind raced ahead, trying to formulate the words she would say, the explanations she would give.

"Ranger Station Eight."

"G-George?"

"Just a minute, I'll get him."

After a moment of silence, a familiar voice boomed through the receiver. "Pembroke here."

"George?"

"Yes?"

Ellen couldn't utter a sound.

"This is George Pembroke. Hello? Is anyone there?"

She tried to speak, but great gulping sobs began to choke her. She drew a shaky breath. "It's... it's Ellen."

"El? It can't... you're not... El?"

"Yes, George. It's me."

"But how? The fire... good God, I thought you were dead! Sweetheart, where are you?"

"In Denver."

"Why didn't you let me know? All this time..."

"Please, I want to come home, George."

"Oh, darlin'. You know your cabin's gone."

"I know." Her voice cracked beneath the weight of her desperation. "I just can't stand the city anymore. It's dirty and noisy and the people..." She swallowed the swirl of panic the memories stirred. "There are so many people in this city, all talking and laughing at the same time. No one cares. No one really cares." Ellen took a deep breath. "Can I stay with you until I can find another place in the mountains? Please?"

"Of course," he said immediately. "There's always room for you. I'll come get you. Just tell me where you are."

She wiped the tears on the sleeve of her sweater. "I'm living in a boardinghouse on the north side of Denver. It's not hard to find." She gave directions, which George repeated in a reassuring voice.

"All right, darlin'. I'll be there as soon as possible. You stay put. Okay?"

She wanted to sound strong and confident, but her words came out in a strangled whisper. "Thank you, George."

Ellen waited in the front room, standing by her meager belongings, which she'd packed into a couple of cardboard boxes provided by Mrs. Pritchard.

The landlady joined her at the window. "Tess...er, Ellen, I'm gonna miss you around here."

"You can't possibly mean that, Mrs. Pritchard, considering how much trouble I've been."

"I do mean it. Most of my tenants think I'm just an old busybody. But you made me feel wanted, letting me do what I could to help you. I needed a chance to do some good for somebody else. Thank you.''

Ellen blushed, not knowing how to respond. ''You're welcome,'' she said simply.

''And I understand why you don't want anyone to know where you're going but—'' the woman stopped and fiddled with the lace doily draped over the back of the threadbare chair ''—maybe you could write every now and then? I realize you couldn't use a return address, but—''

Ellen pulled the woman into an embrace. ''Of course I'll write. And I'm the one who needs to say thank you—for the kindness you've shown a total stranger.''

Mrs. Pritchard wiped her eyes on a faded, flowered handkerchief. ''I better leave now before I start the major waterworks. You take care, now.''

They shared one last hug, then the woman bundled up and headed out into the elements. Ellen settled in an old rocking chair by the fireplace and watched the traffic along the busy street. She tried to imagine she was in her cabin—safe, isolated—indulging in a fantasy under the guise of a plotting session.

Once, her imagination had soared; now it remained grounded. She was empty, bereft. There were no more fantasies. She hadn't been able to write a word since the fire. Thank God, she could still draw.

Her heart skyrocketed as a battered truck pulled up to the curb. When she saw George climb out of its cab, tears clouded her vision.

Suddenly he was holding her tightly. ''Ellen, you're here. You're real. I almost thought I'd dreamed your call.''

''I'm real, George.''

He pushed her back at arm's length and gave her a critical once-over. "You look different."

She self-consciously reached for her missing braid. "It's my hair, George. I had to cut it."

He shook his head, still eyeing her. "No...not that. Something different." He leaned forward and placed a kiss on her forehead. "No matter, sweetie. Let's just go home."

George said little else as they loaded up her boxes. Once she climbed into the front seat, he took a moment to give her yet another long perusal.

"I look different because I'm tired, George. It's hard to sleep here. Horns, sirens, voices..."

"Not like on the mountain?"

"It can never be like the mountain. There's no place like the mountain."

"You sound like Dorothy. You know...in the *Wizard of Oz*? 'There's no place like home...there's no place like home.'"

Ellen squeezed his arm. "So who needs a pair of ruby slippers when you have a tin woodsman with lots of heart?"

George smiled, then started the engine. She admired how he maneuvered through the traffic with a talent evidently born years ago when he, too, lived in the city.

She glanced behind at the downtown skyline. "George, do you miss living here?"

"Me? Not really. I'm glad I live in the mountains now."

She settled against the snug embrace of her seat belt. "But you come into town sometimes to visit, don't you?"

"Yes."

She hesitated for a moment. "Do you think maybe I could come with you next time? To visit...friends?"

He glanced up at her, wearing a look of surprise. "Why, of course, you can. If you think you'll be safe," he added.

She drew a deep breath. "I don't think I'll ever be completely safe, George. But I'm willing to take a few small chances." She stared straight out at the mountainous horizon. "Still, I'm glad we're going home."

She leaned her head against the window, feeling the chill of the glass numb her cheek. *Going home... going home... going home...*, the engine droned. The tension slid from her body and mind, and she fell asleep.

"DAMN IT, REID! All I want to do is borrow your truck, not relive the Spanish Inquisition." Alec's voice echoed across the early-morning darkness that still blanketed the company parking lot.

His friend spun the key ring around his forefinger temptingly within reach, only to catch it in his fist and pull his hand away. "Not so fast, Alec. You're headed up to the mountain again, aren't you? Up where you had your accident?"

Alec glowered at him. "Does it really matter to you?"

"Yeah, it matters." Reid stuck the keys in his pocket. "It matters to me because I can't sit back and watch you do this to yourself."

Alec started to protest, but Reid interrupted him. "Don't try to snow me with some half-ass explanation. Caroline told me everything. Jeez, Brody, I'm not some insensitive boor. I understand a lot more than you give me credit for." He kicked at a nonexistent rock in the driveway. "Hell, I understand a lot more than most people give me credit for. But what I don't understand is why you're

willing to put yourself through the pain of losing her...
again.''

Alec stared into his friend's perplexed face. "I wish I
could explain it to you, Reid. I can't even explain it to
myself. All I know is I have to go."

After studying his shoes for an inordinate amount of
time, Reid reached into his pocket and retrieved the keys.
He flipped them into the air, and Alec fielded them with
one hand. He rewarded his friend with a tight smile.
"Thanks."

"Be careful."

Alec opened the door to his own car and whistled. Hermitt ambled out of the passenger seat and followed him to
the truck. The dog hopped obediently into the cab and
took his favorite position on the floorboards.

Reid helped Alec transfer gear from the car to the truck.
"You know, you never told me why you got this mutt."

Alec shrugged. "I'm not sure whether I got him or he
got me." He stared at Hermitt, who was already em-
broiled in a fidgety dog dream.

Reid shifted from foot to foot. "Well, do you think you
have everything you need?"

"Yeah." Alec held out his hand. "Thanks, Reid. I appreciate it."

His friend's face reddened, and he kept his fists stuffed
in the pockets of his jacket. "I'll shake your hand when
you come back and all this mess is over." He aimed again
at the phantom rock. "And by the way...if you scratch my
Bronco, I'll kill you."

Alec returned his friend's sheepish grin. "I'll keep that
in mind. See you later."

A steady stream of traffic accompanied Alec on his westward trek. Judging by the ski racks on the car roofs, he knew almost everybody had one main activity in mind. Although he'd grown up in the heart of the Rocky Mountain resort area, somehow the magical appeal of skiing had passed him by. Obliged to accompany "the guys" on numerous weekend trips during his high school and college days, Alec hadn't been on skis in the ten years since and hadn't missed it at all.

In typical Colorado fashion, a late-spring snowstorm had given the local skiers one last wild weekend to practice their sport before the slopes closed. Alec grimaced as the traffic slowed before the Eisenhower Tunnel, the expedient solution concocted by the interstate highway department engineers who had taken the phrase "traveling through the mountains" to heart.

A few miles past the tunnel, he turned off the interstate, following a state highway which became a series of switchbacks riding the topography of the landscape. He passed through the small town of Copper Springs and continued north.

Snowplows had heaped tall banks of dirty snow along the roadside, creating an inadvertent barrier between the edge of the asphalt and the hundred-foot drop-off. Looking out the window at the magnificent but deadly view, Alec wondered how he could have handled the vehicle on the same curves only one day after being released from the hospital. The sense of purpose which had driven him that day must have allowed him the degree of oblivion he'd needed to succeed at such a monumental task.

Succeed?

He couldn't in all honesty use the word. He'd won the battle but lost the war. He'd lost Ellen.

Alec parked at the trail head, feeling an eerie sense of déjà vu. The last time he had parked there, hope and anticipation had filled him. This time, expectation had already broken under the burden of mourning and grief. Alec hefted the backpack onto his shoulders. *At least I can say goodbye and let that chapter of my life end.* "C'mon, boy."

Hermitt roused and stumbled from the car. The old mutt stretched, then his black nose lifted. He sniffed and became suddenly alert.

"You know where we are, don't you?"

The dog's tail hung low and he gave a small whimper.

"There won't be any fire this time, old buddy. No one's going to hurt you." Alec reached down and ran his hand along the dog's back, then clipped the leash to his collar. "We're just saying goodbye."

A few cars dotted the sloped parking area, but Alec saw no one else along the trail. He paused by the path that branched off to the ranger station. Some small irritating sense of propriety urged him to follow it. The irritation grew to the point where Alec felt compelled to at least acknowledge, but not necessarily explain, his presence on the mountain to the ranger. After all, the Pembroke man had been her friend.

Hermitt sniffed at the cabin door, his tail wagging expectantly.

Alec knocked. No answer.

"No one's home. C'mon, dog." Hermitt remained rooted to the porch, refusing to budge when Alec stepped away. He fought the urge to jerk on the dog's lead. "You heard me. Come!"

Not even Hermitt could miss the sense of rigid command in Alec's tone. The animal gave the crack beneath the door one last sniff, then obediently followed his master back to the main trail.

The sun skimmed the bare treetops, casting skeletal shadows on the ground. In the city some of the trees had begun to bud, but on the mountain winter still reigned supreme, except for the places where patches of sunshine had melted some of the snow-packed trail. In those spots, firm footing had turned into treacherous mud, creating areas which seemed instinctively to draw Hermitt's attention. The dog plowed through the muck, his attentive nose and tail betraying his growing sense of familiarity.

When they rounded the final curve, Alec wondered why the scene stopped him cold once more.

Nothing had changed.

The stone foundation still delineated the original boundaries of the cabin. The monolithic fireplace still stood at one end of the ruins. All the site lacked was a curl of smoke to duplicate the first time he'd witnessed the evidence of destruction.

Hermitt roused Alec from his uneasy reverie. He reached down and unclipped the leash, letting the animal free. Hermitt darted around, but Alec ignored the dog and concentrated on the volcanic emotions erupting from deep within his soul. The intensity surprised him, and he found himself suddenly searching for someone to blame.

Who had the right to tear him away from something that had been so good, so right?

Why did Ellen have to die?

Why did he feel as if her death was on his hands?

Alec stripped off his pack and knelt, laying it on the ground. He unfastened the top flap and reverently lifted out the flowers. Red roses.

The type of flower he would have loved to have given her in person. Flowers were supposed to signify love and hope, but expectations had turned to regret long before the blossoms had started their hothouse life as small green buds.

He stepped over the small wall of stones and picked his way to the fireplace, where the charred mantel had survived partially intact. He placed the flowers on the scarred wooden plank. When he heard a noise behind him, he spun around and spotted a figure standing beside the cabin's crumbling foundation.

The man wore a guarded expression. "Sorry, sir. I didn't mean to frighten you."

Conditioning and control allowed Alec to keep the surprise out of his voice. "That's okay." Alec sized up the man in an instant, figuring much of his impressive build came from the bulk his thick green jacket added to his frame.

The man remained polite in the face of Alec's obvious circumspection. "This is private property, sir."

Alec stepped over fallen beams and moved closer to the man, noting with a small sense of relief the emblem on the man's ball cap: U.S. Forest Service.

"I'm just here to . . . to pay my final respects."

The ranger stared at the bouquet of flowers on the mantel and nodded. "I understand." The authoritative note dropped from his voice. "Haven't we met somewhere before?"

Alec looked at him carefully. The man was right. They had met. But where?

Before Alec could respond, the man smiled. "I remember you—the lost hiker from last fall." He paused. "So you knew Ellen?"

Alec nodded, unable and unwilling to verbalize just how well he knew her.

The man released a sigh. "She was a real special lady. I miss her."

"Me, too." It was a noncommittal answer, restrained enough for decorum's sake and close enough to the truth to satisfy Alec's needs.

"I'm afraid I don't remember your name. You were in and out of our station so quickly." The man stuck out a gloved hand. "I'm Harlin Banks."

"Brody, Alec Brody. Pleased to meet you." Alec returned the man's hearty handshake.

A puzzled look filled Banks's face as his eyes deepened in color to match his jacket. "I don't remember Ellen talking about anybody named Alec."

Alec stared at the tips of his mud-encrusted boots. "She called me . . . by my nickname, Jack."

"You're Jack?" Banks gaped. "There really is a Jack? Jeez, she always was telling some sort of stories about you! You've done everything! I mean—"

Alec raised his hands and gestured for the man to slow down. "No, that's not me. I mean, I'm not that Jack. I only met her a week or so before . . . the fire."

The ranger nodded. "That's too bad. I'd known her for a long time and I'll tell you, I was impressed with her. Quite a talented lady. Did you know she was an artist? Ellen could create an entire world of people with nothing more than pen and ink. She got her talent from her father. Now that guy was great. I saw—"

As the man continued to speak, Alec began to feel uneasy. It was disconcerting to hear the man speak of her in the past tense when Alec thought of her as alive in his memories.

Banks pulled off his hat and swiped his sleeve across his forehead. "I remember one of her dad's pictures. It was a field of flowers on a mountain very similar to this, with a cabin in the background and beyond, those three peaks." Banks pointed over Alec's shoulder at the view of three snow-topped mountains forming an even, staircaselike effect. "I remember the flowers in the field. They looked so real, you could almost smell them. The guy was really good and so was Ellen."

Alec stared at the mountains, unwilling to turn around and let the ranger witness the very private emotion that controlled his thoughts.

Banks's voice held a note of quiet reverence. "She was a great artist. It's such a waste...."

A low rumble caught Alec's attention. He pivoted and saw Hermitt standing behind the ranger. The dog's teeth bared as a threatening growl filled the air.

The man turned around, then blanched. "Oh, my God! Hermitt, is that you?"

ELLEN WALKED along the path, feeling no comfort from its familiarity. George had wanted her to wait until after his partner, Harlin, had returned before she went back to the cabin. George had even offered to accompany her to the site, but she had told him no. It was her duty, her lone responsibility, to face her past and accept it, and if she didn't do it now, she'd never get up enough nerve to do it. George had rescued her from the city, but it was her job to make a new life on the mountain. But could she do it without Tess?

Or Jack?

Always before, her alter ego had remained strong when she'd wanted to weaken. Then, when Ellen felt strong and safe, she allowed Tess a chance to cry. But now, Tess was gone, faded away to nothing more than a half memory.

And what about Jack?

Ellen would have to live without the fictional Jack or the real one. Back in the truck, George had begun to tell her something about Jack, but she cut him off short. She couldn't give herself the luxury to care, to wonder, to dream.

She stopped just shy of the cabin after she heard a voice riding the soft, cool breeze.

"...could create an entire world of people with pen and ink...talent from her father...remember one picture of his she showed me. It was a field of flowers on a mountain...."

The voice sent an avalanche of fear crashing over her. *Hank!*

She peered from behind a shadowy stand of trees, straining to hear and see without being seen.

"...a cabin in the background and beyond, those three peaks."

That's how he found me. From the picture I showed him. The one Daddy did back when we used to spend summers here.

Beside the cabin ruins, Ellen could see the backs of two figures. One wore a green jacket and what looked to be a

Forest Service hat. The other wore a dark coat. She recognized the puckered edges of her uneven sewing, the rip she had tried to repair.

Jack? Or Hank?

She heard the hideously familiar voice but couldn't see who was speaking.

"...a great artist. It's such a waste...."

Run! Tess screamed, coming to life suddenly.

Run! Ellen told herself. Curiosity didn't need to be satisfied at the price of danger.

The words rang out loud and clear from one of the two men: "Oh, my God! Hermitt, is that you?"

The man in green turned slightly in her direction, affording her a view of a familiar profile, unchanged by plastic surgery, altered only by the passage of time.

Hank.

Chapter Fifteen

"C'mon here, boy." The ranger knelt and clapped. "This is Ellen's dog, isn't it? Hello, Hermitt." The dog refused to take a step closer, standing his ground with another barrage of snarls and rumbles. Hackles rose across the ridge of the animal's back.

For a fleeting moment Alec didn't know what to think of Hermitt's unusual behavior. Reaching down, Alec slipped his hand under the dog's collar, but the animal surged toward the ranger. "Cool it, Hermitt!" Alec shrugged apologetically at Banks. "This isn't like him at all. I've never seen him act..."

Suddenly the significance of the dog's reactions hit Alec like a fist in the gut. Between Hermitt's uncharacteristic demeanor and the extraordinary amount of personal detail the man knew about Ellen, the answer became evident. Alec's stomach lurched at the ugly face of truth.

Harlin Banks.

Hank Bartholomew. It has to be him!

The side of Alec trained in security jumped into control, assessing the situation, running through his options. He could play dumb, showing no reaction, or bide his time and wait for a chance to catch the man off guard or, the most satisfying of the three, go ahead and jump the bastard.

Despite a gut reaction to strike first, Alec knew the element of surprise would serve him better. He needed to stay in control of the situation. He tried to look genuinely puzzled as he stroked Hermitt's head. "That's strange, Mr. Banks. He's usually a friendly dog. Sit, Hermitt!"

The dog reluctantly settled back on his haunches.

Alec repeated the command and let go of the collar. "Maybe he's spooked by being back at the cabin. You know...remembering the fire and all?"

"Maybe so." The ranger slowly straightened and stood. "It's hard to believe Ellen's dead."

"Yeah." Alec knew he had to keep from telegraphing his feelings through his words or his expression. "We didn't part in the best of conditions. I guess you could say I'm here one last time to say goodbye."

Bartholomew nodded. "Me, too." He glanced around at the ruins. "The flowers—" he pointed to the bouquet on the mantel "—are a nice touch. She would have liked them. She always liked roses, especially red ones. I remember once when I gave her—" He came to an abrupt stop, and his face reddened. "Uh...were you two... close?"

"So to speak." There was no doubt in Alec's mind that this was Hank Bartholomew.

"Were you—" the man stumbled over the word "—intimate?"

Alec didn't like the question. Or the odd light which crept into the man's eyes, turning them a deeper shade of green. "That's really none of your business."

Bartholomew backpedaled, but his expression had already betrayed him; he'd said too much, and he knew it.

"Of course. You're right. I'm sorry." He stared into the ruins, his eyes glazing over. "She was a beautiful person, Ellen was. Innocent, pure. Such a sweet young girl." He reached down and picked up a rock, tossing it up nervously in his left hand. "She could have had such a beautiful life. I would have brought her a dozen roses every day." He paused and smiled. "Red roses." He allowed the rock to fall from his hand. "Bloodred roses for my American beauty."

Alec's body tensed in anticipation; he wanted a chance to avenge Ellen's life of forced loneliness. And her death in isolation.

Bartholomew stepped onto the blackened hearth. "I'll never know why she did what she did." He pulled one flower from the bouquet and fingered the blossom. Crushed petals slowly drifted to the darkened stones.

"What did she do?" Alec circled to the left, keeping himself in the clearing. If Bartholomew was going to attack, he'd have to negotiate through the ruins first.

"She never told you?" The man slowly stripped off his gloves and stuffed them in his pocket. "She never told you about her ultimate act of betrayal?"

Alec imagined a fissure forming in the man's sanity and madness spewing to the surface. God help him if Hank had a gun. "Ellen told me many stories."

Bartholomew smiled, revealing the true depth of his insanity. "She told you. I can tell. I can always tell."

Time to strike. "No, you're wrong." Bartholomew stared at him and Alec continued. "You're the one who told me a lot about Ellen, 'Dr. Barton.'" Savoring the man's shocked expression, Alec shot him a calculated smile. "Yes...I'm the same Alexander Brody, the investigator you hired to find your long-lost patient. I found her, all right." Alec forced his smile to deepen. "And although we only had a brief time together, it was very... enlightening."

Bartholomew pulled his trembling fist from his pocket, revealing a switchblade. "You *were* intimate, weren't you? She made love to you." The blade flicked into place. "I can see it in your face."

Alec obeyed the first rule of self-defense: exploit your opponent's weakness. "Yes, we did."

The man stepped forward, and the blade caught the glint of the sun. "It's not right, you know. She always refused me when I made romantic overtures. 'No, Hank. I'm not ready for that, Hank.' It was all a lie," he spat. "She was willing to bed every Tom, Dick and Harry she ever dated but not me! They didn't deserve her love... much less her body. She belonged to me! Mind, body and soul. And in the end, I got all three."

He flipped the knife up and deftly caught it, demonstrating his deadly skill. "I suppose it's time to take care of you, too." He lunged forward, ready to attack.

Hermitt growled and lowered, struggling to get free. "No, Hermitt." Alec tugged at the dog's lead. *I'll take care of him myself.* Hermitt rumbled again, but squatted as if he, too, knew to bide his time for the right opening.

After years of security work, Alec knew how to disarm an attacker. He shifted, preparing to take on Bartholomew, but before Alec could begin his counterattack, a voice called out, destroying his momentum and concentration.

"No! Stop it!"

A figure stepped out of the shadowy undergrowth, and for a dangerous moment, Alec almost forgot about the man with a knife.

"My God..." For a second treacherous moment, his heart misfired, and hope flared where despair had existed for a long cold winter. "Ellen?"

He stared into the face which had haunted his days and nights, living in his dreams and dying in his nightmares. He knew he didn't believe in ghosts, but at this moment he wasn't so sure about believing in reality.

Hermitt's guttural noises subsided, and the animal lunged toward his mistress, all dangers forgotten in the heat of discovery. Alec yanked back the leash. "Hermitt—stay!" The dog crouched, obviously torn between loyalties to two masters. Alec unwillingly dragged his attention back to Bartholomew.

The man stood still with his arm raised in midswing. His face grew slack in shock, and the blade wavered, then lowered. "Ellen? But I thought I'd killed—"

Alec watched her recoil from the man with stark terror etched across her features. He celebrated Bartholomew's gross error while berating the folly of his own actions; the man had a new target now: Ellen.

Before the man could take a step toward her, Alec spoke in a hushed voice. "So, Ellen's haunting you, too, eh?"

Hank stared at her, then gave Alec a quick glance. "Haunting? What do you mean?"

"Her ghost, Ellen's ghost. Do you see it, too?" *Please, Ellen—for your sake—play along with me.*

"G-ghost?" Hank stuttered. He turned to glare at his "spectral" victim.

To Alec's relief, Ellen gave him an almost imperceptible nod, then turned toward Bartholomew and spoke in an ephemeral whisper. "Why? Why did you destroy my life, Hank? Why did you kill me?"

The knife slowly lowered. "I—I had to, Ellen. You weren't pure. Fire purifies the soul."

"It doesn't purify. It consumes. I died in that fire . . . a horrible, painful death."

Good girl. Alec circled around the side of the man, keeping a watch on the knife. *Keep going,* he gestured to her behind Bartholomew's back.

"Why did you hate me so much, Hank?"

"Hate you? My God, Ellen . . . I loved you. With all my heart and soul!"

"I—I didn't deserve to die." She curled her hand into a threatening fist. "I had a . . . right to live in peace!"

"What about my rights?" Bartholomew's voice rose in emotion. "You put me in that damned hospital, with the shrinks and the crazies. I had no freedom. It was as bad as dying!"

"I didn't put you there." She took a brave step forward. "You wanted what you couldn't have. You were obsessed."

He raised his hands, cowering against her ghostly approach. "No. Don't say that word. They were wrong. I wasn't ob-obsessed. I only wanted what was rightfully—" Hank stopped, lowering his arms. His expression changed as his gaze dropped to her feet, then trailed to the shadow she cast over the snow. He covered his sudden burst of gleeful laughter with one hand. "You know, I might be crazy, but I'm not stupid." The laughter took on a maniacal edge. "Ghosts don't have shadows."

He lunged at her, but Alec grabbed him from behind. "Run, Ellen!"

Bartholomew made a complicated move which sent Alec flying. Training allowed him to dilute the force of the landing with a tuck and roll. As he flipped to his feet, he realized Ellen hadn't taken advantage of the diversion to escape. "Get out of here!" he shouted, shifting his attention from his attacker to her.

Bartholomew took advantage of Alec's split concentration and made another attack, this time with the knife. Down filling spilled from the white slash in Alec's dark jacket. The knife sliced the air again, aimed at the arm Alec used to protect his face. He felt the blade bite into his forearm, but he ignored the pain in order to catch his opponent in midswing and kick the knife out of the man's hand. The weapon flew away, embedding itself in the snow.

To Alec's surprise, Bartholomew performed a spectacular flying dive from which he sprang back to his feet, clenching the switchblade. The rapid recovery revealed years of martial-arts training, an annoying fact that cut into Alec's concentration.

Crazy but well trained.

A deadly combination. And a painful one.

"You don't stand a chance," Hank taunted.

"You're losing your touch, Hank," Alec replied, hoping to keep the man off balance. "From what I hear, you used to be a pretty efficient killing machine. But you missed Ellen—and now me. Face it—you just don't have what you used to. You're a failure, Hank, a complete failure."

The madman's smile was brilliant. "Nice trick, but it won't work. Too obvious."

Alec fended off a well-placed kick, furiously trying to formulate a new plan. "Obvious? Maybe. Lucky? Definitely. Much luckier than you." *Ellen, please forgive me.* "I got something in just a couple of days that you tried to get for years but couldn't. She made the first move, you know, jumping my bones like a twenty-dollar hooker.''

Hank stumbled over an exposed tree root, demonstrating the relative success of Alec's psychological tactic.

"She's a real hellion in bed," he continued. "Did you know that? Extremely talented and very eager to please. God... what things that woman can do!" He forced himself to smile as if savoring a fine memory. "Of course, you wouldn't know anything about that, would you? You were never man enough to interest her."

Hank's smile faded, and a look of anger took its place. As his control began to slip, rage threw off his timing and blunted his judgment. Alec was able to kick the knife into a protective tangle of thorns, and the odds shifted in his favor. He played on Hank's physical weaknesses, a blind spot from the left and a tendency to keep his weight on his right foot.

Finally Alec threw one perfect punch, a product of dumb luck more than talent. That single, well-placed right cross to the chin connected.

Hank went down. And didn't get up.

Alec wiped one sleeve across his face. The material was soaked in blood from the cut on his forearm. He knelt beside his fallen opponent, fumbling with the man's belt buckle. *He won't be out long. I've got to fix it so he can't—* Suddenly, he felt Ellen's presence behind him, and he turned around, forgetting the important task awaiting him.

She was shaky, looking as if she was on the verge of becoming sick. "Jack..."

He said the first words that rushed into his mind, voicing them rather than the ones from his heart. "Why didn't you run when I told you to?"

Ellen didn't offer any answer as she knelt beside him. She lifted a hesitant hand to touch his sleeve. Fear remained in her face. "You're bleeding."

He pushed her hand away. "You were in danger. You should have run when you had a chance."

"I...I knew I couldn't keep running from my problems, and I couldn't leave you here. With him." She stood, acknowledging Bartholomew's presence with a furtive glance and a visible shiver.

"He won't bother you anymore." Alec dragged his gaze from his fallen opponent to the pale woman standing in front of him. "I came back for you. Three days after I—"

Hermitt interrupted them with a throaty growl. Ellen screamed. "Look out, Jack!"

Pain exploded behind his eyes, radiating into his vision like a thousand sparks of light. He thought he was falling toward her but instead he plunged into a gaping, black void.

ELLEN SCREAMED her warning too late, and Hank hit Jack squarely across the back of the head with a piece of charred wood. Jack stumbled toward her with the force of the tremendous blow, and she fell backward as his body slammed into her. Pinned to the ground, she struggled under the deadweight, vaguely aware of Hermitt's growls, which changed to painful yelps. When she could focus, she saw Hank towering over both of them.

"Oh, God..." she prayed.

He kicked Jack, and the dull sound made her throat close. Hank pushed the limp body off her.

"Sweetheart..." Hank held out a hand, but she squirmed back, trying to get away from him. The mere thought of his touch made her stomach revolt. "Now, Ellen..." he chided. "Is this any way to greet the man you love? I don't mean this jerk." He kicked Jack again. "You could never love him. I know you still love me."

"Get away from me, you bastard," she rasped.

"Not on your life, darling." Hank stood over her, offering his hand to help her up. When she tried to kick him in the shins, his offer of assistance turned into a backhanded swing aimed at her face.

She tensed in anticipation of the blow, but before the hand reached her face, Hermitt sprang forward, clamping his teeth into Hank's wrist. Hank screamed as the dog tightened his jaws and twisted his head, trying to drag the attacker away from his prey.

Ellen turned to Jack, praying she could rouse him before Hermitt lost his advantage. "Wake up, Jack! Please!" Tears blurred her vision as she shook him, slapping at his face.

Jack looked groggily past her to the altercation between man and beast. Determination pushed the blank look from his face. He stumbled to his feet, shoved her out of the way and lunged at Hank just as the man broke loose from Hermitt's grip. As Jack tackled Hank around the legs, Ellen heard her dog's anguished yelp of pain and watched the animal land in a crumpled heap.

Jack managed to grunt a single word at her as he fended off Hank's punches. "Run!"

This time Ellen obeyed, heading for the trail. She could hear the sounds of the fight behind her splitting the silence of the forest. Fists striking flesh, grunts of exertion and pain, anonymous noises that painted a frightening picture in her mind's eye.

She stumbled down the muddy path, praying she wouldn't lose her footing. How long could Jack keep Hank at bay? How do you win a fight with a mad—

"Ellen!" For one unforgivable moment, she couldn't tell their voices apart. She stopped.

"Damn you, Ellen!"

Hank! She veered off the trail, tripping over the saplings. Bare branches whipped behind her as she pushed her way through the trees and underbrush. Behind, the sounds of curses gained on her. She glanced down, seeing the rocky soil beneath the snow. Ahead of her a break in the trees became an ominous sign.

Ellen realized the stupidity of her tactic; instead of slowing her attacker down by leaving the established trail, she'd boxed herself in. She remembered too late the stone outcropping, a flat rock shelf that jutted out into open space with a fifty-foot drop beyond.

A great place for a picnic.

A lousy place to die.

"There you are." Hank emerged from the trees and stopped, smiling when he realized she was trapped. "What a lovely spot." He pretended to admire the view, then leered at her. "Well, sweetheart, it's just you and me." He stuffed his hands into his pockets and gave her a broad smile.

"Stand back, Hank. Or I'll . . . I'll jump!"

Hank began to laugh, and the small canyon amplified the sound in demented echoes. "Don't make me laugh, Ellen. That's exactly what I want you to do." He paused, and the smile faded away. "I want you to die."

She ran through her options at a furious pace. Deadly inspiration came quickly. "No, Hank. You want to kill me. If I jump, then I rob you of the satisfaction you want . . .

that you've wanted for years. I might die, but you won't be able to claim any credit for it. You would have failed." She paused and added, "Again."

"I'm not a failure!" he screamed, his voice becoming unnaturally shrill. "You won't jump. You'd have to be crazy to jump."

"Crazy? Like you?"

"Why, you—" He took a step forward. "You won't do it, Ellen. I know you won't."

Ellen wasn't sure where the serenity came from, but it flooded her soul, taking away the fear. If she actually jumped, she would most undoubtedly die. If Hank thought she was willing to jump in order to rob him of his warped sense of justice, then she might be able to use his own fear against him. She glanced to the right, spotting a thin path between the cliff's edge and a stand of bare bushes. There was a slim chance for survival, one on which she was willing to gamble.

The element of surprise, she reminded herself, *is the best strategy.*

"You've forgotten one important thing, Hank." She stepped closer to the edge and was able to give him a calm smile. "I'm not afraid to die."

"No!" Hank bellowed, lunging forward to grab her.

Jack exploded from between the trees and flew toward Hank, hitting him behind the knees. Ellen sidestepped their tangled bodies as they rolled toward her. She watched helplessly as the two men struggled for a brief moment before disappearing over the edge of the rock cliff.

Her scream split the silence and ended in a dying echo.

She fell to her knees, listening to the eerie silence. Choking back the terrible sobs which shook her mind and her body, Ellen stared into the infinite blue sky beyond the cliff's edge. A lone cloud blotted the sun.

Oh, Jack, a voice whispered in her imagination. *Maybe it didn't happen this time. Maybe Jack's not dead.* As hope returned, so did fear. *Maybe... maybe Hank's alive, as well.*

There was only one way to tell. Unable to trust herself to walk, Ellen crawled to the edge of the cliff. When she tried to peer over the rim, vertigo made her ravaged senses reel. She pulled back. *No one could have survived the fall.*

How could she assure herself of Hank's death without viewing Jack's demise, as well? Morbid curiosity and sorrow battled for control, and she eventually relented, knowing she had to assure herself of the brutal truth. She gazed over the side with a tear-blurred gaze.

Two bodies were intertwined on a smaller stone outcropping about twenty feet below her. A pool of blood had formed in a shallow depression in the rock. Lying on his back, Hank stared up without blinking, his face appearing strangely inert in death. Jack's body was draped over Hank's chest, and mercifully Ellen couldn't see how death had transformed his features.

Ellen inched back from the edge, unwilling to look any longer. She would never forget the scarlet stain across the rock ledge. The open-eyed stare of death. The weight of guilt.

She heard a noise behind her. When she turned, the burden of blame lightened a little. Hermitt limped toward her from the woods. He whimpered when she leaned forward and threw her arms around his neck. Her companion's black fur absorbed her tears as she wept for death, justified and unjustified.

A quiet scraping sound commanded her attention in the space of a single heartbeat. Hermitt located the noise for her, glancing in the direction of the cliff's edge. She heard rock strike rock, then bounce away. An anonymous groan...

Someone on the ledge was alive.

Her imagination supplied the answer: Hank, popping back like a character from a horror movie, a demon freak who wouldn't stay dead. Ellen crawled toward the trees, trying to coordinate her legs to support her. Hermitt approached the edge cautiously.

"Ellen..." The hoarse whisper was unrecognizable. She waited.

In fear.

In dread.

In hope.

She saw fingers, clutching the edge of the rock.

Then a hand, feeling around for a hold.

A blood-streaked face.

Hermitt's tail began to wag.

Chapter Sixteen

Imbued with newfound strength, Ellen helped pull Jack up until he sprawled across the rocky ground, gasping for breath. She knelt beside him, giving thanks for the miracle of his survival. "Jack, I—"

He opened his eyes and started to grin, but pain took sudden control of him, making him draw in a raspy breath. His bloodied hands tightened into fists. "He's d-dead, Ellen."

"We've got to get you to a hospital, Jack."

He coughed again. "Listen . . . Ellen. Hank's dead."

She brushed a curl from his forehead, recognizing the thin scar which led into his hairline. The scar represented another painful dose of reality. "I'm not worried about him anymore. I'm worried about you. You're hurt. We don't know how bad."

"Not ba—" His words turned into a sudden gasp for air. His face turned a pasty white beneath the dirt and blood.

She dared to touch his cool cheek. "Stay here. I'll go to the rangers' cabin and get help."

"No!" He placed an iron grip on her arm.

His sudden burst of strength startled her. She tried to keep him from sitting up. "But, Jack—"

He gritted the words between clenched teeth as he tightened his hold on her. "We go—together. Or not—at all. It can't be like last time."

It surprised her that she understood both the logic and the urgency of his request. She finished his thought from her own perspective. "When I came back to the cabin with help, you were gone." The moment Ellen spoke, she realized the fatal implication of the word *gone*. She swallowed a lump of panic. "I understand. Together. No matter what." She slipped behind him, hoping to brace him. "Can you stand?"

"Sure." He closed his eyes, then pushed to a sitting position with a raspy groan.

"Jack, I don't think—"

"I *will* make it, Ellen."

She positioned herself behind him, reaching under his arms. Then she sent up a hasty prayer. "One, two..." Ellen lifted on "three," and his eerie silence scared her worse than the earlier sounds of discomfort. They were upright, but their stance was unsteady. "Jack, this isn't such a good idea. You might—"

"Together or not at all," he repeated in faint resolution.

Proceeding at an agonizingly slow pace, they traveled in silence, interrupted only by her occasional direction or warning about their footing on the trail. At one misstep, she felt Jack shudder in pain. Her sudden flare of bravado faded. "Why don't we rest for a few minutes, Jack?"

"No!" He grimaced as he spoke. "Gotta keep moving." A few steps later, his low words caught her by surprise. "Ellen... tell me a story."

Her heart wedged itself in her throat. "A what?"

"A story. About Tess and Jack." A spasm of pain crossed his face as they took another jarring step together. "Tell me how happy they were."

"Happy?" She thought for a moment.

"Did they ever . . . ever get married?"

"I guess so." Her mind painted a quick picture of a wedding scene: Tess in a beaded silk dress holding white orchids, and Jack in a tuxedo. The picture dimmed when blood began to stain Jack's crisp white shirt.

"Tell me more . . ."

"I can't," she whispered. "There are no more stories. They're gone."

"Then who do you dream of?"

Her eyes felt hot and dry. Where were the tears to wash away the pain? Where was Tess to absorb the brunt of the emotion to protect poor Ellen? She heard her own voice utter the simple, unvarnished answer. "You."

She took several steps before the dam began to crack within her. A trickle of emotion dripped from the widening fissure in her control. "Why did you leave?" As soon as she spoke, she regretted how accusing she sounded. "No . . . no don't answer that. Just keep walking."

He astounded her with the strength in his voice. "When I woke up, I didn't know where I was."

"I said, be quiet."

"I can't, Ellen." He stumbled to a stop in the middle of the trail. "You deserve to know the truth. When I woke up, I had no idea how I got in the cabin or what had happened to me. I didn't even remem—" A shuddering barrage of coughs interrupted his explanation.

Her panic rose to an almost unmanageable level. "Please, Jack. You can tell me all this later. We need to concentrate on getting you to the cabin." She drew a deep breath, hoping to calm herself. "It's not far now," she added with false encouragement. "It's just around the next turn." *And the next, and the next...*

"But you need to know—"

"No, don't try to explain. You wouldn't be in this condition if it weren't for—" She couldn't finish the statement; it would mean admitting all her solitude, all her trouble, was for nothing. Isolation had failed to protect the innocent from the lethal. Ellen choked back a sob, letting the needs of the moment outweigh the accusations of the past.

"Maybe George can hear me from here." She took a deep breath, then yelled her friend's name. Hermitt reacted to her sense of urgency with a flurry of barks as he rushed ahead. She could hear a voice in the distance.

"What the... good God, Hermitt! You ol' son of a—"

"George! Over here. On the trail!"

Once she saw her friend lumbering toward them, it became difficult for her to see through the sudden curtain of tears. Jack sagged against her, his weight almost making her knees buckle. "Hurry, George! Jack's hurt. I think it's bad."

The ranger slipped beneath Jack's other arm. "What happened?"

"It was Hank."

George stopped, shifting his hardening stare between Jack and her. "He's Hank?"

"No!" She gestured frantically toward the cabin. "Hank attacked him. Please... he needs a doctor." With George's help, they reached the cabin in a matter of seconds.

Once inside, Jack gestured away their help as he lowered himself to the edge of the mattress. "I'm...ok-kay," he said, stuttering. His face reflected the agony of the movement.

Ellen stood beside the bed, trying to convince herself they had reached safety and everything would be all right. One look at Jack's face reminded her of the difficulties that still lay ahead. She shuddered as she flashed back to a mental image of two bodies entangled on the stone outcropping.

"You just take it easy, son. After I radio for a chopper for you, I'm goin' to get my shotgun and put that bastard Bartholomew out of his misery. Once and for all."

Ellen grabbed George's arm before he could charge into the radio room. "That's how Jack got hurt. Hank attacked me and Jack knocked him over the stone outcropping." She swallowed hard as the image of Hank's death swam before her eyes again. "They fell together, and Hank broke his neck when he landed. He's...dead."

The big man paused. "Dead? You sure?"

Until that moment Ellen had been asking herself the same questions. Was Hank truly dead? Or would he rise like a specter to torment her again? She reached out to identify the sense of trepidation that had always accompanied any memory of Hank.

It was gone.

Hank was gone, and she was at peace.

Ellen closed her eyes and took a deep breath. "I'm sure. He'll never bother anyone ever again."

"Then I'll get on the horn and get the Medivac chopper for your friend. He's not looking too good."

Panic replaced her momentary sense of serenity. Ellen rushed back to the bed to discover Jack no longer sitting but slumped over, his eyes closed. She knelt on the floor beside the bed and reached up with a trembling hand to brush a lock of hair from his dirtied forehead. "Everything's going to be all right, Jack," she whispered. "George'll get help here soon. Just hang on."

He opened his eyes and gave her a pale grin. "If I had hung around the cabin when I was supposed to, I wouldn't be feeling so lousy now. Don't look so scared, Ellen. I don't feel as bad as I did the first time you found me. And I came back. I really did. I came back, but it was too late. The cabin was gone. I thought you were gone, too. Even when I found Hermitt, I figured he was the only one to survive the fire."

When the big dog heard his name, he placed his broad head on the bed, sniffed Jack's jacket, then wagged his tail.

Ellen stroked the dog's muzzle. "I thought he died that night. I searched for him the best I could." Guilt washed over her as she admitted her darkest thought. "After the fire started, I thought I'd discovered the awful truth—you had to be Hank. After all, you were the only one who knew I was there. And the fire happened the night after you disappeared. I truly believed you were Hank...until I saw the two of you standing there at the cabin. Face-to-face."

A dark flush added color to Jack's otherwise whitewashed features. "Do you remember our conversation about Hank? You said he considered himself an expert and he would never have hired someone to perform a task he thought he could handle himself?"

Her stomach began to churn, seeing the obvious direction of his confession. When the floor began to tilt, she was glad she was sitting on it rather than a chair.

He reached blindly for her hand. "Hank contacted me by phone eight months ago, saying he was a doctor at Mountain Point Hospital. He said he was concerned about a patient of his, and I had no reason to believe he was lying. He checked out completely."

His grip tightened on her hand. "That's why I was on your mountain—looking for you. Maybe it was luck... maybe instinct, but no matter which, once I pinpointed your location, I decided I needed to talk to you before I reported back to him. Ellen, I—" He drew a ragged breath that disintegrated into a wheezy gasp for air. His grip loosened and his eyes drifted shut.

"Jack? Jack!"

He forced his eyes open again. "When I woke up by your fireplace, I didn't remember how I got there. I didn't remember anything about him or you. Or even myself. F-forgive me, Ellen."

She placed a gentle finger across his bruised lips. "How can I not forgive you, Jack? After all you've done..."

To her relief he rallied enough energy to smile at her. "Thank you," he whispered.

George walked back into the room, carrying a large tackle box marked First Aid. He placed it on the floor beside the bed. "Chopper'll be here in a half hour. Can you hold out till then?"

Jack managed a small nod. "I'll have to."

"Meanwhile I'll see what I can do." George began to paw through the medical supplies. "El...that night—how *did* that fire start?"

She sagged against the mattress, resting her head on the scratchy army blanket covering Jack. "I'd just fallen asleep when I smelled smoke. The fire started in the pantry, then suddenly filled every door and window."

George nodded. "As if someone had planned to methodically cut off all the escape routes."

Tears began to form in her eyes. "I thought Hermitt had gotten trapped in the cabin. I never dreamed..." She reached down and rested her hand on the dog's sleek back. "I'm so glad you're back," she whispered to him.

George pulled a knife from his pocket and split the torn sleeve of Jack's jacket. "Have you figured out how Hank found you?"

She shared a hooded glance with Jack before turning toward George. She drew a deep breath. "Jack's an investigator. Hank hired him to locate me."

George's careful ministrations came to an abrupt halt. "You told him where she was?"

Jack stiffened. "In a way... I did. Right after he hired me, I started to have second thoughts. Something about him just wasn't right. So, I came here to talk to Ellen first, before I gave away her location. Even after I... 'escaped,' I didn't remember anything about having him as a client until long after the fire. However Hank found out where she was, it wasn't because I told him. But it's not that hard to figure." Jack closed his eyes as if conjuring up a mental picture. "I met him in this room on the day I—I ran away from your cabin. Ellen, you saw the insignia he was wearing today, didn't you?"

George stiffened. "Met him here? What the hell are you talking about?"

Jack splayed a hand across his lower chest as he struggled to inhale. "When I met him the first time, either he didn't tell me his name, or I forgot it. But today at the cabin, he introduced himself as Harlin Banks."

The red flush drained from George's face. "Good..
Harlin? My partner? He's..." George stopped and looked
at Ellen.

She felt her throat close. *Harlin Banks.* Though she'd
never met the man, she'd heard George talk about his
partner, Harlin.

George continued to stare in shock. "He's dead?"

She couldn't speak, answering him with a nod instead.
She found solace in the silent grip she shared with Jack.

The awful truth washed all the strength from the ranger's body. They watched him age ten years in mere seconds. After a few moments he looked up at Ellen with
anger and confusion. "If he was here all the while, why did
he hire an investigator to find you? It doesn't make sense."

She glanced at Jack. "It makes perfect sense... in the
warped way Hank's mind worked. He'd been looking for
me for four years but couldn't find me. He finally broke
down and hired a professional. Yet he still couldn't stop
from looking for me himself. He must have figured out
from one of Dad's paintings that my family had a cabin in
this area. Maybe he even knew you were a friend of Dad's.
It made sense for him to station himself in this area and
watch and wait."

"Dead..." George rose to his feet. "I've got to see it for
myself, Ellen." He reached over and grabbed his shotgun,
his face grayed with anger.

As the man thundered out the door, Ellen covered her
face. It wasn't fair. Even after death, Hank could still
cause pain to the innocent.

"Ellen?"

She felt Jack's hand flutter against her arm. Wiping
away her tears, she turned to him, taken aback by the
startling lack of energy in his eyes. She brushed her lips

cross his forehead. "Hank has hurt so many people. You, eorge..."

"Don't forget you. What he did to you was..." He oughed, unable to finish.

She dragged the medical box closer to the bed and pawed arough it. "Right now I'm more concerned about you. our injuries."

He shrugged. "I'll heal." He faltered several times before finally raising an unsteady hand to caress her cheek. Ellen, it's over. You're free now."

"F-free?" Ellen straightened, riveted by his words. he'd been so busy dealing with the past and the present, ne hadn't had time to examine her future. With Hank ead...

"You can go anywhere. Do anything."

She glanced up at him, trying to read her future in his azel eyes. The flicker of energy she saw there kindled a ew flame in her. "I want to—"

"No. Stop." He reached for her hand. "Before you say nything, I need to tell you what I feel. Ellen...I love you. 'll take you anywhere you want to go. I'll help you reuild the cabin or find you another one. Just tell me. I'll o it."

Ellen closed her eyes and pulled his hand to her lips. She emembered saying the words once before at a time when ope seemed gone...when the admission of her true feelngs was her way of saying goodbye. Now it meant the opposite.

"I love you, Jack."

He shot her a strained smile.

"Did I say something wrong?"

"No, of course not." His forced manner belied his ords.

The truth made a cold shiver crawl down her back
"Your name... it isn't Jack, is it?" She heard the slap o
approaching rotors; the helicopter had arrived.

"No, it's... it's not. I'm almost afraid he's the guy you
love rather than me." His eyes fluttered and closed.

"Jack? Jack!" *You idiot... that's not his name!* "Wake
up. You can't go to sleep now!"

"T-tired," he mumbled, not opening his eyes.

"Please wake up! How can I tell you I love you if I don'
know your name?"

A weak smile flashed across his face. "Tell me again."

"I'll tell you I love you," she taunted, "if you tell me
your name."

His eyes opened and his smile grew stronger. "Only
when you agree to marry me."

Her heart skipped a beat. "M-marry you?"

"I'd get down on my knees if I thought I could make it.'

"Marriage?" She stopped and repeated the word to
herself several times. She swallowed hard. "If I marry you
then I'll become Mrs....." She trailed off, hoping he'd
supply the answer.

"Nope." He drew a painful breath. "No name until you
answer my question. Will you marry me?"

She closed her eyes and listened to the approaching
voices. "Yes." She waited for a moment. "Then I'll be
come..."

"Mrs. Alexander J. Brody, Jr."

"Alexander Brody." She tested the name, trying to se
what reactions she felt when she heard it spoken aloud.

"Alexander J. Brody, Jr.," he corrected.

"What does the *J* stand for?"

He smiled. "What do you think it stands for?"

Epilogue

The Denver Post

The Tattered Volume invites the public to a book signing by local Denver author/illustrator, Ellen Brody, on December 8, 7-9 p.m. Ms. Brody's latest work, *Once upon a Mountain,* from Pantomime Press is the first in a planned series of romantic-suspense novels concerning the adventures of Tess and Jack Phoenix.

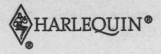

HARLEQUIN®

INTRIGUE®

**HARLEQUIN INTRIGUE AUTHOR KELSEY ROBERTS
SERVES UP A DOUBLE DOSE OF DANGER AND DESIRE
IN THE EXCITING NEW MINISERIES:**

THE ROSE TATTOO

At the Rose Tattoo, Southern Specialties are served with a
Side Order of Suspense:

On the Menu for June

Dylan Tanner—tall, dark and delectable
Shelby Hunnicott—sweet and sassy
Sizzling Suspense—saucy red herrings with a twist

On the Menu for July

J. D. Porter—hot and spicy
Tory Conway—sinfully rich
Southern Fried Secrets—succulent and juicy

On the Menu for August

Wes Porter—subtly scrumptious
Destiny Talbott—tart and tangy
Mouth-Watering Mystery—deceptively delicious

Look for Harlequin Intrigue's response to your
hearty appetite for suspense: THE ROSE TATTOO,
coming in June, July and August.

HARLEQUIN®

I N T R I G U E®

What if...

You'd agreed to marry a man you'd never met, in a town where you'd never been, while surrounded by wedding guests you'd never seen before?

And what if...

You weren't sure you could trust the man to whom you'd given your hand?

Look for "Mail Order Brides"—the upcoming two novels of romantic suspense by Cassie Miles, which are available in April and July—and only from Harlequin Intrigue!

Don't miss

#320 MYSTERIOUS VOWS
by Cassie Miles
April 1995

Mail Order Brides—where mail-order marriages lead distrustful newlyweds into the mystery and romance of a lifetime!

HARLEQUIN®

Don't miss these Harlequin favorites by some of our most distinguished authors!
And now, you can receive a discount by ordering two or more titles!

HT#25577	WILD LIKE THE WIND by Janice Kaiser	$2.99	☐
HT#25589	THE RETURN OF CAINE O'HALLORAN by JoAnn Ross	$2.99	☐
HP#11626	THE SEDUCTION STAKES by Lindsay Armstrong	$2.99	☐
HP#11647	GIVE A MAN A BAD NAME by Roberta Leigh	$2.99	☐
HR#03293	THE MAN WHO CAME FOR CHRISTMAS by Bethany Campbell	$2.89	☐
HR#03308	RELATIVE VALUES by Jessica Steele	$2.89	☐
SR#70589	CANDY KISSES by Muriel Jensen	$3.50	☐
SR#70598	WEDDING INVITATION by Marisa Carroll	$3.50 U.S. $3.99 CAN.	☐
HI#22230	CACHE POOR by Margaret St. George	$2.99	☐
HAR#16515	NO ROOM AT THE INN by Linda Randall Wisdom	$3.50	☐
HAR#16520	THE ADVENTURESS by M.J. Rodgers	$3.50	☐
HS#28795	PIECES OF SKY by Marianne Willman	$3.99	☐
HS#28824	A WARRIOR'S WAY by Margaret Moore	$3.99 U.S. $4.50 CAN.	☐

(limited quantities available on certain titles)

	AMOUNT	$
DEDUCT:	**10% DISCOUNT FOR 2+ BOOKS**	$
ADD:	**POSTAGE & HANDLING**	$
	($1.00 for one book, 50¢ for each additional)	
	APPLICABLE TAXES*	$_____
	TOTAL PAYABLE	$_____
	(check or money order—please do not send cash)	

To order, complete this form and send it, along with a check or money order for the total above, payable to Harlequin Books, to: In the U.S.: 3010 Walden Avenue, P.O. Box 9047, Buffalo, NY 14269-9047; In Canada: P.O. Box 613, Fort Erie, Ontario, L2A 5X3.

Name: _____

Address: _____ City: _____

State/Prov.: _____ Zip/Postal Code: _____

*New York residents remit applicable sales taxes.
 Canadian residents remit applicable GST and provincial taxes.

HBACK-JM2